THE

CLEARING

DAN NEWMAN

DIVERSIONBOOKS

Diversion Books
A Division of Diversion Publishing Corp.
443 Park Avenue South, Suite 1008
New York, New York 10016
www.DiversionBooks.com

For more information, email info@diversionbooks.com

First Diversion Books edition April 2016.
Print ISBN: 978-1-68230-050-3
eBook ISBN: 978-1-68230-049-7

For Laura

1

All three of the boys knew Richard was dead.

His limp form lay at their feet, his eyes wide and unblinking, and his left hand waving an eerie goodbye as the river tugged at his arm in a regular, unsettling rhythm. They stood in a loose semicircle, their wet clothes dripping on the riverbank, watching for something to happen but knowing nothing would.

"He's dead," whispered Pip, his mouth suddenly and completely dry. He looked up at the others; his eyes had none of the boyish bravado that had been there only moments before. Now he was just a frightened twelve-year-old. "I want to go home."

To his left stood Nate, eyes and face pleated, chest heaving but finding no air in the tropical humidity.

Tristan stooped beside Richard and nudged his cousin's shoulder with a tentative, outstretched foot. "Wake up, Richard." But nothing happened, save the gentle lolling of the boy's head and the vacant expression that hung there. Tristan rose slowly, never moving his eyes from the boy at the water's edge. "Shit. He's really...dead." And because Tristan said it, it was finally true.

"What are we gonna do?" Nate began to rock slightly from side to side.

"It was an accident, right? You saw it—just an accident?" said Pip. He clutched his hands in a tangle against his chest. "We shouldn't be here. We shouldn't be this far out." And then, in a voice weakened by looming tears, "I'm scared."

Nate looked at him blankly but said nothing.

It was getting late. The sun had already gone down over the tops of the trees, and the woods had begun to take on a darker shade of green as the first hints of nightfall set in. In the rainforest, the days ended quickly, and the trees seemed to gather and hide the pathways and trails, crowding their shoulders and linking limbs in some ancient pact of secrecy.

The boys were far from the house. Current horrors aside, they knew they had to move. There were things you didn't want to come across out here in the night. Things that were better avoided. And that wasn't the only problem—they would need to get back to the plantation house or Tristan's dad would have a fit. The same thought seemed to run through them all at once, and like a single twitch, the real problem reclaimed them. At their feet lay the dead boy, and at their backs a darkening forest.

How the weekend at the old plantation had come to such a horrible and complete full stop no one knew—at least not right then.

Tristan was the first to move. His feet were bare but callused heavily from a lifetime of shoeless island living, and as he moved up the slope toward the path he dug his toes into the soft earth like hooks. Around the boys the mass of the tropical forest—the vines, broad leaves, ferns and flowers, the thick ground covering succulents and the bougainvillea—all of it crowded together to hasten the onset of night.

Tristan looked back at the others and drew his lips into a hard white line. At thirteen, he was already keenly aware of his role in the group. "Get moving!" he barked, followed by a sharp curse in patois—a French Creole language native to the island. Neither Pip nor Nate understood the words, but the message was clear.

Pip looked up the bank at Tristan, whose form was merging with the darkness. "We can't just leave him." Pip's voice was thin, hesitant.

Nate wiped at his eye as sweat crept in at the corner and knew instantly it would draw fire from Tristan. He saw the older boy's lips curl, saw locks of his dirty blonde hair move as his head shook—almost imperceptibly—in disapproval. It said *cry baby* without the need for any words at all.

The three stared at each other in a silent standoff. "Fine," said

Tristan defiantly. "Stay if you want. But remember what we heard last night. Remember what we saw. It lives 'round here. If you want to get caught out here after dark, that's *your* problem."

The two boys cut sharp glances at the gathering gloom around them, then at each other, looking for courage that neither could find. Tristan's goading was enough. Richard would have to wait.

In 1976, St. Lucia was something of a pet project for international aid, with countries from around the globe pouring resources and people into the island in an orgy of philanthropic one-upmanship. Both Nate and Pip were sons of international development workers—Pip from Holland and Nate from Canada— and both had lived on the island for a little over three years. They didn't know everything about this raw island paradise, but they knew enough to take Tristan's words seriously—especially when it came to the forest. Tristan and his family had lived on the island for generations, and the deeply tanned boy with wild, dirty blonde hair looked entirely at home surrounded by the rainforest's mass of green.

The boys scrambled to the top of the bank, stopping only long enough for each to cast a single glance backward. Then they turned away, one by one, leaving a darkening scene where a small, cold boy was left alone at the edge of a river being swiftly reclaimed by the night.

"Come on," said Tristan, tugging at Pip's shirtsleeve. "We need to go. Now."

The boys pushed on silently along the path at a trot, past landmarks that only Tristan could see, racing the daylight. They covered at least a kilometer of thick jungle pathway, batting vines and forearming broad leaves as they wove their way through twists and turns of green. Ahead, Tristan slowed, then stopped, then turned to the others. He was sweating heavily, and beads of moisture had gathered on the tip of his broad nose. "Wait up," he said, heaving for breath. Tristan squatted down on his haunches, and the two others followed suit. The little group stared at one another, heaving for breath and chewing at nails and lips.

"What?" asked Nate, itching to keep moving.

Tristan only stared at him hollowly.

"What!? Let's go! I want to go home!"

"Home?"

"Yeah. I want to go home. Now." To Nate's left, Pip bobbed his head up and down frantically in agreement.

"Home," said Tristan, as if remembering something long since lost. "You can't just go home now," he said.

2

He had never fully understood what triggered these moments—but it happened the way it always did: a bright and sudden surge of panic, fresh beads of sweat prickling across his skin, and a flush of heat that threatened to smother. The sensation had been more intense lately, but it would leave as quickly as it came.

Nate braced himself and waited for it to pass. For the moment it owned him, as it always did—for as far back as he could remember. He steadied himself against a seatback, drawing in a half-dozen deep breaths, and the sensation slowly ebbed away.

He filed toward the open door of the airplane, shuffling with the other impatient passengers, and breathed in the heavy wash of tropical air, the warm, almost oppressive quality of the island's moisture-laden breath. As he passed into the daylight through the curve of the aircraft doorway he paused for a moment, just for a beat or two, long enough to slip a pair of old Wayfarers over his eyes, before descending the rickety truck-mounted stairway to the tarmac below.

As he set foot on the island, he knew that at least some part of him had come home. But then there was that other part: that low-slung and heavy stone stitched roughly into the pit of his gut. It amassed gravity now, and pulled downward with a dread so tangible he almost reached down to cradle it. His mind sprinted ahead, through the airport terminal, past the well-pressed customs officers, past the colorful tour buses, and straight on through town. It arced through streets lined with third-world commerce, past vendors ebullient with wild fruits and brightly colored parasols, across the Morne and into the real heart of the island, then plunged into a thick and wet rainforest that so easily hid whatever it wished.

And Nate understood that amid that unyielding tangle of vines, the broad leafed Tanya, the thick plantain shoots and banana trees that knotted tightly into that gush of botanical life, something was waiting for him. Out there in the lush, humid hills, at the end of that roughly hewn dirt road that winds blindly through the mass of green, it knew he was coming. It always had.

"Passport please." The voice popped him from his daydream and he complied, muttering something that never quite saw fruition.

The black man in the black uniform smiled broadly. "Fers time in St. Lucia, Mr. Mason?"

"No, no," he said. "I grew up here as a kid. But I haven't been back for… Jeez, I guess thirty years or so."

The customs agent smiled, stamped the passport and handed it back. His Caribbean accent was a lullaby. "Then let me be the fers to say *welcome 'ome.*"

During the taxi ride through town, he became aware of the tension in his shoulders, a tension that had been there all day, all week—Christ, all his adult life. And so he lowered his head to stretch the muscles that ran down from the back of his head and into his shoulders. In the back of the taxi, he looked much like a man in prayer.

The driver chimed in, his voice melodic with island inflection. "Why you pray, man? You dun arrive in paradise already."

Nate Mason smiled and looked up, rubbing at the back of his neck. "No prayers for me. Just a stiff neck is all."

"We can fix dat fuh you. We can fix dat fine." He laughed and flashed bright white teeth that filled the rear-view mirror.

"I'll be okay," said Nate, brushing the comment aside, until he saw that the driver was holding up a small bag of what appeared to be weed.

"Island remedy for *eeeeveryting.*"

Nate had an instant vision of drug busts and sting operations, being bent over the hood of the taxi in handcuffs and hauled off to some airless hole. "No, really, I'm good," he said, embarrassed at some level for his complete lack of cool. The driver shrugged and didn't press the issue.

At the Breadfruit Tree Inn, he paid the taxi and was left standing on the street in the center of Castries. The inn sat squarely in front of him, and a thousand sharp memories clamoring for attention from behind. He turned slowly. Much had changed, but among the changes, hiding like frightened children, he could see all that had remained the same.

In his room, he splashed his face with water and sat on the bed, drinking in the smell of the place and letting memories wash over him. The bed smelled very slightly—almost imperceptibly—of mold, as if the odor existed only at the very edges of the human olfactory palette. The smell transported him to his first summer on the island, to those days when he traveled around the island with his father, mother, brother, and a glassy-eyed embassy official, visiting houses they might live in. He remembered the newness of the experience, the intensity of the sunlight, the lush setting, and of course the subtle smell of dampness at every house they visited.

And he remembered his mother, crying late at night, unable to fully process the magnitude of the changes before her. His heart sank at the memory, but then he thought of her in later years, in a better house, in a better part of the island, laughing and mixing drinks for a collection of expats clad in kitschy afro-shirts, loud plaid pants, and blouses in shades of orange that haven't been seen again since that part of the '70s.

From the balcony of his room at the inn, Nate watched the early evening foot traffic around Derek Walcott Square, a near perfectly preserved piece of the island that he remembered fondly as a child. From his second story perch, he could see the massive and sprawling tree that had dominated the square for decades, the lush gardens and the pavilion set at its center.

All the buildings that surrounded the square back then were made of timber. They were two- and three-story structures with balconies at each level, each adorned with intricate swirls of woodwork where the uprights met the roof. They had a Victorian

DAN NEWMAN

feel, and as he looked at the collection of buildings that lined the square now, he saw that much had been preserved. There was a bit more concrete and glass dotted here and there, but the old square had not lost its charm.

In the park itself, couples drifted to and fro, enjoying the warm gloaming as the day's tropical heat waned. There were benches and low walls for perching on, tangles of bougainvillea that created private partitions and rooms, and at the center, the great tree. A few tourists ambled through the park, branded loudly by their cruise wear, and a vendor at a small cart flipped fish cakes on the orange glow of an open fire. Nate could feel his shoulders loosening, his big city tension getting ready to slip, and yet something there would not let him fully enjoy the moment.

Inside his room, the light on the phone beside the bed blinked. Had it been blinking when he came in? He couldn't remember, and it occurred to him that he was tired, wilting like long forgotten back-of-the-fridge lettuce. He was too tired to pick up the message waiting there, too tired to let his mind begin churning on the great wheel that the call would set in motion.

Tonight he would simply go to sleep. He would permit himself one more night of delusion, one final investment in nihilism and the decision that for the next eight hours at least, everything in his world was just fine.

In the morning, the light was still blinking. He showered slowly, dressed, and hung the few clothes he had brought with him in the closet. In his small suitcase sat a worn and well-aged brown paper bag, folded over at the opening. It had seen many years and many miles. It was creased and wrinkled, and bore the vague outline of the precious cargo it had held for so long. Nate placed a hand gently on top of it just to make sure its contents were safe. He felt the bulk there, and satisfied, closed the suitcase and placed it back in the closet.

Downstairs, he sat by the window in the small, nearly empty dining room overlooking the street, and he ordered a half grapefruit. He never liked grapefruit, even as a boy, but it was part of the fabric of being here, part of the memory. He ate the tart, pink flesh slowly, and watched as the square began to wake. It was a peaceful moment, and he felt a rare pang of joy as thoughts of Cody flashed through his mind. In that moment Cody was three—maybe four—sleepy-eyed and glowing with just-woke-up warmth, and cuddled impossibly into the crook of Nate's arm in the big chair in the den. It would have been a Sunday, dawn barely broken, perhaps in winter with the snow landing silently on the ledge outside. It was as near perfect a moment as any he could recall.

It seemed memories were coming thick and fast this morning. Nate spied the old Rain Restaurant building across the square. The restaurant was long gone now, but the building had persisted. He could almost smell the Wednesday night fish and chips special and the feel of his dad's hand on his shoulder as they all walked toward the front door, bellies growling and spirits high.

He dipped into his grapefruit again and wanted so badly to look up and see his father sitting there, across the table, eating his own grapefruit. He wanted to reach out and touch his hand, then point across the square and say something like, *Can you believe it, Dad, the Rain building is still standing thirty years later...*

A man walked slowly past on the sidewalk, and thoughts of Cody and his father evaporated. As the man passed, he pitched his head slightly to the left and glanced in. Their eyes connected through the open window, and the man held Nate's gaze for what seemed a beat longer than appropriate between two complete strangers. Finally he looked away and swept past. A spark of concern flared through Nate. Was that more than a casual glance? Was the man looking at him? Was he looking *for* him? He shook his head gently. *Get it together, man. No one knows you're here.*

Nate finished his coffee and went back to his room. The light was still blinking, and he finally accepted that he could delay no more. Answering the message meant it was all beginning in earnest, but the reality was that it had begun a long, long time ago.

He took a deep breath and dialed the voicemail.

• • •

Smiley Edwin was named well. He smiled brilliantly as he walked up to Nate, arms fully extended and fingers splayed. His welcome was obvious, unabashed, and completely genuine.

"Mr. Mason!" he said in the kind of tone normally reserved for old friends. "I am so glad to meet you at last!" He was easily two hundred and fifty pounds, but he carried it remarkably well, despite his five foot nine frame. He wore a starched white shirt under a navy blue blazer, and his necktie was cinched up as far as it would go against a top button that was destined to never meet its neighboring hole. Smiley was a reporter for *The Word*, a small and relatively new local newspaper that was working hard to make itself a name.

The two men stood in front of Smiley's battered white Honda, in the shade of the almond trees that lined Vigie Beach. In front of them was the Caribbean sea, and behind them a tangle of sea grape bushes wrapped itself around tall, swaying coconut trees as if to beg them not to leave. Beyond that ran a road parallel to the long beach, bordered on the far side by a chain link fence around the grass apron of Vigie Airport. The beach had its share of sprawling all-inclusive hotels, but they were well spaced, leaving this part of the pristine coastline to the St. Lucians. Dotted around were people in ones and twos, mostly locals, save the odd pairing of tourists venturing past the boundaries of their expensive waterfront real estate.

"I'm sorry I didn't get back to you last night," Nate said, "I was pretty worn out from the flight in."

Smiley waved the comments aside with a meaty paw. "No problem, no problem," he said dismissively. His skin was a light brown, the color of hazelnuts, and he had a spray of black freckles across his nose and cheeks. "I jus' pleased you here, man—dat I get dis chance to meet you."

Nate smiled uncomfortably. The meeting was something he wanted now, but that position had come at a tremendous cost. Smiley continued. "So tell me, man," he said, panning his outstretched hand at the beach before them, "has much changed?"

"You know, I've been wondering that myself. The roads are better—still a lot of potholes, though."

Smiley nodded in recognition.

Nate went on. "The cars are newer, and there's a bunch of new buildings and hotels that were never here when I was a kid, but it still *feels* the same. Does that make any sense? It just…I dunno, it just still feels like that quiet little island I remember it to be."

Smiley pointed down the beach to a wall that marked the property line of a huge hotel. "Dat prob'ly wasn't dere in '76."

"No," Nate nodded in agreement. "Back then it was just beach and almond trees. I used to walk this way home from school, and back then the beach was practically deserted. There was only one hotel here—the Malabar—but that was way down the other end."

"The Malabar! Yes…you know I had forgotten 'bout dat place. Dem had a pointy red tin roof you could see from de road…"

"That's the one."

"I think it was blown flat in a hurricane in de '80s. It a Sun Spree now."

They chatted aimlessly, the island's past their common ground, all the while both men fixing their eyes on the horizon where the arc of the planet was scribed in perfect blue against the sky.

In his mind's eye, Nate recalled the stretch of beach they now gazed upon, and could see himself, thirteen years old, running home along the sand in uniform gray flannel pants and a white button down shirt—untucked now that the school day was over. He remembered dropping the green canvas backpack he carried, and stripping down to his boxers, splashing into the brilliant blue of the Caribbean just to cool off. There was a freedom to that life that seemed so foreign to him now, and as the memory strove to reconnect him with the moment, with the sensation of a thirteen-year-old's carefree romp across a sun-bleached beach, something else in him wanted it all to stop.

Smiley, to his credit, felt the shift. "So, de research. You want talk 'bout dat?"

"Yes, sure. That'd be great."

Smiley went round to the back seat of his car and returned with a thick manila envelope, stuffed to bursting with paper and photographs. Smiley grinned, and then pulled the documents out and laid them on the hood of the car.

"All this research," Nate puffed out his cheeks. "You were able to pull it together without too much, well…fuss?"

Smiley understood exactly what Nate was asking. "This was all assembled very discreetly, let me assure you. Nuttin' to worry 'bout."

Nate felt suddenly foolish for his insistence on secrecy. "Yeah, sorry about being so cloak and dagger. I just wanted all this handled quietly."

"For now," said Smiley, smiling empathetically.

Nate nodded. "Right, for now."

"Well, man, just as you reques', I have told no one 'bout your visit. Dat will remain confidential, until you ready…"

There was an awkward pause, and it was now Nate's turn to steer the conversation to safety. "Smiley, just as I said in the emails, you get the exclusive. I promise. Professional code and all that," he said, smiling conspiratorially.

Smiley nodded. He turned back to the hood of the car and lifted a photograph that sat underneath the pages. He handed it to Nate and watched as it transformed the man's face, seeming to age it instantly.

The photograph captured a blond-haired boy, ten or eleven years old, smiling brightly. He was leaning against the upturned hull of a small sailboat—a Mirror dinghy—itself sitting atop a pair of wooden work-horses and having its hull repaired. The boy was slight, small even for ten, but his face was the kind that makes mothers clutch their hands to their chests and let out long, wistful sighs. It was Richard, captured at his most ebullient, bursting with life and gushing happiness from the page. It saddened Nate more than he was ready for.

Without looking up from the boy by the sailboat, and without fully understanding himself where the question came from, Nate quietly asked, "Do you believe in the Bolom?"

3

"Can I get you some water, sir?"

"No, no."

"Is there someone we can call? Someone you'd like to be here?"

Nate nearly laughed at that one, although there was nothing funny about the scene around him. *Christ*, he thought. *There's not a single goddamn person.* "No. There's no one."

The police officer patted him once on the shoulder. "Okay, just sit tight and someone from VS will be here shortly," he said. Nate was sure he could sense relief in the man's voice. He watched as the officer left the living room, pushed the screen door open and went outside. And what was VS? He didn't care enough to ask. He was too tired.

From the couch where he sat, Nate looked around the living room, taking it all in like a man suddenly waking up to find himself in a foreign land. Of course, he'd been here hundreds of times before. He'd sat on the couch, often in this very spot, on more occasions than he could remember. But gazing around the room that night, Nate felt it was the first time he'd really looked at the place, the first time he'd really taken it in.

On the table at the end of the couch was a picture frame. He'd seen it before, but had he ever paid it any real attention? The corners were chipped and the photograph inside was an old Polaroid—square and bordered in white, the colors and images gently fading with time. Nate had a million of them at his own apartment. Everyone his age had a box of them somewhere—refugees from the days before digital, when photographs were something you actually had printed. You kept them handy for a while, maybe even filled an album or two, but eventually they were consigned to the dusty box.

The photograph in the frame was Nate's mother dressed in a simple orange summer dress with a matching band in her hair—it was unmistakably '70s. She was smiling, holding a cigarette high in her left hand and leaning against a railing. There were no other reference points in the photo, just the wooden railing and a bright, clear sky. Nate knew unequivocally it was the house at Vigie.

In front of him, on the wooden coffee table, was a small stack of magazines, a set of coasters, and an empty 40oz vodka bottle. To his right was the old man's La-Z-Boy, complete with the woolen blanket that had covered it for as long as Nate could remember. It was an ugly brown shade that hid its stains well, but as he stared at it he saw there was much the color couldn't mask. He had always meant to wash that damn thing. It probably reeked of his father; for years he had sat on it, drooled on it in his sleep and wrapped it around his bony shoulders during the countless times he had passed out right there on the chair.

Nate looked around the rest of the room, at the few sticks of furniture that sat there, and suddenly the simplicity, the functionality of it all struck him as entirely cold. How could he have lived like this? The furniture was tired and worn out; every piece was different, unmatched and impersonal—consignment store remnants. The drapes were there when he moved in years ago, and their once-white chiffon was now yellow with dust and age. It occurred to Nate that the whole place was rundown, just south of filthy, and furnished with nothing that offered even the slightest nod toward comfort. But when his eyes settled again on the photograph of his mother, he realized he was wrong. That was what passed for comfort here. At least in this room anyway.

"I gotta wash that thing," muttered Nate, staring at the blanket.

"Pardon me?"

The voice to his left startled him and when he twitched around he saw a small woman with sandy hair do the same thing. "Oh, sorry, I didn't…"

She recovered her composure quickly. "It's okay," she said.

"I was going to wash that blanket."

The woman nodded.

"I'm sorry. Who are you?" asked Nate.

The woman stepped forward and seated herself next to Nate on the couch. She placed her hands on his in his lap. "I'm Kathy Taylor from Victims Services." She smiled briefly, then patted his hands twice and let them go. "Can I get you some water?"

"What? No." What was the obsession these people had about getting him water?

Kathy continued unabated. "Is there anything I can do for you right now? Someone you'd like me to call, someone you'd like to be here with you?"

"No, I'm good." Nate was getting annoyed— unreasonably so, he recognized. "Why are you here, exactly?"

Kathy shifted uncomfortably and as she did so Nate was able to look past her, to the open door of his father's bedroom. Nate recognized the slippers—they were a gift to his dad last Christmas, wrapped, he remembered, by a pretty woman at the mall. They were gray and lined with sheepskin, and as he stared past the lady from Victim Services, Nate could see three inches of his father's shins protruding from them before they disappeared under his flannel pajamas.

The slippers made a wide 'V' with their heels together against the carpet, and the toes pointing up and out toward the ceiling. That was all he could see from the couch; the rest was inside the bedroom.

Just the slippers, three inches of shin and a bit of flannel pajama.

4

The question took Smiley completely off guard. Bolom. He realized he had not thought about it since he was a child himself. And on cue his mother's voice chattered away in his head from some place far in the past. *Boy, it gettin' dark out dere—you get inside dis house now before the Bolom dun take you!*

The man from overseas had surprised him. After the hour they spent at Vigie Beach, Smiley had come to the conclusion that Nate Mason was in fact just a regular fellow. Perhaps a little dark, a little doleful. But quite regular. But this was different. Still, Smiley had to admit that right from the beginning, right from that first email four months ago, he had known this journey would be a dark one for Nate. "What you know 'bout dis?" Smiley asked. It came out unexpectedly short and cold.

"Well," Nate said, and then teetered for a moment on the edge of a full explanation, a mea culpa of sorts, perhaps for Smiley's benefit, or perhaps for someone else's. "It's nothing. Fairy tales. Just some nonsense we heard about as kids is all."

Smiley eyed him guardedly as the moment between them stretched into infinity. Finally he spoke. "Dis ting—Bolom—dis perhaps not as trite as you think." His mood became suddenly serious, and the playfulness in his voice, a staple of the St. Lucian accent, departed like smoke before a stiff breeze. "Our little island has all de conveniences of de modern worl', for sure, but we are fond of our, how shall I put it, our indigenous culture. It be very well rooted here. And very real."

Smiley's tone pulled Nate from the photograph and he realized his remark had perhaps been interpreted as a slight. He backpedaled awkwardly. "Smiley, I didn't mean any offense. I was just—"

"No problem, no problem," Smiley's meaty paw came up in mock defense. He smiled, the sun shone, and the lazy waves ran up the beach in a perfect blue. "Come," he said. "You must be hungry. Le' we get some good West Indian food into you. You like accra? Fish cakes?"

Nate smiled and nodded. Accra was one of the things he remembered keenly—soft golden cakes of battered fish, deep fried and heavily spiced.

"Good, good. Hop in. We'll run down to Gros Islet. The best accra in St. Lucia."

• • •

The drive to Gros Islet, a local community just north of the capital, Castries, was short, but a virtual time capsule for Nate. They passed Choc Cemetery at the far end of Vigie Beach—a boneyard on prime beachfront real estate that Nate remembered passing (at a run, just in case), every day after school. They passed the old school itself, CCSS, a sprawling structure made of breezeblock and tin roofing, and the memories came flooding back. Gray pants, white shirts, plantain chips, and orange Fanta. He could remember the smell of the place, the sugary scent of mango in the many trees throughout the school. In summer, they would droop with heavy fruit the color of sunburns, some of it feasted upon by students, much of it left to fall and spoil beneath the trees in the sweltering heat.

He watched houses flick by, many seemingly untouched by time, still built in that open and airy style of cinderblocks set widely apart to let the Trade Winds waft through. The stray dogs still bounced along as they had in his youth, chickens still darted into the road, and the lianas and ferns still choked at telephone poles and the edges of houses, still trying to assert the rights of the island's lush botanical heritage wherever they could. There were new structures, too, glass and smooth concrete, while alongside them third-world commerce in the form of rum shacks with rusting tin roofs seemed to chide them for their opulence.

Smiley stopped the car and the two men found a table outside of a small wooden shed. Above them a hand painted sign bleached heavily by the sun said *Bozu*, and before long a stringy dog appeared and curled into a black and white circle at Nate's feet. He reached down and scratched the mongrel behind the ears, and the little dog began to murmur and groan with pure satisfaction. It made Nate smile and slip into a private memory.

In front of them three puppies climb frantically over each other, stretching their thin necks and whimpering in excitement. Cody squats down like only five-year-olds can, his hands wrapped tightly about his knees, a smile the size of the Grand Canyon splitting his face in two. He looks up at his father for approval, then reaches into the cardboard box to pet the head of the little black-and-white one. But it's too fast and begins madly licking the boy's hand. Cody dissolves into giggles and pulls his hand back.

Cody leans in and fearlessly scoops the black-and-white puppy into his arms. Its tail spins like a propeller and it licks at the boy's face, squirming to get closer. Cody giggles in delight, his shoulders bunched about his ears and his eyes shut tight.

The boy is in an entirely altered state, and Nate knows he cannot—must not—stop the moment. And as he looks on he begins to smile. *Mom is gonna kill me*, he thinks to himself, watching as Cody falls backwards onto the ground, puppy clutched tightly in his arms while it clambers, wild-tongued, over his face. *When we come through that door with a puppy, I'm as good as dead.* He smiles again. He knows she won't be upset for long; the boy and his dog will win her over quickly. She'll melt, smile and hug them all. Hopefully.

"Dat ting gone give you fleas, man," said Smiley. Nate gave the dog a final pat and let the present reclaim him, but thoughts of Cody lingered on long after the dog had loped away.

At the door of the shed a large black woman with a larger voice boomed, "Smiley, you jus' limin' or you gwan have sometin'?"

"Ah, Ma Joop, come out here, girl!" He briefly introduced Nate, and then dispatched her in patois, laughing as she went. "You'll see," he said to Nate conspiratorially, "de best accra in de West Indies."

And, true to his word, the food was incredible. Fresh, decadently rich and dripping with spice-laden oil. When they were finished eating, the two men worked at another set of Heinekens and the conversation eventually turned to the envelope Smiley had brought to their meeting at Vigie. It sat at the table's center, and Smiley pointed at it with the green bottle in his hand.

Nate raised the empty bottle to Ma Joop who was puttering about at the edge of the shed, and asked for two more. "Let me ask you something," he said to Smiley, "and I'll go over everything in the envelope tonight—but is there anything else you've dug up that's not in print? I mean, in my experience there's often a whole bunch more being said and felt than hits the page. You know what I mean?"

"Sure do," said Smiley nodding. "I know exactly what you sayin', and yes, there be more. But man, it's goin' take a few more of these," he said, taking a bottle from Ma Joop's tray.

Above them the sun arced its way across the sky and made a run for the horizon to the west. In an hour it would be dusk, and with that dusk would come fruit bats by the thousand, screeching in delight as they gorged themselves, sweeping in enormous windblown sheets of black above the tree line. In the all-inclusive hotels, at the swim-up bars and al fresco mezzanines, pink-skinned tourists would be sipping umbrella-laden drinks and watching for the million dollar sunset. But here, on the side of a well potholed road in a part of the island that tourists never saw, the sunset only darkened Smiley's already somber tale.

• • •

Smiley peeled the label off the Heineken and laid it with the others. The sun had set now, and the two men were alone at the rickety table at Bozu—save the impressive collection of moths that swarmed the naked bulb above the sign. It was a warm night, but a breeze gently fanned the coconut trees and their fronds rustled in approval. Smiley went on. "The De Villiers are a prominent family on de island.

Always have been. But on de day dat boy died, their family…well, dey lost two. His mother, Collette De Villiers, she never recovered from it. She blamed her brother-in-law, Vincent, who owned the plantation at the time."

"You mean Ti Fenwe Estate?"

"Yes, Ti Fenwe. It still in de family today. Anyway, she nearly tore de place apart for the two weeks it took to find the body. She had great influence at the CID."

"CID?" asked Nate.

"The Criminal Investigation Division. De task force within the police department responsible for dis kind of investigation."

Nate nodded, and something in his memory squirmed.

"Anyway, de De Villiers had most of de police force up there day and night, combing through the rainforest, looking. And eventually dey found him, or at least what was left of him. Two weeks will almost completely destroy a body in de tropics—never mind de animals and de other things.

"When de CID found de remains, Mrs. De Villiers insisted on coming out to Ti Fenwe, and it was in the middle of the night, too, but she was determined to see her son. De constables tried to stop her, I mean, dat body in a very advanced state of decomposition an' had been partially consumed. But don't no one say *no* to a De Villiers.

"And so Mrs. De Villiers go and see her son, or what was lef' of him, and me think she simply could not bear it. She'd been looking for dat boy all these weeks, her little boy with blonde hair—and what she found was a nightmare." Smiley shook his head in reflection, and then tipped the bottle to his lips.

Behind him, dotted on the hillside, lights began to flicker to life in the small houses made of wood and tin. "In her grief she apparently swore she would take revenge if she found someone had caused her little boy's death. Here," he said, pulling a photocopy from the document pile on the table and passing it to Nate. It was a copy of the front page of *The Voice* from 1976, with the bold headline: *I Will Take a Life in Payment.* It also had a small, grainy picture of Collette De Villiers. It was a posed shot from another time, and in it she was calm and composed. It seemed to jar with the headline. Nate was transfixed by the words. It felt like Collette was speaking out directly to him across the years. Finally he placed the sheet down, and without realizing it Nate gently brushed his hand against his hip, as if to dislodge something unwelcome that had stuck there.

Smiley hooked a finger into his collar and tugged at it gently, then went on. "Dey sedated her, took her back to Castries an' she was hospitalized dat night. After dat she was jus' plain inconsolable. According to daughters of one of their housekeepers from back den, Mrs. De Villiers began walking the house in a constant state of panic, calling out for Richard. This went on for days, weeks. In the end the family flew her out to de US, to some clinic where she dun stayed for 'bout a month. When she come back dey said she was a ghost. She would never speak. Never cry. Barely eat. What was it dem said? She was like a blank page."

"And the rest of the family?"

"Dey took it hard, too. And there was a bad patch for dem after that. They were caught up in *désann asou pwi*—you know, like um, a price slide. Nutmeg, copra, bananas—it affected a number of the staples of their export business, and I think de family's net worth really shrunk. Many De Villiers properties around de island were sold off, a few of their smaller businesses closed, as well as a couple of de big ones—a banana plantation in the south near Vieux Fort, and the Slips."

"Slips?"

"Dry docks. You know, where you can pull your boat out de water for repairs to de underside. It was good business for De Villiers because their slips were de only ones in the Windward Islands large enough to pull out the expensive pleasure craft that sailed 'round here. Apart from DV Dry Docks, the next closest were six hundred kilometers away in St. Kitts. So they commanded top dollar for services."

"So why'd they get rid of it?"

"Hmm. Cash flow, perhaps. Maybe somethin' else. All up, things went from bad to worse for de family, and in…" he paused and reached for the envelope between them and fished out a single sheet. "Ah, here it is. In December of 1977, Mrs. De Villiers killed herself."

Nate did not know this, and the news stopped him cold. The information was more than thirty years old, but it struck him like breaking news hot off the press. It made him feel small and awash with well-aged guilt. "I had no idea." In his mind he saw endless bouquets of yellow flowers, candles in brass holders and rows of dark wooden pews. The images were borrowed from other funerals, and brought with them a sadness he recognized all too well.

"Yeah man, it was a bad time for de De Villiers for sure. She lef' behind a husband, but him now loss both a son an' a wife. He a shell of a man today. Never recovered himself."

Smiley's words landed like medicine balls on Nate. Was this really possible? Could so much destruction come from that one foul moment in the forest? And the echoes had rung out across oceans, across time, and were drawing parallels that were almost too much to bear. He could feel the sadness coming back, unfurling inside him in dark canvas sheets that would blot out the light.

This nightmare for the De Villiers clan and the lengthy reach of an event thirty years in the past and on the other side of the world. Lives were still collapsing. And all he could think about was Cody. Smiling, beautiful Cody. For Nate, the pain was suddenly as sharp and as present as it had ever been.

Smiley was still staring at the page in his hands, unaware of the effect it was all having on Nate. He went on. "How so many bad things can come in such a string, one after de other—it make a man wonder."

"Makes you wonder what?" he asked gently.

Smiley arched his back and a series of small pops rippled through his spine. "Man, how long we been sittin' here?" He reached up to his neck and loosened the tie, then pulled it free in a single motion. "Back at Vigie, you asked me about de Bolom. You called it, a kid's tale?"

"A fairy tale," said Nate sheepishly.

"Right, a fairy tale. Well, tell me what you remember 'bout this fairy tale. From when you were a boy here on dis island. When did you leave here?"

"1976."

"Okay, tell me what de boy from 1976 remember 'bout dis Bolom."

Bolom. The word had such a powerful effect on Nate, something that he would forever associate with the island and the deep reaches of the forested interior. He thought about what he should tell Smiley, and wondered whether the telling of it would demean him in Smiley's eyes and reveal him as just another gullible *vwayaje*, here for a week of sun and then gone. And if he did think that, would it matter?

Bolom. Nate rolled the word through his head like a child fumbling with a marble set deeply in his pocket. The word had the usual effect, and within seconds he began to hear it. It evoked two sounds: one setting a hollow background note in the darkness, and the other, laid over it sharply, a staccato of intense and hurried footfalls from something solid, soft-footed and wild. He knew exactly what the first sound was—he'd seen it himself as a boy: hundreds of thousands of nutmegs, all wrinkled and hard like dried walnuts, laying in a sprawling, empty old attic on hard, wooden floor boards. Through them runs something unseen in the darkness. It is short, quick, and stocky, and while the sound of its footsteps are soft, presumably unshod, they land firmly. Almost arrogantly. And as it darts through the nutmegs they begin to roll, rattling along the wooden flooring in their thousands, sending up that singular note: an empty, soulless drone.

And as it scurries through the attic, the nutmegs roll and roll and roll.

5

Island life for the expats was good. Very good.

Nate's mother came through from the kitchen carrying a tin tray crammed with Piña Coladas. She wore a bright orange floral print dress with a matching band in her hair, and swept a wayward lock from her face. "Refills!" she announced, and the crowd in the sprawling balcony area of her home rose with smiles and hurrahs from white wicker furniture, through a haze of blue tobacco smoke, to collect the icy drinks.

The evening was humid, but the house was situated on the tip of Vigie, a headland that jutted out into the Caribbean and caught the cooling breezes that once propelled great Galleons and Men of War through the azure waters that the house now watched over. There were about thirty guests at the party: teachers, socialites, barristers and politicians. Bellbottom pants, space age polyester in brave plaid patterns, afro shirts, and wide swept collars—all were in goodly supply. On the record player, the Carpenters cranked out a fresh hit and told everyone they were *On Top of the World* and *Looking Down on Creation*, and indeed creation seemed to be listening.

Moths fluttered in their thousands around Chinese lanterns, those rice paper lampshades that hung like glowing planets in every room, and in the darkness around the house a chorus of a million insects, frogs and toads kept rhythms of their own. Between the *peep-peep* of fruit bats, the chirping and clicking of umpteen yet-to-be discovered genera of insects, between the laughter, the sound of crushed ice and swizzle sticks and the spinning '70s vinyl, the St. Lucian nights were thick and brimming with life.

The kids darted in and out of the large balcony area, artfully breezing through the crowd of glowing guests, sneaking off with cans of beer and half-finished glasses of rum and Coke. They were barely noticed, and when they were, it was with a pat on the head in mid-conversation and nothing more. Talk among the grown-ups was of the QE2 visit set for the following week: who would be invited aboard, what dignitaries might hold a reception, and whether such rarities as potatoes, white sugar and fresh milk might surreptitiously find their way off the boat and into expat homes.

Between forays into the party to raid for booze, peanuts, and the ultimate prize, Bugels (crunchy, cone-shaped treats that Nate's dad had flown in specially), the boys watched from the sidelines as they always did. Their spot was perfect: they sat in lawn chairs in the garden just beyond the circle of light cast by the house, and to anyone who looked their way, they were little more than shadows. The parties were every weekend, rotating from one expat's house to the next, but Nate's parents held more than their fair share—thanks to the ideal entertaining qualities of the house on Vigie.

It was in a well-to-do part of the island, and the neighbors were people of influence. Behind them lived a judge. To their left, through the trees and hidden by gangly knots of hibiscus bushes down toward the water, was the Dutch ambassador. And behind him were four houses belonging to various members of the De Villiers family. All the houses in Vigie were well spaced, set on large plots of land and set among lush thickets of ever-blooming flowers and sweet-smelling fruit trees.

The house was not the one originally issued by the government to the Masons, but Nate's dad was well liked and well connected, and the right set of moves—and perhaps a few hundred well-placed EC dollars—saw the family ensconced in the beautiful house on Vigie.

It was built on the site of a gun battery dating back to the 1800s, and the house itself was basically two large blocks—the bedrooms and the living room/kitchen area—set on a huge reach of polished flooring, then covered with an expansive roof. The structure was cut into the natural grade in the land as it sloped down toward the point, with the front of the house sitting up well above the grade to catch the sunsets. The net effect was that the house appeared to be one huge balcony, surrounded by polished teak banisters, and open to cooling breezes and breathtaking views.

The lawn at the front of the house was dotted with coconut and mango trees, and came to a point a hundred yards further on where the Vigie headland ended and dropped off into the sea thirty feet below. From this vantage point, gunners of old could defend access to the harbor in Castries, lobbing cannon balls and musket fire on potential invaders. Now, all that was left was a cavernous gray concrete bunker, overgrown and filled with spiders and bulbous red hornets the boys called Jap Spaniards. Set back from that, toward the house on the flat, open lawn, was a huge circular pad of concrete where the big canon once sat. It was empty now, the gun long since removed, the only lingering threat now from lizards stalking their insect prey.

The boys sat on the lawn chairs at the edge of the concrete pad, watching the party from the shadows. Nate put an elbow into Pip, and pointed at the bowl his mother had just set down among the guests. It was Bugels.

"Oh, we have to get some of those!" said Pip, holding a half empty tin of beer. He didn't like the taste—none of them did—but still they each held a tin, and occasionally made the gesture of lifting it to their mouths.

"We've got no chance now," said Nate, flicking his chin toward the large, sweaty man scooching forward in his seat and dipping his fist into the Bugels.

"Aw, man," said Pip. "I love those things."

Nate put up his hands to calm the little Dutch boy. "Wait," he said. "Here comes Mrs. Patterson." There was music in his voice.

Mrs. Patterson was the kind of woman all the boys dreamed of. She was in her early thirties, heavy chested and always without a bra. She was the stuff of fantasy, commanding awestruck stares from all the boys. But her power was not limited to the boys alone; Nate noticed that she had an effect on all the party regulars—women, too. As she wandered back into the group he knew the odds of snagging a few Bugels were greatly improving. "Her drink's on the guardrail on the other side of where everyone's sitting. When she goes to get it, you go, Pip."

And, sure to form, all eyes followed Mrs. Patterson and her pendulous breasts. Without a word, Pip was up and running, and Nate watched as the small boy slipped quietly in and took not just a handful, but the whole damn bowl. At the guardrail, Mrs. Patterson leaned with her back against the teak, her hands pressed palm-first into the top of the railing. The effect was to push her elbows out past the line of her back, tightening the thin, white fabric of her blouse against her large, unrestrained breasts. Pip could have turned a cartwheel while stealing the Bugels and no one would have noticed. Mrs. Patterson, or more accurately, Mrs. Patterson's boobs, were mesmerizing.

"*Tete en pain!* Now that's a pair of tits!"

Nate and Pip almost shrieked at the voice behind them in the darkness. It was Tristan, of course, and he had already drunk one of the beers the boys had liberated from the party and was in the process of finishing the second. Once he had recovered, Pip thrust the Bugels in front of Tristan without question, an offering, really, and the big thirteen-year-old mashed his fist into the bowl. Nate scrunched his face up. "Come on Tristan, quit it. Those things are like gold."

Born on the island, Tristan was a white St. Lucian. He was descended from generations of French landowners stretching back to the days of buccaneers and tall ships bristling with cannons as the English and French fought for control of this sparkling Caribbean jewel. His family, and others like them, had become the island's wealthy, owning huge plantations that grew bananas, nutmeg, coconuts, and dozens of other crops—just as they had for hundreds of years. His life was one of privilege, although to look at him in his cut-off jeans and sleeveless top, you'd assume he came from much poorer means. "Why do you guys love these things?" he said, emptying a crushed handful into his mouth. "Salty fuckers." Tristan took the bowl and ate another handful. Pip reached for some and

Tristan simply waved him away.

Even at night, Tristan wore no shoes, and Nate could see in the half-light that the soles of his feet were black and cracked, hard as shoe leather. He watched as Tristan assumed possession of Pip's lawn chair, and felt a small prick of annoyance at the way the little Dutch boy squatted dutifully beside him. Pip was a genuinely nice kid, and being Nate's neighbor the two had struck up an easy friendship. But it was different whenever Tristan was around; Pip's personality seemed to shrink in Tristan's shadow, and Tristan knew it, too.

Still, like all the other kids, Nate acknowledged that Tristan had something that none of the others had. There was no name for it at their age, but they all recognized it, and fell in line behind Tristan whenever he was around. It was that way for all the kids. Well, almost all.

"Tristan, give the *garçon* his crisps," came yet another voice from the darkness. This time all three boys jumped and at least two of them yelped—loud enough to draw a handful of quizzical glances from the party.

Richard stepped into the light and laughed. He was the youngest of the group, and all the boys smiled when they saw it was him.

"Richard, you doofus!"

"Jeez—you almost killed us!"

The undersized blonde ten-year-old smiled brightly and shook his head. "You're a tough bunch." He looked at Tristan and then flicked his eyes only briefly at the bowl. It was enough. Tristan sucked air in through clenched teeth to produce a brief squeaking sound—an iconic island gesture of displeasure called *chups*—and then roughly pushed the bowl into Pip's hands.

Nate felt a pang of satisfaction but let it go as quickly as it came. Tristan could be an ass sometimes, but he was still an okay guy. And he always had interesting things on the go. Nate looked at him and noticed the boy was wearing a homemade slingshot around his neck: the Y of a branch, a leather pouch and two rubber strips cut from an inner tube. And when Tristan noticed Nate looking, he casually swung it over his shoulder so that it dangled out of view behind his back. Nate pretended not to care, but what he really wanted was to hold it, maybe even try it out.

"What took you guys so long?" said Nate dismissively. "The party's half over."

Tristan was watching Mrs. Patterson, his eyes locked on her while he spoke. "Maria's having a sleepover. We had some watching to do first." A moment later Tristan and Richard dissolved into a fit of half-stifled giggles.

Nate raised his eyebrows. "You guys were spying on your own sister?"

Tristan objected. "Hey, it's Richard's sister—she's just my cousin."

"Oh, that's so much better," said Nate.

"You're both perverts," said Pip. And then, "What did you see?"

"Smokes," said Tristan.

Pip's face folded in confusion until he realized Tristan was watching the party again, and a box of cigarettes in particular. They belonged to Sweaty Scoocher, and sat on a side table at the very periphery of the party, not far from the shadows hiding the boys.

Nate threw up his hands. "Don't do it, Tristan. My mom will freak if she catches you stealing. She'll call your Dad for sure."

"Ooh! Gonna tell your mama!" Richard teased. Pip laughed, and on some level he knew, as did the others, it would have the desired effect. Everyone wanted Tristan to do it. Even Nate.

Tristan stood and rubbed his hands together. "Is there anything you guys aren't scared of? *Jenn fi.*"

Richard, as usual, obliged with a translation. "He called you little girls."

Nate and Pip played it up and giggled like schoolgirls, but they got nothing more from Tristan.

He was making his move.

6

Smiley sat patiently while Nate wrestled with the question.

It would be easy for Nate to just tell him what he knew about the Bolom—what he'd heard, what he'd read in the years since he left the island, and what he knew from firsthand experience. It was simple, really. It was nothing more than just a series of statements about what Nate believed—knew, as a child—to be true. But the thought of even the smallest detail added yet another, and then another. And before he'd finished drawing a single breath, that simple series of statements had taken on so much more substance, so many more layers, like the base of a snowman rolled across a long stretch of perfect packing snow.

"Ma Joop!" called Smiley over his shoulder. In the rickety building, the large woman who had served accra and beer peered around the door jamb. "Ma Joop, we need more beer here, please!"

Nate looked over to the woman and took her in for the first time. He had seen her a few hours ago when they first met, of course, but he'd merely said hello, eager to get back to what Smiley had to say. But now, in the blush of a half dozen cold Heinekens, and while Smiley joked with her and laughed out loud, he took his first real look.

Ma Joop was a woman of generous proportions. She was probably in her late forties, and moved in practiced, deliberate ways, as if each move cost her greatly. Her hips were wide and as Nate watched, it became clear that she was favoring one leg. While she bore no evidence of it on her face, Nate was sure she was enduring pain of some sort hidden beneath her skirts and smiles. But despite her size and weight, her real defining factor was her booming voice, with which she exchanged easy and natural remarks in Creole with Smiley.

Temporarily outside of the conversation, Nate focused his attention on the envelope sitting among the empty beer bottles. He turned it so the opening faced him, pulled out a small handful of papers and laid them on his lap. The very first one stopped him cold.

It was an obituary, cut from the local paper, announcing the untimely passing of Tristan De Villiers.

Nate sat back heavily in the chair and scratched at his chin stubble; it never occurred to him that Tristan might not be alive all these years later. But did it matter? He wasn't sure, but there was a new and sudden hollowness there. First Richard, then Collette, and now Tristan, too? It seemed that over the years the De Villiers family had been decimated. He looked up for Smiley, but the man was still deeply ensnared in laughter with Ma Joop. There were a thousand new questions Nate wanted to ask, but they would have to wait.

He dipped his head and read the obituary again, searching for details but finding scant few. It merely said that there would be a closed service for immediate family only. The obituary was dated at the top; it had run just over three years ago. Certainly coming back here wasn't about confronting Tristan—that was never the plan—but now that he was gone, Nate sensed that something within him would remain forever unresolved. Maybe he *had* expected to see him. It wasn't part of the plan, but he admitted it was something he might have been secretly relishing.

Something in the tone of the conversation happening around him shifted suddenly, like a brief jolt of turbulence at thirty thousand feet, and snapped him back. He looked up to a strange and uncomfortable pause in the conversation between Smiley and Ma Joop.

When the dialogue resumed a moment later, Nate thought he recognized a single word among the string of Creole consonants and vowels that Smiley was issuing. He saw an immediate change in Ma Joop. She broke from the conversation and stood suddenly upright, placing her hands against the top of her buttock at her back. "Come again?" she said in clear English.

Smiley's reaction was both telling and instantaneous: no matter the language, his face was that of a man who had crossed an invisible line and either had, or had come very close, to offending a woman—a woman of whom he was at least a little bit frightened. His first defense was to wave his hands in that dismissive way designed to minimize the preceding comments, but Ma Joop was having none of it. She chattered back at him sharply, and the inflection at the end of her Creole torrent told Nate it was a question—one delivered in the form of a demand.

Smiley's posture changed instantly. He became apologetic, diffusive, and while the string of words was lost on Nate, the man's tone and actions said volumes. Smiley's smile was gone, and he was now a picture of contrition, his pitch repentant and at the edge of pleading. The word popped through again, the one that seemed to have changed the entire conversation for Ma Joop, and this time Nate was convinced he had heard it clearly: *Bolom*. It was Ma Joop who said it this time, and as she did she cut a single and searing glance at Nate. It was venomous, and her eyes burned with anger.

When at last she spoke, it was in an eerily calm and quiet tone, and in English, perhaps for Nate's benefit. "Don't fuck aroun' wit dis," was all she said.

She then turned, smiled briefly at Nate, and moved off in that deliberate and unhurried way that was all her own. When she had disappeared inside, Nate let out an almost inaudible whistle. "Whoa. What was all that about?"

Instead of explaining Smiley said simply "You mus' be tired. I think it time I took you back." It was a definitive moment; the evening was over.

An hour later, Nate lay on the bed in his room at the Breadfruit Tree Inn, watching as the ceiling fan turned in lazy, ineffectual arcs. It was out of balance and the whole hub moved as the blades turned. There was no off switch to the thing, and no speed control that he could see; it was perpetually in motion, a repetitive, looping circle with no chance of stability.

He glanced at the envelope, and at the corner of a photograph peeking out. He reached down and pulled it out slowly—just enough until he could see that it was indeed the photograph of Richard, and then he pushed it back in. But it was enough. The thoughts began tumbling in: first it was Richard and Pip and the dense green of the forest, but then it was Cody.

The memory was Cody as a one-year-old, all warm and bundled in a soft yellow sleeper, and sleeping the impossibly peaceful sleep only afforded to infants. Cody was perfect in that moment, as he was in all Nate's moments. But there was a pattern here, and the memory would be followed, as it always was, by a crushing reality.

He tried to steel himself against it, but there was no use. Nate knew exactly what was coming next. In his mind's eye Cody was six, and their faces were pressed closely together, nose to nose. He could smell Cody's breath, his hair, the scent of his clothes. And his perfect boy asked the question again, as he always did, in that innocent voice still untouched by the horrors of the world: *Will I be okay, Daddy?*

Fully clothed, Nate reached under the lampshade beside his bed and snapped off the light, rolled onto his side and drew his knees up tight. And then, like so many times before in the quietness of a day's end, he began to cry.

7

Kathy swivelled her gaze to follow Nate's and saw the feet—the slippers—through the bedroom door. She turned back and shifted slightly, obstructing Nate's line of sight. "I know this is a very difficult time for you, Mr. Mason…"

Nate looked away from the room and into Kathy's eyes. "You can call me Nate," he said flatly. He was so tired. Not just sleepy, but body tired. Life tired.

"Have the officers spoken with you yet?"

"No—just the guy who said to sit tight."

"All right. If you'd like, I can explain the process from here on in."

"The process?"

"Yes—this can be overwhelming."

Nate nodded. He knew all about overwhelming.

"An officer, or maybe a detective will want to sit and ask you some questions," continued Kathy. "They'll get you to make a statement if you're up to it, but you don't have to right now if you don't want to."

"That's fine. That's okay," said Nate, looking again at the La-Z-Boy. That blanket. That goddamn blanket really needed to be washed.

"…and there will be some men here to collect your father. They'll bring a gurney in, and they'll take him to…"

Nate stood and walked over to the La-Z-Boy, gathered the blanket and put it to his nose. It smelled stale and dusty, with a sharp edge of something long since spilled and dried. And it smelled of his father.

"Mr. Mason?"

"I gotta wash this," he said quietly, heading for the kitchen.

Kathy followed, but didn't try to stop him. "Are you sure there's no one I can call to come and be with you?"

Nate stopped and the unreasonable agitation swept over him again. She was there to help, he knew. She was there to bridge the gap between law enforcement and family, and in all fairness she was doing a pretty damn decent job. And so when he turned and snapped at her he knew she didn't deserve it. "I already told you, there's no one!"

Kathy nodded calmly. "I understand."

"Everything okay here?" asked the policeman from before, edging his head around the kitchen wall.

"We're fine," said Kathy.

Nate turned away and shoved the blanket into the small stacked washer/dryer in the corner, and busied himself figuring out how to turn it on.

"Sir, I need to ask you not to do that just now," said the officer. He spoke in calm, almost apologetic tones. "Just not until the detectives have had a chance to check everything out. It's just routine, but they'll want to talk to you."

Something in that reached back into Nate's own experience and echoed through him like a ghost in a far off canyon. *They'll want to talk to you.* It bounced hollowly around inside him, and then finally landed home: policemen in pressed uniforms, bright lights and ceiling fans, parents with pinched, frightened faces anxiously imploring him to tell, tell, tell. For a brief moment he could almost feel the heat of the room, taste the moisture in the tropical air, and hear the anxious thud of his almost-thirteen-year-old heart.

"Sir? Could I ask you to leave the blanket be?" repeated the officer.

Nate let the present reclaim him. He seemed almost surprised to be standing there, looking down into the machine with the old brown blanket sitting inside. "Sure, sure," he said, almost silently.

Nate went back to the couch, flanked by Kathy from VS and

the police officer, and sat quietly, thinking about his father, thinking about how tired and worn down he felt. *This might all be too much*, he thought. *It might all be too much, too soon.* He knew he hadn't processed it yet, not really, and he knew from experience that that would come later.

He closed his eyes for a moment and felt everything sag. Sleep was there if he wanted it. There were men at the door now, talking. He didn't care. Nate kept his eyes closed and leaned back into the sofa. It was old and sprung, and sucked him in deeply. He felt himself going.

The screen door banged and a voice cut through: "You gotta be fucking kidding me... Sarge, come here."

Nate could hear it, but he was too tired, too close to sleep. He let his eyes stay closed.

The same voice: "Sarge, it's that guy again."

Then another voice, quieter this time, as if trying not to be heard: "Oh shit," said the second voice. "You're right. It's that same poor bastard..."

• • •

Nate's dreams were alive with images. He found himself at the foot of a set of old concrete steps leading up to a sprawling and dilapidated plantation house. It was set among a thick and encroaching jungle, and the sun broke through occasionally in great shafts of softened yellow. He could see windows high above in the wooden structure set atop a great concrete foundation of arches, each yawning with darkness in the spans between the uprights. Some of the windows were sealed and closed, some partially covered with old wooden shutters, worn and peeling and hanging at tenuously odd angles, while others were vacant and hollow like dead, black eyes. There was peeling paint along the wooden boards, warping sills and rusting sheets of corrugated sheet metal streaked in red, and all around a sense of bleakness and senescence.

And with it all went an unexplained sense of threat, something hovering just out of view, and as Nate roused from his troubling dream the sense of unease stayed with him. Was it the house in the dream? Was it the sense of decay that hung on everything in it? Or was it the figure standing silently at the foot of his bed in the dark?

The sight at the foot of Nate's bed was too impossible, too outlandish for his brain to accept. And so where there should have been fear, there was only confusion. He blinked heavily and struggled to understand what he was seeing. The room was dark, lit only by the glow of the street lamps in Derek Walcott Square, and filtered again by the chiffon drapes at the window's edge. Where it did fall into the room, the light pooled at the foot of the bed in a soft, diffused shimmer, backlighting the figure of a large man. He was bathed in perfect black on a background of *almost* black, and the effect on Nate's eyes was an illusion where the silhouette appeared and disappeared with every blink and twist of his head.

Finally the figure moved, just a tiny adjustment of balance, but enough for Nate's brain to solve the puzzle. The figure came into sharp and sudden focus, and an instant later Nate's conscious mind understood the gravity of the situation. The shadow raised its left arm, and light from the Square glinted once across a broad blade in its hand; it was the trigger Nate needed to move.

He lurched left on the bed, rolling once across the floral bedspread, just in time to hear a heavy grunt from the intruder and the muted *thwap* of something driven hard into the bedding.

"Help!" shrieked Nate as he struggled to find his feet at the side of the bed. "Help!" His hands went instinctively to the bedside table for something to defend himself with, and he launched the first thing he touched at the shadow with as much force as he could muster. The clock radio missed the target but forced the man to duck, buying Nate a precious few seconds to reload. Next he threw the lamp, but the cord pulled taut in mid-air and pulled the lamp up short, as if striking an invisible force field around his assailant. It fell vainly onto the bed and Nate shrieked again, this time something less comprehensible, more primal—it was half yell, half scream.

In the light from the window he saw the blade flash again,

long and broad like a swashbuckler's cutlass, and the figure made a sudden move around the edge of the bed toward Nate. Like a kid at a sleepover, Nate bounded over the bed, scampering across the sheets with an agility that he'd not seen in himself in years. The bed jarred suddenly and the man with the blade grunted as his knee drove solidly into the steel frame. It took the air out of his advance. The figure paused, uncertain and undecided, until he suddenly turned and bolted to the door. He heaved it open and darted through it in one motion, and ran headlong into the door on the opposite side of the corridor. He recovered quickly, and was out of sight in seconds.

Nate stood stunned in the shadows. He stared at the open door, and his eyes were drawn to the green glow of the clock radio sitting against the wall near the closet. Miraculously it was still showing the time—3:37 in the morning—and Nate could not understand why no one had come to see what was going on in his room. Surely they would have heard his cries for help? Someone would have called the front desk, even if they didn't want to come out and see what bloody murder was being committed themselves.

At last he moved to the door, the light from the hotel corridor pouring into his room and painting a perfect rectangle of light on the floor. At the opening he paused, half expecting the intruder to be waiting in the hall, then cautiously he pushed his head through.

The blow hit him hard in the chest, drove him back into the room and sent him sprawling onto the floor. The man followed through with his full weight and landed squarely on top of Nate.

Nate screamed, but nothing came out; there was no air in his lungs. He thrashed as best he could, but the intruder was large and powerful, and soon Nate was almost entirely immobilized by his attacker. Understanding that it was hopeless, Nate stopped moving and looked, for the first time, at the man who was clearly going to kill him.

The man from the shadows was dressed entirely in black, his face covered with a balaclava that left enough skin around his eyes and mouth for Nate to tell only that he was black. By the force of the man's grip and the solidness of the flesh Nate could feel under his hands, he could tell that the man was well muscled and athletically toned. The man was breathing hard, and brought his face down close to Nate's. He looked directly into Nate's eyes, and watched as Nate struggled for breath like a newly landed fish. The big man then dropped his head lower still, and Nate could smell the sweetness of rum on his breath as he whispered almost silently into Nate's ear. "*Sòti la!*" he said, and then he raised something in front of Nate's face. Nate's mind raced with panic, terrified of the heavy blade that the man had tried to kill him with earlier, but as his eyes focused, he saw something else.

The thing held in front of his face was some kind of animal part. At one end, the skin and bone was sliced through neatly—the action of a sharp blade, no doubt. But, where the cut ended, the skin was partially torn, as if sheer brawn had finished the job that the blade had started. Beneath the flap of skin white bone shone through, and something dripped off it and spattered on Nate's forehead. He blinked wildly, and focused again on the object, and saw that at the other end, about eight inches from the cut, was a large cloven hoof. It was too broad and thick for a goat; a cow or bull seemed more likely. It spattered again on Nate and the floor around his head, and once again the man on top of him whispered, "*Sòti la! Go now!*"

Nate knew this was when he would die. The man stood up, towering over him, with a severed bloody hoof in one hand and a large cutlass in the other. He reached down and put the tip of the blade on Nate's chin.

Nate closed his eyes; he didn't want to see the end coming.

8

Tristan never got the cigarettes. At least, not for keeps.

He made it to the edge of the party, out of the shadow and into the booze-hazy penumbra inhabited by the guests. He watched carefully as Mrs. Patterson leaned on the back of her husband's chair. As she did her breasts fell forward and hung down in great looping arcs, and the wide neck of her blouse spilled invitingly open. Every man at the party looked over to see. Tristan knew that was the moment, and he reached from behind the wicker sofa and took the cigarettes in a smooth silent motion, then set off back into the shadows.

"Tristan De Villiers! Stop right this instant!" Nate's mom had delivered a commandment, not a request, and Tristan could do nothing but comply. He stood rooted to the spot, his back to the party, dropped his head, and cursed under his breath. In the shadows, the other boys froze in horror, and despite the fact that they knew they were all but invisible to the party-goers, they understood that Tristan's infraction was something for which they all might pay a price.

"Nathan! Are you back there? I said, *Are you back there?* Nathan Alexander Mason come out here right this instant!"

And so Nate, too, dropped his head, and walked zombie-like into the light. Behind him he heard a stifled giggle, and knew that Richard and Pip were already headed for the hibiscus bushes and relative safety. It would be Tristan and Nate alone on this one.

The two boys were called to the edge of the party, which had virtually stopped save the Steve Miller Band and their advice to *Take the Money and Run*, and they were forced to stand guiltily in front of the guests. Tristan, true to form, stood with his chin defiant, eyeballing the guests and radiating contempt. Every one of them caught a look from him. Everyone except Mrs. Mason, of course. Nate, on the other hand, studied the grass at his feet, and could feel the crimson creeping up through his face.

"Just what do you think you're up to, young man?" asked Nate's mother with her balled fists pressed firmly into her sides. She was talking to Nate, but the scolding was designed for two. "Since when is thieving acceptable behavior?"

All the guests were watching now, many with expressions of amusement hiding behind feigned adult concern. "Come on now, Patty. The boys are just having a bit of fun. No harm no foul." Oddly enough it was Sweaty Scoocher who had come to their defense, but his protest was short-lived once he took a sharp glance from Patty Mason.

"David, I'll thank you to keep your nose out of this," she said, and the gallery of gently glazed guests let out a collective *ooh*. It was enough to break the tension and finally Mrs. Mason cracked a smile and shook her head. "Tristan, you get on home. And you'll be lucky if I don't call your father in the morning."

And then she turned to Nate. "And as for you, young man, march yourself inside and into bed. We'll discuss this tomorrow." Nate looked up and caught his father, to the right of the group, beer in hand, looking at his son with a bemused expression on his face. He knew that later, when the moment was right, his dad would come in, smile and tell him everything was okay. He had the power to do that, and with a few kind words everything would be made just fine again. Nate would suck it up for now, take the heat, and wait for his father.

An hour later, Nate, lying on top of his sheets watching geckos stalk their prey on the high bedroom walls, tried hard to ignore the antics at his window. All three of them were there—Tristan, Pip and Richard—ducking down low and popping their heads up and doing anything that came to their minds by way of getting a reaction from Nate. It was a silent pantomime conducted through the wrought iron burglar-bars.

"Can't you guys see I'm in enough trouble already?" He was whispering as loudly as he dared, but in truth there was no way the partygoers on the other side of the house could hear a thing. "Jeez, if my mom finds you out there she'll kill me—and you guys, too."

Tristan scoffed. "Come on, you big baby. You're free and clear now. You're busted and jailed—everyone's forgotten about you. Come on. Come on out. We'll go spy on old Judge Harding."

"No way, guys. I'm staying put."

Tristan pressed on. "Come *oooon!*"

"Naw. I can't."

"Pussy."

"Screw you, Tristan."

And then Richard chimed in from the windowsill. All Nate could see of him was his eyes, a tuft of blonde hair and a set of fingers on either side. "Leave the guy alone, Tristan. He doesn't have to come if he doesn't want to." Richard's eyes flicked up and over to Tristan's, and the reaction was instantaneous.

Tristan reached out and clipped Richard at the back of his head with an open hand, hard enough to make Richard's head pitch forward and hit the window sill with his mouth. Tristan laughed and Richard's head sunk below the sill. In the background, Pip took a step away from the action.

Nate watched the exchange and, inside his head, called Tristan an ass. He would do something about that one of these days. He would do something about the way Tristan always treated Richard.

Just not today.

• • •

The voice was somehow familiar, Nate knew, but that wasn't enough to pull him from the edge, away from the promise of heavy, dark sleep that offered an escape from all this—from everything. It was the tone in the voice that opened his eyes.

At the door he saw two officers; the one who had been there

earlier and another—a large man with an unruly mustache and a spray of sweat about his forehead. He wore sergeant stripes on the sleeve of his blue police uniform, and he held his hat in both hands the way people do at funerals. It took Nate a moment to place him, and then he remembered.

Sergeant Cole walked slowly into the room and sat on the coffee table in front of Nate. It was a solid piece of furniture but still creaked under the weight of the big man. His holstered gun made a dull *thunk* against the table top, and the officer wiped at the perspiration on his forehead. "Mr. Mason…" He spoke softly, as if to a child. "Do you remember me?"

Nate looked at the man and somewhere inside a dam began to fracture.

"Hello, Sergeant Cole," said Nate. A moment later he began to cry.

The big policeman placed one hand on the Nate's shoulder. "Ain't this a son of a bitch," he said quietly. "Ain't this a goddamn son of a bitch."

Kathy looked on, puzzled, but calm. She produced a tissue, almost magically, and handed it to Nate.

"Thanks," he muttered, taking a deep, steadying breath. He knew the loss of his father would shake him, but this reaction— these tears and the sudden emptiness inside him—that was all tied to the sudden appearance of Sergeant Cole.

Cole took a long breath and began. "The officer there," he said, pointing at the policeman by the door. "He tells me you found your dad? Just like he is now?"

Nate nodded.

"You didn't move him at all?"

"No. Well, I covered him up. Covered his head with a towel."

Sergeant Cole nodded. "And the gun. Did you touch it?"

"No." he said hollowly.

"What about the box of papers and things? All that stuff he had around him. Did you touch any of that?"

"No," said Nate. It was a lie, but a small one. "I just came in here and called you guys."

"That's good, that's good," said Cole, putting his hand again on Nate's shoulder. "Has your dad been going through tough times lately?"

Lately? thought Nate. *Sure, if lately meant the last thirty years.* "Yes, he's been struggling for some time. He had some problems with alcohol."

"Okay. Okay." Sergeant Cole looked around the room. "And what about relationships? I gather he lived alone, but is there anyone else we need to notify? Your mother perhaps?"

Nate shook his head gently. "They're not together anymore, not for a long time."

Nate thought about that quietly. *His mother. When was the last time he'd seen her?* He couldn't remember. *Someone should probably tell her,* he thought. Nate knew it wouldn't be him.

Behind Sergeant Cole two men in overalls came through with a stretcher. Cole raised his hand and the men retreated silently from the doorway. "Those guys, they're from the Coroner's office, they're gonna take the body away when we're all done, okay?"

Nate was still thinking about his mother. "Sure. Okay," he said vacantly.

"Right. I'm going to go take care of things in there. You sit here with…"

"Kathy."

"…with Kathy, here. She'll help you with whatever you need, all right?"

"Sure. Okay," said Nate, watching the big man heave himself up from the coffee table.

The Sergeant nodded to Nate, then retrieved a small device the size of a harmonica from his breast pocket. He turned to the bedroom and brought the black digital voice recorder to his lips, speaking as he went. "Today is June twenty-seventh, the time is 6:22 pm. This is the audio log of Sergeant Eugene Cole. We are at the private residence of one Mr. David Mason at number twelve, Morningside Drive…" His voice trailed off as he rounded the corner into the bedroom, followed by the other officer.

In his mind, Nate had disappeared to a time long ago, huddled under the sheets in Cody's darkened bedroom and cuddled into a tangle of arms and legs, deep in a bedtime story. His son absolutely loved them. Nate made them up on the spot every night, and Cody would gleefully retell the stories to his mother the next morning, details and characters jumbled, but with an enthusiasm that filled every corner of Nate's heart. He remembered his wife standing at the door as he crept from the boy's room. *I can't believe how much he loves your stories, Nate.*

Really?

I don't know if you can see his face when you're telling them to him, but he's just sitting there, beaming. I mean, he adores them. He might be the only kid in the world that actually looks forward to bedtime.

It's gonna suck when he gets too old and doesn't want them anymore.

You ever thought that writing for kids might be your thing? They're great little stories, Nate. You should record them. If not for you, for Cody.

You think so?

I do, he might want them for his own kids one day. In fact, I'm going to get you boys something that will help.

And so, in time, the small digital voice recorder she bought them was added to the nightly bedtime story—which Cody officiated over, looking very serious and stern when pushing the record button. They recorded hundreds. Some were put on the family computer, and some were recorded over, being mostly just the breathy sounds of a father and his five-year-old son sleeping.

It was a warm, calming memory, and as it ended, Nate had no idea how long he had hung there.

The men from the Coroner's office were coming out of his father's room, and on their stretcher was a heavy shape zipped into a thick black plastic sack. He had expected a crisp white sheet, like in the movies, and somehow the blatant practicalities of the black bag seemed cold and on some level cruel, even disrespectful.

"They're all done now, Mr. Mason," said Kathy. "Let's get your things. We can take you home and have your car sent over."

Nate smiled thinly. "No, thanks. I can take myself home." They stood, and Nate looked once again around the room. Across the room the bedroom door was still open.

The slippers were still there, on the floor, but his father was gone.

9

With the man's weight suddenly off his chest, Nate was able to suck in at least half a lungful of air. He waited for the thud of the blade, the grunt of the man wielding it, and the muted crack as it splintered through bone.

But it never came.

He lay on his back and finally opened his eyes. The man was gone, and once again the light from the corridor poured through in a perfect rectangle on the floor, this time interrupted by his own legs from the knees down. Soon a face peered round the edge of the door. It was an older man in pajamas, bleary eyed but startled nonetheless, and soon he was joined by a woman in a housecoat, and then others.

Lights were flicked on and people flooded the room: guests, staff, and a man who seemed to be a doctor, or at least somehow medically trained. Nate could hear voices, high strung with concern, *What happened? Oh my God, what happened?* but his panicked mind couldn't connect the sounds with the faces. He sat up and became aware of the wetness about him, and when he looked at himself he saw that his clothes, the ones he had fallen asleep in and still wore, were spattered with blood. He reached up to his face and his hand came away red. Panic flooded through him and his hands flittered desperately around his face in search of gaping wounds.

Someone passed him a towel and he wiped frantically at his face, and the man who might have been a doctor spoke in calm, reassuring tones. *It's okay—it's not your blood.* More staff arrived and the guests were herded out. The door closed and Nate took a hand that helped him to the edge of the bed. Then he remembered the sensation of something spattering his forehead as the man had held him down, and with a pang of relief he put the pieces together— the severed hoof, the spatter. Blood from an animal part—not his own. Nate forced himself to calm down. He was not cut. He was not going to bleed to death from some yawning wound at his neck.

Finally, he became fully aware of the people in the room with him. He recognized the man from the front desk, and another from breakfast. The other two were strangers, and one held a cell phone to his ear. The man with the phone snapped it closed and took Nate by the elbow. "Come, come. We take you to hospital. Just in case."

Nate did not want to go anywhere. It was all happening too fast, too loosely and altogether too far out of his control. "No, I'm okay. I don't…"

"Mr. Mason, we must go. Just to check, to make sure."

Nate shrugged out of the man's grip. "No, I'm okay, really."

"But Mr. Mason…"

"No!" said Nate sharply. He regretted the outburst the moment it left his lips. "I'm sorry. I'm okay, really. I just need some time to gather myself. I'll take myself to the hospital tomorrow. I promise. But right now I just need to…I just need a bit of time."

"Are you sure, Mr. Mason? I can drive you."

"No, honestly. I'm fine." It finally occurred to Nate that the man with the phone was the hotel manager. "But I appreciate the offer."

The manager nodded in understanding, then knelt beside Nate and spoke gently, as if to a child. "Can you tell me what happened?"

Nate wiped his face again with the towel and looked at the blood that stained it. "I'm not sure. I was asleep. There was a man. At the foot of the bed. He had this sword thing, like a cutlass or something. He attacked me, had me on the ground and I thought he was going to kill me."

"Did he take anything?"

Nate cast his eyes around the room. It hadn't occurred to him that this might have been a robbery, and he suddenly wondered if his wallet and watch were gone. "No, I don't think so," he said, seeing everything where he had left it the evening before.

"I think you must have hurt him. Cut him," he said, pointing at the blood stained towel.

"No," said Nate. "That's not his blood either. He had something else with him, part of an animal I think. That's where all the blood came from."

The manager's brow furrowed deeply. "An animal?"

"Yes, a cow's foot I think. A hoof. He held it over my head and…"

There was a solid rap on the door and two men came through without being asked in. The police constables were wearing smart navy blue uniforms with shiny buttons and clasps, and each was armed with a pistol strapped to a broad and polished leather belt. They waved the manager aside, cleared the room of everyone but Nate, and curtly asked, *Are you hurt?* Nate shook his head, and wondered why he felt no compassion from the two officers.

The larger of the two men dragged the chair over to the bed and sat down. He leaned in close enough that Nate could see the small veins that ran through the whites of his eyes. The officer stared at Nate for a long moment, and then asked in a tone that was just short of accusatory, "Why was this man in your room?"

Before Nate could answer, the other officer barked his own question. "Were you buying something from this man tonight?"

Nate was incredulous. First he's attacked in his room and now the police were going to blame him for it? "What? No! I was sleeping!"

"And yet here you are fully dressed at three o'clock in the morning."

"I was tired and fell asleep in my clothes…"

"So you've been consuming alcohol as well."

"I was with a friend and…"

The other officer was looking at the door and cut him off. "The door here is in fine condition. No one forced it and the window is not accessible from the street. You let this man in?" It was more accusation than question.

Nate felt his chest tightening. "I didn't let anyone in. I was asleep. What the hell's going on here?"

The seated officer reached over and picked up Nate's wallet from the desk and fished out a fistful of American dollars, about $60 in all. "And what about all dis currency?" He waved it at Nate accusingly.

"Currency? "Nate's face twisted incredulously. "Christ, that's just my money. I'm a tourist, for fuck's sake!"

The officer flipped through the wallet again, eyeing Nate suspiciously. It fell open and a photograph of Cody appeared in the inner plastic photo sleeve, upside-down and facing Nate in silent appeal. The picture was of Cody holding up a small book—small even in his five-year-old hands. He was holding it proudly, right after having given it to Nate as a present—not for a birthday, Father's Day, or Christmas. It was what Cody and his mother called a *just because* present.

The book was called *Thanks, Dad* and each page had a simple stick-figure drawing of a father and son doing different things together, each captioned with a tribute, like *Thank you for always carrying me when I get tired, Dad,* and *Thank you for taking me on big adventures.* It was mushy, sappy stuff, but Nate remembered it hitting him like a freight train.

The officer followed Nate's stare and looked at the image, turning it round for a better view. He snorted once and cast the wallet dismissively onto the bed. Then, in a strangely choreographed manner, two officers exchanged serious glances and turned in unison toward Nate. The one on the chair stood and Nate watched in disbelief as he unclipped the leather handcuff holster.

Nate stood abruptly. "You're kidding me, right?"

• • •

By morning, the incident at the party was all but forgotten. It was Sunday, and Nate woke late to find his parents sitting on the balcony eating halves of freshly sliced grapefruit. The place had already been cleaned up; the chairs were all returned to their usual spots, the ashtrays emptied, the glasses cleaned and the beer cans swept away.

"Morning, sunshine," said his father.

Nate smiled at him in secret camaraderie. The chat had come late the night before, when the party was nearing its end, and his father had left him with a kiss to the crown of his head and the whispered magical words, *everything's fine.*

His mother smiled, oblivious to the silent exchange. "Want some breakfast?" She proceeded to put a bowl of the tart pink fruit in front of Nate's spot at the table. He never liked grapefruit, but it wasn't worth the argument so he ate it anyway.

Nate's dad flipped through the paper he was reading and folded the broadsheet into a manageable rectangle. "I had an interesting call this morning," he said, peering over the top of the paper at Nate. It was clear he wasn't going to go on unless Nate played along. It was corny, but Nate secretly liked it.

"And?"

His father looked over to his mother with feigned concern. "I don't know, dear, should I tell him? I don't want to get him too worked up."

"Oh, stop teasing the boy," she said.

"Dad! Come on!"

"All right, all right. Seems you've been invited to a sleepover—a two-nighter."

Nate sat up straight. A sleepover! Now that was some news. In two weeks, he would be thirteen, and for almost a year now it hadn't been cool to be too openly excited about anything, but this...this was a sleepover. "With who?" he asked.

His parents were glad to see the child in him return; unabashed enthusiasm was an increasingly rare commodity in Nate. "Tristan's dad called and invited you up to the plantation," said his dad. "Sounds like a boys' weekend: You, Pip, Richard and Tristan. That is, if you want to go."

"Yes! Yes! Yes!" cried Nate, hopping up from the table. "It's soooo cool up there!"

The plantation. It was the stuff of legend in their little group.

Tristan had been there a million times; he'd grown up on the island and Ti Fenwe Estate was a second home for him. But Nate had never been. He'd heard the stories. Ti Fenwe had taken on a mystical quality among the boys thanks to three important facts: One—it was in a very remote part of the island, deep in the bush like a secret hideout—probably discovered by pirates. Two—Tristan had two mini-bikes out there, little dirt bikes with fat wheels and chrome frames that the kids were allowed to zoom around the expansive estate on. And three—the place was steeped in spooky stories.

To hear the older De Villiers kids tell it, there was plenty out there to get you delightfully creeped out: there were relics of the island's grim past, including a wall with rusted and rattling chains still waiting patiently for the next cargo of slaves. There were the unexplained deaths of almost every former owner of the property—every one of them a male heir of the De Villiers clan. And there were the obscure forest spirits that were rumored to roam that particular part of the remote St. Lucian rainforest. For expat kids marooned by their parents on a tropical island paradise, it was nothing short of Disneyland.

Nate tucked into a second piece of grapefruit. The sleepover would be next weekend—Friday and Saturday night—and that would make for a mighty long week in between. He thought for a moment about the timing of the invitation. He'd never been asked before, so why now? And then it came to him. This would be Tristan's doing. As mean as that boy could be, you had to admire his audacity. The invitation was a pre-emptive strike designed to throw Nate's mom off-balance. She'd never complain to Tristan's dad about the incident the night before—not while he was calling with such a gracious invitation for her son. The move was daring, genius stuff.

Nate wanted to bolt over to Pip's, to scream and shout, and to run through the bush at full speed with airplane arms.

He was finally going to Ti Fenwe.

10

When he woke it was dark outside.

Nate swung his legs off the bed and rubbed his face with both hands. The stubble was thick and scratchy. It had been that way for days, weeks even, but he didn't care. There was no reason to shave. No reason to clean the place up. Around him the apartment was in disarray, and he supposed it had been that way for a long time, too. But now, after the hours he spent with Sergeant Cole, the lady from Victims Services and his cold, dead father, he realized his own surroundings echoed his father's in a horribly similar fashion. He could almost hear the apple thud to the ground, resolutely sitting there mere inches from the trunk.

In truth, his furniture was only marginally better than his father's, but it was pieced together with the same utilitarian eye— something he'd put down to necessity after the divorce. His apartment screamed bachelor—one who didn't care. His living room consisted of a worn, tan-colored couch and a well broken-in leather chair that had once been black but was now something much grayer. There was a particle board coffee table that had seen service in his college days, and two lamps that looked like refugees from an old-age home. Everything else had gone with the house. Christ, he'd never noticed how transient it all looked—it seemed temporary, like a student's dorm. Here for a semester then gone.

The similarities between his own apartment and his father's house were suddenly too sharp and uncomfortable; he needed a distraction. In the fridge he found a bottle of cold water, and when he sat down at the tiny kitchen table to drink it, he saw a pair of business cards sitting there, one from Kathy Tailor at Victim

Services, and the other from Sergeant Cole.

Nate picked up Sergeant Cole's card and stared at it. There was a matching one around here somewhere, he remembered. And it was enough to start it all again. His head sank slightly and the hollowness began to creep back in. He thought of his father's house again, about the questions Cole had asked him there. *What about the box of papers and things? All that stuff he had around him. Did you touch any of that?*

No, he had said.

He slipped his hand into the pocket of his pants and found it all still sitting there, bunched up and folded. Why had he lied to Cole? He wasn't sure, but it felt like it was none of the policeman's business.

When he found his father, he knew right away the old man was beyond help. There was no mistaking the damage the gun had done to his head. The complete finality of it all—punctuated in crimson along the far wall—had stopped Nate from running for the nearest phone and crying for help. Instead he had sunk slowly beside the old man, and then covered his shattered head with a towel from a nearby laundry pile.

He had just sat there for a time—it seemed like hours but it was probably only minutes—with his brain in a flat stall. He could see what his father had done, but it didn't register.

Around him were the upturned contents of two shoe boxes: papers, documents, and letters that he had apparently poured into his lap just before putting the pistol in his mouth. Nate picked up a random handful—a dismissal letter from the Foreign Service, his parents' marriage certificate, letters from Nate's mother—long since estranged. There were copies of his father's military record, his honorable discharge, a raft of legal papers associated with the dissolution of his marriage and, among everything, a stack of airmail envelopes with a rubber band around them.

In his kitchen, Nate had to stand to pull the folded wad of paper from his pocket, and when he placed it all on the table he did so carefully. Somehow the letters were now more valuable than he had appreciated when he first stuffed them into his pocket. He smoothed each one out, and laid them in two columns—one set that was addressed to his father, and another set addressed to Nate. There were six envelopes bearing his father's name, and two with Nate's. All were the same kind of airmail envelopes with blue and red chevron borders. Nate carefully arranged them in order of their postmark date. Of the letters sent to his father, the earliest one arrived in 1978, with the other five arriving in intervals of about five or six years. The last one, the most current one, had arrived only a week ago.

In the other group, the letters addressed to Nate, the postmarks showed one sent in 1980, and another in 1982. Nate ran the numbers through his head. He would have been seventeen when the first arrived, and nineteen by the time the second showed up. Both were sent to his father's address, and both remained unopened. Nate had never seen them before, didn't even know they existed, but he knew right away what they were about.

He knew he would read all eight of the letters, but not today. No, that would be too much for now, in the immediate wake of his father's death. He already knew the broad strokes of what was in each of them, so it was really just a question of details. When did he last talk to his father? He couldn't bring it to mind, couldn't bring the specifics into view no matter how he tried. That, too, felt like a failure, but there were so many.

First there was the career. He had over a decade of journalism under his belt, a degree that said he had the requisite training, but what he'd been covering was drab, spiritless stuff. He had worked for a string of local dailies across the country covering winter fairs, local elections and Santa Claus parades. But it wasn't news. Not really. It wasn't the important, center-of-it-all lifestyle that he had dreamed of.

He'd applied to all of the big national papers of course, but never got so far as an interview. A couple of requests for tear sheets, but then nothing. Silence. And so discouragement would inevitably set in and he'd go back to covering the drama of some hardware store's one-hundredth anniversary. And as real success eluded him, he began to see it in his wife's eyes. It was a shared disappointment at first, but over time it converted, changed into something more defeated, as if she was finally seeing the limitations in the man she had married. She hid it well, but he could see it.

But Nate kept trying. At one point he'd even tried freelancing. He recklessly quit his job at the Oxford Herald and two months later went skulking back, head low, penitent and penniless. A sympathetic editor took him back and suggested there might be a column in the experience. It worked, and then there was another, and another. Something stuck and after a few months he was given a regular four column-inches every week in the "perspectives" section. It was what would pass for the highpoint.

And then there were the novels. There were three of them, each carefully woven together night after night consuming thousands of hours, but none had found the mark. He'd sent them to hundreds of agents and publishers, and one by one the responses came back with polite rejections, and then, after a while, they stopped coming back altogether. At first his wife was sympathetic—*keep trying, it'll break*— but after a while, after the relentless march of his mediocrity in both the job hunt and his great literary career, she eventually stopped caring. Her husband was already the man he would become, and nothing more. Eventually all three of his novels ended up on the same shelf in his spare room closet. Her voice chattered at him from across the years: *Maybe teaching? Maybe you could become a teacher?* Of course, the subtext was clear: *Maybe you should focus on getting a real job.*

It still burned.

He wondered when that happened—when his wife went from *I do* to *I wish I hadn't*—and whether it was a singular event or a series of stacked disappointments. Probably the latter, he thought. When they were first married life seemed so simple, so easy to navigate: see friends, go to work, catch a movie, make love. Repeat.

When had she begun to see him as something other than her equal? He thought of her on their honeymoon, in the hotel pool with her arms locked about his neck, staring into his eyes like there was nothing else in the world worth looking at.

He thought of the divorce, the custody hearings, where everything fell apart so quickly. Crossed arms, pursed lips, dismissive glances and quiet whispers to that bastard of a lawyer. He remembered the awful awareness of knowing he was losing Cody as it was happening. And this thing with his father—the man was already gone, already lying on a slab in some tile-cold morgue, he understood that—but the *losing* felt somehow the same, like a final glance backwards on moving day: it's just a hollowed-out house now, but it used to be a home. He tried again to remember the last conversation he had had with the old man, but there was nothing there.

Will I be okay, Daddy? Cody's voice echoed plainly in his ears, and the pain was as fresh as the first time. The memories were tag-teaming him now, leaping from tragedy to tragedy in some grim orgy of self-pity. Fathers were supposed to protect their sons, to provide for them and shield them from life's hard, jagged edges. He thought about his father back in the days on the island, when his dad used to tell him so convincingly—whenever he needed to hear it—that everything was going to be okay. And for a brief moment Nate could almost feel his father's hand at his back, ushering him to safety. He remembered the surety of his father's momentum, moving him calmly but firmly through the crowd of suits and uniforms in the police station and out to the waiting car—all the while whispering *don't worry, Nate, everything's going to be okay.* And up to a point, it always had been. Up to a point.

Nate couldn't do that for Cody now, and the truth of that cruel fact was an ache that would never go away. Was this something his own father could have ever understood? Perhaps the one he remembered so fondly from those carefree days on the island could. But not the more modern version, and certainly not the version he found lying on the floor with the top of his head blown off.

Enough, thought Nate. He moved to the couch, and scooped up the remote. Perhaps the TV could stop this cavalcade of misery. As he sat down he caught a perfect reflection of himself in the black mirror of the TV screen. He hadn't shaved in days. His hair was unruly and the shirt he was wearing, the same one he had worn all week, looked stained and stretched out of shape. He looked at the black screen and wondered who it was looking back at him.

The question went unanswered as the screen surged into high-color life, mercifully bleaching out thoughts of Cody, his father and the woman he must have once loved.

• • •

The larger of the two policemen motioned for Nate to stand. The man's demeanor was aloof, bored almost, and he held the cuffs loosely by his side as if they were nothing of any real significance. For Nate they had become the center of his world.

"Sir, please turn around," said the one by the door. His Caribbean drawl was rich, and in any other setting would have been a charming affectation. "Dis will be much easier if you jus' cooperate."

Nate was wide-eyed. He could feel his heart racing, and his breaths were coming fast. "Wait, please, can we talk about this?"

"Turn around. Now."

"Please."

The officer stepped in aggressively and spun Nate around. Immediately his partner was somehow there and pressing Nate into the wall face first. His arm was twisted backwards and up, more enthusiastically than needed, and Nate yelped as his arm's range of motion was met and passed. With the pain came an overwhelming sense of dread, and a remarkably rapid urge to cease resisting and do whatever the burly policemen wanted. He had visions of rat-infested cells, consular visits from pale men in wrinkled suits, and uncomfortable realities about the law in the Caribbean and the limited influence of his government far, far away. The handcuffs cinched up and bit into his wrists, and Nate yelped again—in fear as much as pain.

He was jerked from his spot against the wall and turned to the doorway. Now he would face the perp walk, shamefully paraded through the hotel in full view of all the other guests and staff, made to exit in shame and humiliation.

But before that indignity, there would apparently be another—the pat down. Nate was shoved firmly into the wall beside the closed door and rough hands clawed at every part of him. His head was twisted away from the doorway, and from there he could see the second officer stuff the bills into his pocket. He sneered at Nate and snorted once. "Evidence."

Another hand seized the back of his collar and jerked him backwards, popping the top button off his shirt as the garment rode up and into his throat. Strong hands pushed him round to face the door, and Nate could feel the last vestiges of courage slip away. Why was this all happening? His eyes flicked wildly around the room, looking for something, anything that might bring an end to this bizarre and frightening turn.

"Move," said the big policeman, and without waiting for Nate to comply he put a heavy hand between Nate's shoulder blades and shoved him forward. Nate's feet were too slow, and he pitched forward and down, his chest and face hitting the floor at the same time. He heard the *whoosh* of air being forced from his lungs, and the icy burn of the skin below his eye splitting down to the bone.

The two men seized him again, and hoisted him up effortlessly. With muscled arms linked through each of Nate's, they propelled him down the hall, past startled faces of guests and staff alike. In moments he was thrust into the covered back of a small police pickup with a simple padlock door, where he lay on his side struggling to regain his breath as the vehicle bumped through the darkened Castries streets.

Nate was terrified now, but anger was trying to find a way in. He could feel the brightness of the new cut on his cheek, and as he lay on his side with his hands cuffed behind him, he could see the blood dripping steadily and consistently onto the corrugated floor of the pickup. He wanted to call out to the policemen in the front, but he knew they had no interest in his side of the story. He was no longer the victim, and fear, anger and frustration swirled in generous proportions. How had this happened?

The pickup swerved hard and Nate rolled against the exposed wheel-well, grunting as the air was driven out of him again. The men in the front laughed, and stopped the pickup hard sending Nate sliding forward and headfirst against the cab. The two policemen then pulled him roughly out, feet first, and let him fall hard onto the ground. Again the wind was driven from his lungs. His vision was spotty, and he was unable to speak. He wheezed and struggled to breathe, much to the amusement of the officers.

Nate looked around and saw he was in front of a small white building with a police sign glowing blue in the night. Inside there was light, but the street, which appeared to be in an industrial part of town, was dark and deserted.

Inside, grunted the larger of the two, and Nate was shoved forward. As they entered the lobby another policeman looked up and immediately left the room, closing the door behind him. There appeared to be no one else around. Something about the way that officer left, the look of resignation, of his complete understanding of what was about to happen made Nate's heart sink even more.

The room was starkly lit by a single neon tube, and on the two desks in the room sat stacks of papers and tan colored files. There was a water cooler with no water bottle sitting in the corner, two wooden chairs, and a row of steel filing cabinets lining the back wall. The room had not a single nod toward comfort. Nate looked back through the front door and into the street. There was nothing there, save the blue glow of the police sign. Something terrible was about to happen, and no one would be here to see it.

"I didn't do anything. I was attacked in my room."

The two officers exchanged glances. One said something to the other in patois. They both nodded, and turned to face Nate. This was it.

The bigger of the two officers put his face directly in front of Nate's, and stared hard into his eyes. Nate could smell the man's breath, the sweat in his uniform and the lingering odor of tobacco. The policeman held the moment, and Nate became once again aware of the cut in his cheek. He could feel it oozing blood. It coursed down to his chin, where it gathered at the center and ran down his neck to feed a growing arc of crimson at the collar of his T-shirt.

"Dis place here," said the policeman quietly, "dis place can be a terrible, terrible place." He pointed to the single door at the back of the room. "We take criminals from de street—hard, hard fellows, tough-as-nails, seriously bad—and we take dem through dat door. And when dem see de door, dem cry like li'l girls." He took a deep breath and looked at the door. "If you go through that door, you not coming back. Happens all de time here. So I goin' tell you once and only once. Dis island not a safe place for you, I think. My advice—leave before you dun get hurt."

Without hesitation he spun Nate around, unshackled him and shoved him through the front door and out into the night. Nate stumbled and almost fell, and stood confused in the glow of the Police sign looking back at the station. The two policemen were chatting to each other, paying no attention to Nate. He was confused, scared, and sure they would come after him the moment he looked away in some perverse game of cat and mouse.

Nate walked away backwards, into the darkness, watching the front of the station and waiting for the officers to take up the chase. They never did.

Nate had no idea where he was. It was dark, he was disoriented, and there was no one around to ask for help. He walked for two blocks until he found a payphone, and with no money he called the operator and asked to be connected, with the charges reversed, to the only number he knew: Smiley's.

Half an hour later he sat in Smiley's white Honda in front of the Breadfruit Tree Inn. He was still shaken. "It's aright, Mr. Mason. It's aright." Smiley's voice was calm and reassuring.

"The *jandam* gone now." He helped Nate out of the car, and back up to his room. He brought him a towel from the bathroom and pressed it firmly into the arc of red beneath his right eye.

"I don't know what the hell…" He pulled the towel from his eye and it began to bleed again like an open faucet.

Smiley quickly guided the towel back and held it firmly in place. "We'll have to get that seen to right away, Nate. I think you gone need some silk."

"What?"

"Stitches, my friend. You need some stitches to close dat."

Nate didn't argue the point. He just sat and stared off into space. Finally he shook his head. "Christ, I have no idea what just happened. One minute I'm sleeping, then I'm fighting some asshole with a cutlass, and then I'm getting arrested."

"Look, don't worry about de *jandam*, the police, they won't be back to bother you. At least not tonight. You want to tell me what happened?"

Nate struggled to describe the bloody scene in his room. Anxiety was returning like a gathering wave, but Smiley mercifully cut him short.

"It aright, man. It aright." Smiley smiled again. "We do need to go and get you eye fix. And I want to hear about de intruder. We can talk on de way."

"The hospital?"

"Mmm, no. I don't think so. We'll go private tonight, I think."

Nate squirmed uncomfortably. "I don't know if my insurance covers private."

"Dat's okay, man—dat's not the kind of private I talking 'bout."

"…so what kind of private *are* you talking about?"

"The kind where people can't find you."

"People?"

Smiley barged on. "Come, le' we pack you things. You checking out of the Breadfruit Tree. My brother can fix you up. He a doctor. And don't worry 'bout cost."

Nate decided not to fight it. There were many more questions circling nearby, but they could wait. Together they collected Nate's things and stuffed them into his single suitcase, then stood at the door for one last look back. There was blood spattered liberally about the room, and pooled on the floor where the man who had attacked him brandished the cow's hoof. There were so many questions, but they would have to wait.

"Your brother," said Nate as they closed the door to the hotel room. "I thought he was the archives guy."

"He is," said Smiley. "But dis a different brother."

11

The road to Ti Fenwe Estate cut through some of the thickest parts of the island's rainforest, and the dense green expanse of 1976 was much like it had been for thousands of years. The road was little more than a roughly hewn track—two wheel ruts, really. For two hours the tangled tropics scratched at the Land Rover like jade demons clawing at its sides, eager to snatch the occupants and drag them into the heart of its darkness.

The boys squealed with delight with every pitch of the vehicle, every lurch of its rusting frame, especially through the wet spots. Where the track ran through a valley or a dip of any kind, the water pooled and the vehicle's heavy treads churned it into a sticky black bog. Twice they had to stop and run the cable from the winch mounted on the bumper to a nearby tree, and each time the boy's sense of true adventure doubled.

Vincent De Villiers heaved the hood of the Land Rover open and slammed it against the frame of the windshield. "Out, boys!" he commanded. The four hopped dutifully out of the open back and took their spots safely away from the cable as the winch whined and slowly drew the vehicle out of the sticky mess. "Keep back, lads! If that cable parts, it'll slice you in half and your legs will walk off without you!" He announced the horrifying fact the way a pirate might announce the execution of hostages—which of course thrilled the boys even more.

Once clear of the mud, they all clambered back in and the Land Rover continued its jolting progress along the winding trail. "This path was cut by my great, great grandfather," announced Vincent. "It was just a pony track back then, just wide enough for a few horses and a line of slaves in chains. There's many a dead fellow in those bushes, boys," he said, looking back for a moment and smiling giddily. "Any that couldn't make the journey were cut loose and left to die where they lay."

Pip's sense of adventure evaporated and was replaced quickly with anxiety. From his seat on the opposite side Richard reassured him. "Don't worry about Uncle Vince, Pip. He's just trying to scare us. There's nothing in there but more bushes."

"There's nothing to worry about, boys," Vince continued. "Nothing at all." Then he turned and winked at them. "Well, not *much* to worry about—as long as it doesn't take a dislike to you." Then he threw his head back and belly laughed.

"Quit it, Uncle Vince!" shouted Richard, half laughing himself, and the effect was only to ramp up the ham factor in his uncle, who twisted his laugh into the classic villain *mwa-ha-ha*.

"Yeah, quit it, Mr. D.," seconded Nate. "You're scaring your son!"

Tristan smiled acidly at the others, who all started laughing—including Pip. "I got nothing to be scared about—I'm the heir," said Tristan defiantly. "And owners don't get messed with."

The Land Rover trundled on. It took the group further into the rainforest, deep under the canopy that blocked out the sun for minutes at a stretch, and on through a wet lushness that seemed to close in on them more with every turn of the old four-wheel-drive's knobby tires.

The boys all liked Vincent. He was larger than life, and they liked him all the more for the fact that the parents collectively regarded him with mild suspicion. He was the De Villiers family bad boy, married and divorced three times, and as the eldest of three heirs, Ti Fenwe had passed to him on the death of his father—an inheritance rumored to be hotly contested by the rest of the De Villiers clan. He had fathered two sons: William, who died hours after being born to his first wife, Nora, who had herself died later that year in a boating accident, and, of course, Tristan. And with Tristan, it appeared the apple had come to rest just inches from the husky, weather-beaten trunk.

At last, the disorder of the forest—the tangle of broad leaves, the sprawling vines woven through banks of lianas, the knots of bougainvillea tied inexorably to and through trees and tumbles of greenery dotted with splashes of color—finally it all gave way to a strangely ordered scene of monoculture: organized rows of tall and spacious nutmeg trees, each with a sudden and jarring expanse of space around their trunks, and each laden with clusters of woody colored fruit among their waxy leaves. The lush forest had just suddenly stopped, the day washed back in, bright and dry, and the boys all drank in the space.

Behind them, beyond the first few rows of nutmeg, was a green wall of jungle. Were it not for the ruts that had guided them in, those two brown furrows through the short grass, the expansive green snarl would seem an impenetrable barrier designed to let no one leave.

"Not far now, boys," yelled Vincent over his shoulder. "Not far now!" Vincent forced the Land Rover into an unwilling gear and the old box-shaped four-wheel-drive lurched forward with a new determination. The vehicle followed the two dark scars in the earth that rounded the edge of the nutmeg orchard, and then gathered speed as it ran down a gentle slope and through a small river. Once clear of the water, they trundled up again, into a steep grade in the land that peaked in a crest where a series of rickety shacks stood clustered among coconut trees set on shortly cropped grasses. There was an even more welcoming sense of space here, and while the green mass was still there at the edges, somehow the little huts and the people milling around them made it all feel something akin to normal.

Among the ramshackle buildings a handful of women were hard at work, the color of polished mahogany and glistening with sweat, carrying loads balanced precariously on their heads in brightly colored plastic bowls. They turned in measured, careful sways, waved unenthusiastically at the Land Rover and the group within it, then went back to their work. Vincent nodded in their direction and the boys, save Tristan, waved back.

The Land Rover passed the little village of huts and turned right onto a track that was much more serviceable, almost a road in its own right. They picked up speed through the coconut grove, and Vincent pointed a well-muscled arm off to the right. "Swamps are over there. Stay away. All of you—and I'm not kidding."

The boys all turned and looked, and at the far end of the grove they could see a different kind of denseness, a thicker green than that from which they had recently emerged. This was much darker, blacker. From the track they could see the confusion of mangrove trees, an intertwined labyrinth of roots the size of scaffolding tubes, each jostling for position and overlapping as they disappeared into the bog below. The tangle was so thick it was impossible to see past the first flourish of mangrove, and as the Land Rover passed out of the grove the boys were all instinctively glad to leave the swamp far behind. "That place is creepy looking," said Pip, voicing everyone's thoughts.

"And it's out of bounds," added Tristan.

"How come?"

"Pip, it's a swamp, it's dangerous." Tristan's tone was flippant. "Besides, if my Dad says stay away, you stay away, got it?"

"Yeah, sure but…" Pip's comment was lost as the pitch of the engine changed and the Land Rover braked hard.

Vincent let the engine die and the vehicle shuddered to a halt. He threw his arm over the passenger's seat, and twisted to face the boys in the back. He looked at them over the top of a pair of beaten old sunglasses. His face was weathered and deeply lined, and his hair was sun-bleached to a sandy blonde and cropped short around his face. At forty-seven he had aged well, and almost any woman on the island would agree. "You guys already know the rules up here," he began, pointing at Tristan and Richard. "But you two—Pip, Nate— you boys need to listen carefully. This is a great place for exploring, running around, the mini-bikes, all of that. And I want you to enjoy it. But there are things you need be careful of here, too. It can be dangerous. So if I tell you something is out of bounds, it's out of bounds. Understand?"

"Like the swamp," added Tristan.

"Like the swamp," agreed Vincent. He turned back to Pip and Nate. "There's also rules around daylight. When the sun goes down, you all need to be back in the house."

Pip's eyes widened and Vincent saw it. "It's nothing like that," said Vincent, smiling at last. "There're no vampires here… It's just that there's no electricity this far into the bush, just a small generator for the one room where we sleep. Ti Fenwe is a big estate, and it's easy to get turned around if you're caught out in the darkness, so we have a daylight curfew: everyone in by nightfall. Got it?"

"Got it," said Pip. Nate nodded as well.

"Great. Everyone ready for some fun?" He swung back around in his seat and started the Land Rover. "Next stop, Ti Fenwe Estate plantation house!" Vincent dropped the clutch and the vehicle jerked forward, toppling the boys onto one another. They laughed and the mood was once again light and cheerful.

"Tristan, what were those huts? And those people?" asked Nate.

"Laborers," said Tristan. "They've been here since my great, great grandfather's days. They work the plantation, look after the house, all that stuff."

"But they live here, like all the time?"

"Ya, sure. They've lived here for generations. Most of them are the descendants of slaves."

Pip's eyes were as wide as they could be. "Slaves? For real?"

"Of course! Who do you think built this plantation?" Tristan was warming to the conversation now; he leaned in and the others immediately followed suit. "Most of the people here, all the women you saw back there and…"

Pip jumped in. "Where are all the men?"

"Jesus, Pip. Will you let me tell the story? The men are working in the fields. You'll see them later. Anyway, almost everyone who works and lives on this plantation is descended from Africans captured and brought here as slaves in the olden days."

"Back in the 1600s," added Vincent without turning from

the front seat.

Nate was fascinated and listened intently. He'd never heard Tristan speak with such authority before. "The people who lived here before that were the Arawak Indians, and the Caribs—bloodthirsty warriors that could kill you and gut you before you even knew you were dead. They could cut your head off so fast that they could show you your own body lying there before you died."

"No way!" said Pip tentatively. "Come on, that's not even possible."

Tristan went on. "You have Arawaks and Caribs, the most skilled warriors in the whole of the Caribbean—maybe the whole world— and then you add to that a whole mix of ancient Africans, with all their rituals, their secret potions, their millions of years of sorcery and magic, all that cool stuff, and what you get is something that exists nowhere else in the world. There's stuff that happens on this island that is so ancient, so secret, so super-specialized that people from the outside—people like you, Pip—can't even understand it. And you doubting it, shit, that's proof of what I just said. You can't even understand it."

"Jeez Tristan, ease up on Pip, will you," said Richard.

"Mind your own—"

Vincent slammed on the brakes and the boys all tumbled forward into a heap against the cab. "We're here!" announced Vincent triumphantly.

The boys kept laughing as they extracted one another from the heap, and finally Tristan and Richard hopped down and began unloading the duffel bags. Nate and Pip stood transfixed in the back of the Land Rover, staring up at the old structure that stared hollowly back at them.

"Hey, Dad," said Tristan, pointing at the two boys.

Vincent smiled and nodded. "She's got you now, boys. She's laid her eyes on you. Be on your best behavior; she won't stand for any nonsense." Then he laughed and hoisted a crate of soft drinks onto his shoulder. "Come on lads. The quicker we get this stuff unloaded the quicker you can all go have some fun."

Nate and Pip stood for a moment longer, unwilling, or perhaps unable to pull their eyes from the dark, empty windows above them. The house looked abandoned, uncared for, left for the forest to reclaim. Only the entry way seemed tended to. At the front of the house sat a flower bed that seemed to have at least some order to it, but even that had gotten out of control and grown well past its boundaries. Everything else about the place seemed to be in a gathering state of decay.

The whole house was set on top of a large gray concrete foundation made from a series of arches. Each arch spanned about six feet wide and stood seven feet tall at their apex, and the structures ran around the entire base of the house. The wooden building itself sat atop the gray arches, and was at one time painted white with red trim. But that had been some time ago, and now it was all faded and chipped, and some of the siding was swollen and spongy with rot. The tin roof, also once red, was now bleached by the unyielding sun to a rose color and dashed with rusty streaks of brown. The roof was raised into seven steeples set evenly around the building, each with a shuttered window at the peak, hinting at the presence of an upper floor, or perhaps an attic. Below that a series of large bay windows looked out over the yards, with the sill of each window still a good ten feet from the ground. The result was a structure that looked down on new arrivals, and Nate and Pip both felt its heavy gaze.

Centered in the front of the house was a large entryway where a pair of double doors once stood. Now only one remained, and it hung open at an odd angle like a kicked-in tooth. The doorway was accessed by a large concrete stairway spanning a gap between the landing and the yard, allowing enough room for a man to walk along the arches and under the front steps uncontested. To the sides of the front door, and continuing on at the two sides of the house, were verandas with traditional white railings made of continuous 'X's joined together. At some time in the past the house would have been a magnificent example of island architecture, but now it looked as if the island was doing its best to tear it down.

Nate stepped down from the Land Rover. His gaze was drawn to the small window at the top of the steeple directly above the front door. It was partly open, the shutter pushed outward slightly, and through the sliver of space Nate could see only blackness.

There was nothing there, just the dark inside of some upper room, but to Nate it felt like someone, something was watching. Tristan followed his line of sight up to the small window. When he saw where Nate was looking he smiled. "See something?" he asked in a conspiratorial tone.

"Should I?"

Tristan laughed and turned to the house with a box of tinned food. "Nope. *You* can't."

12

"Nate, you must hol' still, man. Very still," pled Smiley. "I understand it be painful, but you must hol' still."

Nate lay on the table with a light shining brightly in his face. Smiley's older brother was bent over him, a curved needle with a blue filament tail in his hand, and lines of frustration gathering in his brow.

"Jesus, that fucking hurts!" Nate cursed, and Smiley's brother stepped back—for the third time—and let his arms fall to his sides. He shook his head gently. Nate apologized immediately. "I'm sorry, I'm sorry—it just really hurts. You sure you have nothing to numb it?"

Smiley's brother, who looked nothing at all like Smiley, shook his head sympathetically. "I can give you something for later, but I have nothing here that can stop the pain for now. We almost done—two or three more and we finish for sure. Can I go on?"

Nate clutched both sides of the narrow kitchen table, nodded and clenched his teeth. He swore again as the needle hooked into the flesh at the sides of the wound on his cheek, and groaned at the sensation of the thread being pulled through. It tugged at his skin and drew the crimson smile below his eye closed. Another two loops and it was done, and Smiley's brother tied it off and taped a fresh pad of gauze in place. "There," he said, wiping his hands in satisfaction. "You gone be fine now, but you will leave de island wit some new character in your face." He smiled and finally Nate saw the resemblance to Smiley.

"You okay now," said Smiley. It was a statement, not a question. He turned to his brother, put one of his meaty paws on the man's shoulder and spoke in Creole, melodic and warm. Nate sat up and thanked him as well.

"No problem, no problem at all," he said, straightening up the small kitchen. "But tell me, what you two going to do now? And what about this thing tonight. You clearly can't rely on the police for help—or for answers."

Smiley agreed. "Ah, don't worry 'bout us. We just needed to get dat cut sorted out, and we'll be on our way. I'll take care of our Mr. Mason." He smiled and shook his brother's hand.

Nate wondered where they would go, but Smiley seemed to have a plan. It was his island, his town, his people, and Nate could feel the effects of the evening catching up with him. He'd slept for a mere two hours at best, been attacked, arrested, threatened, poked, and needled, and now he was temporarily homeless. There were just too many swirling unknowns.

But there was Smiley, and so Nate was content to let Smiley call the shots. He was just plain exhausted, and while there were questions—burning ones—at the moment, a few hours of undisturbed, safe sleep was all he wanted.

They left Smiley's brother and drove out of town and into the countryside. It was almost dawn now, and the glow of first light was silhouetting the island against a sky that was already a promising shade of blue. They stopped at a small village, a cluster of modest houses really, where chickens were already scratching at the yard in search of their breakfast. Smiley led him into a small building made of breeze blocks and wood with a sloped tin roof, and pointed to a cot in the corner. "You'll be fine here. Lie down and get a few hours' sleep. When you wake, we'll talk 'bout last night, and 'bout what to do next."

With a reassuring hand on the shoulder Smiley left, and Nate sat on the cot. There was a small wooden table surrounded by six mismatched chairs, a single window with a brown curtain drawn across it, and a white plastic sink in the opposite corner. It had a faucet connected to a garden hose that ran through a hole in the wall. On the table was a rack of colorful poker chips, several decks of playing cards, and three empty beer bottles. The door had a lock, the cot was soft and the sheets smelled clean. Nate lay down and in the darkness his mind went back, as it always did in the quiet of the night, to Cody. He missed him terribly, but drew courage from the fact that it was in part Cody who had made coming back possible. And soon he slept.

His dreams were sharp, uncomfortable and as palpable as any he had ever had. He dreamt of arches; long spans of worn gray concrete that stretched out one after the other in a perfect line. Behind them, through the archways was a dead blackness; an impenetrable, inky pool of darkness that stank of menace. He found himself walking slowly, parallel with the arches, filled with the utter conviction that someone or something was watching from deep within its shadowy recesses. He wanted to turn and walk away from the arches, but he couldn't. And so he walked, and it watched.

He woke just after eleven in the morning with the sound of Smiley at the door. Either the lock didn't work or Smiley had the key, and he came in with two steaming mugs of sweet tea and a brown bag that smelled of pastry and warm honey. They sat at the table, sipping the tea and licking the honey from their fingers. "Jeez, these are good," said Nate, fishing another of the freshly deep-fried treats from the bag. "I didn't realize how hungry I was."

Smiley smiled and helped himself to another. "So, you ready to talk some?"

Nate nodded while he chewed.

"Aright. Dis fellow in you room, last night. Tell me 'bout him."

"Man, where to begin…" Nate wiped his mouth with a napkin.

"Did you recognize de fellow? De fellow who dun attack you?"

"No, I was fast asleep. I woke up and he was just, well, there. Scared the shit out of me. Next thing I'm jumping around the room and he's swinging some damn sword at me, and I'm throwing everything I can put my hands on at him. He eventually knocks me down and has me there on the floor, and I thought I was a dead man. He could have just hacked me into little pieces right there, but he didn't."

The pause went on too long. "Well?" prompted Smiley.

"Well, I was lying there, and I open my eyes expecting to see this sword, cutlass thing, but instead this guy is standing over me holding a goddamn cow's foot! At least I think it was a cow's foot—and the thing is pissing blood all over my face and the floor. Can you believe that?"

Smiley's face went slack and his mouth fell open, his half chewed pastry there for anyone to see. "A cow's foot? A hoof?" Smiley hissed in a whisper as if speaking only to himself. *"Bondie! My God!"* He staggered up from the chair like a man who had just seen a ghost.

Smiley paced nervously about the small room, and Nate watched with growing alarm. "What is it?" Nate asked anxiously. "What does it mean?"

"A cow's foot? Are you sure?"

"Yes—no. I think it was…fuck, I don't know. I think it was!"

"La jah blesse! Bondie!"

"La ja what? What are you talking about?" Nate was now standing, too.

Smiley made a conscious effort to rein himself in. "I'm sorry—sorry. It's just something that I was not expecting. It might be nothing…"

"Might be noth—Christ, Smiley, what are you saying?"

"It's okay. It's okay…" He paced another lap of the room with his hand pressed into his forehead, then: "I have to go talk to someone—jus' a minute. Wait here and I'll soon come, okay? I'll soon come."

Nate was in no mood to be left behind now. "Screw that, I'm coming with you." He followed Smiley through the door, and for the first time since arriving in the early hours, it occurred to him that he had no idea where he was. He followed Smiley around to the side of the house and it all suddenly gelled. He recognized the small hut, the road where they had parked, and the table they had sat at. It was Bozu, the little roadside bar from the night before.

"Nate, just wait here, man. Seriously, just wait for me. I'll be quick; you wait—sit at de table," he said, pointing to the spot where they had sat the night before.

Nate could feel the nervous energy coming off Smiley, but he wasn't sure if it was because of what Nate had told him, or because of the person he now needed to speak to. A second later the answer swung through the open door of the shebeen.

Ma Joop's eyes fell first on Smiley, and for a moment she didn't see Nate at the table. Her reaction was swift, going from smile to concern in the single beat it took to drink in Smiley's face. A second later she glanced over at Nate—a purely intuitive reaction—and it was enough to change her again. This time her face went from concern to outright horror. She squealed in Creole and threw her hands up to her face, and then backpedalled through the door she had just come through. Smiley followed her with hands outstretched as if to catch her, and Nate was left alone with a sense of dread pooling in his gut.

Inside, he could hear Ma Joop and Smiley. Ma Joop was near hysterics, and her voice was ratcheted up and held many octaves higher than what he had heard from her the night before. Nate couldn't understand a word, but the tone spoke clearly. He could hear her slowly winding down, then occasionally regrouping into the full blown timbre of panic, then gradually working down again toward something akin to calm.

He listened as Ma Joop and Smiley went back and forth. Smiley's voice was sometimes cast in appeasing tones, sometimes forceful and finite, but all the while helping Ma Joop down like an outstretched hand over a steep and rocky path. Finally there was quiet, and for many minutes there was no sound at all. Nate stood halfway up from his spot at the table, caught firmly between two minds: Should he go in and see if everything was okay? Or should he sit tight and wait to see what it all meant? The longer the silence in the little shack persisted the more he was convinced that something awful was about to happen, that someone with another machete would come barrelling out of the doorway and finish the job started the night before.

Eventually, with none of the fanfare of a sword-wielding madman, Smiley came through the doorway. He walked slowly with one hand on top of his head and a tangled look on his face, and Nate knew without question he was coming with bad news.

"What? What is it?" he asked.

Smiley blew out a lungful of air through puffed cheeks. "Ma Joop," he began. "Ma Joop has seen somethin' on you. Somethin' dat took her by surprise, dat's all."

Nate sat and blinked. "I don't even know where to start asking what you mean by that."

Smiley tugged at his chin. "Ma Joop, she...she is a very special person to me, to many of us. She need some time. We have to...*you* have to go away for a little bit."

"What do you mean, Smiley? What do you mean *I* have to go away?"

"She jus' need a little time, man, dat is all."

"Are you saying *I* need to leave, that you're ditching me?" This was starting to feel like last night all over again, and Nate instinctively glanced around, half expecting to see his two favorite constables and their shiny new handcuffs.

"No, no, nuttin' like dat, man. But me need to help her. Me need to be here for a while. I want you to take my car," he said reaching into his pocket and retrieving the keys. "I want you to take a drive, man. See de island, see de places from when you were a *lightee* here."

Lightee. Nate hadn't heard that expression in more than thirty years, and for a blissful moment he remembered the older kids scorning him and Richard and the others: *Stay away from the drink table—you* lightees *are not even supposed to be at this party. Stick to the lime juice.* It was a warm and inclusive memory; he was part of a clan, the little kids, the *lightees.* It was a piece of island slang that drew him instantly back to that perfect thirteen-year-old state of being. But almost as soon as the memory formed, it was gone.

"Nate, take the keys, man." He pressed them into Nate's palm and looked him straight in the eye. "Stay away from downtown Castries, and from de Police. Come back 'ere tomorrow afternoon, 'round five. We'll sort everything out."

"What about tonight?"

"Jus' find a small inn, there's many. But pay cash and use another name, jus' to be safe."

Nate suddenly became aware of how ludicrous this all seemed. "Smiley," he said in a forced half-laugh, "what the fuck is going on?"

"Tomorrow at five. Here in Gros Islet. Everything will be fine. You have to trus' me, man."

"Can't I just stay here in the back room?"

"No, no. Dat won't do. We need some time. Jus' find a place—there's many up near Reduit Beach. You remember dat area?"

Nate nodded. He knew the name. There was a yacht club up there—at least there was in 1976 when he was a kid—where all the boys would sail Mirror Dinghies in Sunday races.

"Good, good. Get a room, stay inside and jus' lock you-self in for tonight."

Nate was bewildered. Something inside him was teetering between fear and ridicule, but he wasn't quite sure which way it would all go. "You know this all sounds way out there, right?"

Smiley shook his head in mild agitation, but Nate was well past worrying how other people felt. "Nate, jus' do as I ask. You have a car for de day, some free time, jus' enjoy de island. Please."

Nate raised his hands in surrender. "What choice do I have?" Another boot was set to drop; he could smell the damn leather.

"One more thing, Nate," Smiley began uncomfortably. "If you begin to feel not so well later, not to worry, it's de tea and de sticky buns. Dey can be hard on you system if you not used to local spices. You might feel a little sick, you know, maybe have some bad dreams or something." He smiled but there was no warmth in it.

And then, with one hand outstretched as if to parry any advance Nate might make, Smiley walked slowly backwards and through the door to Ma Joop.

13

For Nate, Ti Fenwe lived up to his every expectation.

The older kids, the ones who had all been there before and who told stories about the Estate, about huge spaces to run through, about a jungle riddled with mysterious pathways and secret hiding spots, about trails to tear along on the little mini-bikes belching blue smoke, those kids—they were bang on.

Once the supplies were loaded into the kitchen, the boys poured out of the house, down the front steps, and plunged into the forest. Tristan lead them through a maze of pathways, ducking under vines, through tunnels formed by dense, overhanging tree limbs, and over rocks worn smooth by generations of scramblers. He took them to the clearing, a natural circular opening deep in the bush about the size of a generous living room. The green walls of the jungle rose up on all sides like a dome, almost touching at the top and leaving a thin veil of leaves and creepers for the light to stream through.

Over the years, kids had dragged old bits of furniture into the clearing, and now the area was dotted with a ragtag collection of cast-offs: four plastic chairs, a camping cot, two wooden stools and the remains of what was once a couch. At one side of the clearing there was a dusting of tiny white polystyrene beads; they littered the ground and clung to trunks, leaves, and roots with static fanaticism. Above them in the tree branches themselves were several pieces of thick polystyrene blocks—the kind used for packing materials—and although they were largely intact, their odd, product-specific shapes were smashed through with holes, and chunks were missing along the edges.

On the ground lay candy bar wrappers, bottle caps, ripped and faded comic book pages, empty Coke and Fanta bottles. And at the center of the clearing, like the hub for the ragtag bits of furniture, sat a large wooden industrial-wire spool laying on its side. Its four-foot diameter dominated the clearing like an altar, and on top of it sat an old wooden box with a hinged lid.

With as much drama as he could muster, Tristan opened the box and produced two Wrist Rockets and a bag of chrome half-inch ball bearings. Like a well-choreographed response, Nate and Pip stepped forward together and said the same thing at exactly the same time: *No way!*

The two boys were in nirvana. Wrist Rockets: For Nate and Pip there was nothing more wondrous than this. This was a slingshot made in a real factory, not some forked tree branch rigged with a slice of inner tube. No, this was the real deal. The ultimate slingshot. It had steel uprights that dropped through a moulded plastic pistol-grip handle, then bent 90 degrees and back, extending over the top of your wrist for real torque. It had a genuine leather pouch, two heavy-duty surgical tube elastics, and it could fire a stone into a tree and make it stick. These were legendary. They were also illegal, or so everyone said, because (according to Tristan), they could kill a kid at a hundred paces.

Nate and Pip were awestruck. Tristan tossed one to Nate, and he held it like a revered work of art, turning it in his hands and taking in every part of it. He'd never held one before, but he'd seen them often on the backs of comic books. Everything about it was perfect: the knurling on the grip, the words *genuine leather* branded on the pouch, and the raw power he could feel waiting to be unleashed by the hard yellow elastic. He was about give it a test stretch when Tristan took it back, loaded a ball bearing into the pouch and drew the tubing back to his chin. His hands quivered with the force of the elastic. *Thwack!*

The ball bearing rocketed forward and punched a hole clean through one of the polystyrene blocks in the tree, and a small cloud of white pellets floated to the ground from behind it.

Pip and Nate squealed with delight, and when Richard let

fly with the second Rocket, the sound of it cracking through the polystyrene block made them jump. Tristan joined in on the laughing, and the boys spent the rest of the afternoon firing shiny ball bearings through the blocks in the trees and then searching for them to fire again.

Finally Tristan looked up through the top of the clearing. "We need to get going soon."

"Just a few more shots," implored Nate, stretching the elastic to his chin and taking a bead on a small piece of polystyrene in the tree. His tongue crept out of the corner of his mouth, and finally he let the ball bearing fly. "This is *soooo* cool!"

"Okay, last five shots," said Tristan, and the boys each took their turns, marvelling at the amazing hits and wild misses with equal enthusiasm. When the last shot was fired, Tristan placed the two Wrist Rockets, and what ball bearings they had left, back in the wooden box on the wire-spool table.

The boys watched somberly as the Wrist Rockets disappear into the box. "Can we come back and do some more tomorrow?" asked Nate.

"Yeah, can we?" Pip joined in.

"We'll see," said Tristan, drawing in a full breath through a raised nose. He was enjoying the control the boys were heaping on him.

Richard put a good natured elbow into Pip's rib. "We'll come back, but there's tons of other stuff to do up here."

Tristan set off down the path with the others in tow, winding through the darkening shades of afternoon green. "You *did not* touch them, you liar!" said Richard, shouting to the head of the single file line to Tristan who was leading up front. The conversation had turned, as it often did among the boys, to boobs.

"I did too. Just ask her when we get back," he boasted. "Maggie will tell you it's true." The path eventually wound down and out of the green mass, and deposited them on the track about four or five hundred meters from the plantation house. They could see the grassy lawn area up ahead, but for a moment the house itself was obscured by bush. The boys turned and formed a line four abreast, and ambled on toward the house. "I bet Nate's touched Rachael's boobs, right Nate?"

Nate felt a crimson rush at his neck and fought it, unsuccessfully. He didn't want them talking that way about Rachael.

"Yeah, look he's blushing! He did it for sure!"

Nate tried to shrug it off. "Shut up, Tristan." But there was no stopping it now.

"Come on Nate. Fess up!" said Pip, prodding him in the back with a stick he had picked up from the side of the track. Nate swung his arm at the stick and missed.

Tristan turned to Richard. "Are you going to stand for this? That's your little sister's friend he's been feeling up." He laughed and shook his head. But there was no rise coming from Richard so he moved on.

Up ahead, about halfway between the boys and the plantation house stood another structure. It was an almost perfect cube, about the size of a single car garage. It was made from old and heavily whitewashed brick, and topped with a flat, rusted tin roof that sat propped up about ten inches above the top of the brickwork on cinder blocks at each corner. There were no windows, just a single and oddly-wide doorway on one side of the building.

Beside it sat an aging hand cart and a pile of fibrous coconut husks as high as a man's waist. Nate didn't remember passing the building on the way in, but it must have been there, as it sat at the side of the road a mere two hundred meters from the house itself. "What's that for?" he said, pointing at the building. He didn't really care; he just wanted everyone to stop talking about Rachael.

"It's the copper oven," said Richard, "They use it to roast the coconuts and turn it into copper."

Tristan was on it instantly. "*Copra*, you twit."

And again Nate felt it. He knew instinctively that Richard's mistake was deliberate, and that the boy knew full well the difference between copper and copra.

"It's a copra oven." Tristan shook his head at Richard and swallowed the bait whole. "Come. I'll show you guys." He led the boys over to the wide door, and as he wrestled it open, Richard and Nate exchanged a secret glance. It wasn't quite a smile, but it was something very, very close.

The heavily rusted hinges on the door groaned in protest, and finally Tristan folded it back flush against the outside wall. Inside, there was an empty room the size of a single car garage with a dirty floor that looked like the bottom of a fireplace after a hasty cleaning. Exactly halfway up the building was heavy wire mesh that extended across the whole structure like a horizontal chain-link floor. The only place where it wasn't connected to the building was against the wall where the boys stood in the doorway. "That," said Tristan pointing at the wire mesh mezzanine, "is the rack. We put freshly split coconuts on it, across the whole thing, then set a fire with old husks down here underneath," he said, pointing at the floor. "The husks kind of smoulder all night, and in the morning the laborers come and clear out the husks, let everything on the rack cool and then bag the copra for market."

"So copra is just cooked coconut?" asked Pip.

"The boy's a genius!" declared Tristan, but no one really laughed.

Instead Nate asked a question as well. This was all new to Pip and him, and all so, well, fascinating. "What do they do with copra?"

Tristan switched gears easily into the role of information provider. "Suntan oil," he announced.

"Really?"

"Yep. Monday the copra oven, Tuesday the market, Wednesday some tourist's fat white arse."

The boys all burst out laughing and spilled out of the oven, but once outside the laughter quickly evaporated. Before them stood a slender black man with a very serious face. The man's clothing was worn and stained with sweat, and on his head he wore a tattered hat woven from dried palm fronds. His hands, large, callused and black-nailed, hung loosely at his sides. He eyed them each with an expression that told them that he was—at the very least—agitated by their presence. Finally he turned to Tristan and began to speak.

What was being said was a mystery to Nate and Pip, but they

noticed that Richard looked down and away as the stringy man spoke his Creole in slow and measured tones. Tristan listened and did not talk back, even though it was clear that the man was in some way reprimanding him. Seeing Tristan in this apparent state of subordination was something Pip and Nate had rarely seen, and in truth it was a little unnerving.

Finally the man gave the group one last disapproving glare, then turned and strolled off down the track toward the laborer's quarters.

"What was all that about?" asked Nate.

Tristan clenched his jaw tightly. "Nothing," he said. He turned and set off toward the house ahead of the others.

With Tristan out of earshot, Pip whispered to Rich. "What was all that? What did that man say to Tristan?"

"It's nothing, really. Just that Tristan was supposed to do some chores and he's forgotten to."

It felt vague, and Pip pressed him harder. "What chores?"

"Nothing, forget it."

Nate joined in. "Come on, Rich, what chores?"

"It's no big deal."

Nate and Pip exchanged glances with well-raised eyebrows. "What?" asked Pip.

"Nothing, seriously. Just leave it alone, okay?" He gave them a forced half-smile, and then set off toward the house. "Come on. It's getting late."

14

It took a few kilometers and at least one close call, but Nate eventually got the hang of driving on the wrong side of the road. He ran Smiley's car down through Reduit Beach, north along the road that would take him past the manmade Rodney Bay and on to Cap Estate. In his youth Rodney Bay was an empty lagoon with brown water and choked with weeds, but today it was Millionaire's Row.

In the years since Nate had left the island, developers had seized upon the area, and now condos and private villas lined the shores of an inland water system that was calm and clear and littered with expensive pleasure crafts. Nate drove the car slowly through the development, watching as an endless stream of well-heeled tourists strolled happily about and perched in front of natty coffee shops. It was as welcoming a place as could be: bright, shining, dotted with perfectly straight palm trees and alive with smiling people whiling away their holiday hours, and yet Nate felt entirely alone.

He swung the car into a parking lot in front of a line of condos, and sat quietly trying to calm his spinning thoughts. Finally, he shook his head in disgust. *Come on, Nate, what the hell are you playing at?* The wallowing had to go, and Nate decided that the whole incident with Smiley and Ma Joop was just too ridiculous, too bizarre to explain, and the best thing to do was to simply forget it. If only for now. He would take Smiley's advice. He had wheels, a beautiful Caribbean island underfoot, and hours ripe for the spending. He decided, for the second time since landing, that for the next eight hours at least, everything in his world was just fine.

And for a brief sliver of a second, he marveled at the capacity within himself that permitted such a definitive parsing of reality.

It was an ability he'd used often in his lifetime, and one, he was aware, that tended to have ramifications that weren't always the most comfortable. Still, even as the thought came he shuffled it aside, too. For now, everything would be just fine.

Nate reached into the back seat, and among his hastily thrown belongings, found the manila envelope Smiley had brought him when they met yesterday. He thrust it under his arm and slipped out of the car, round the front of the condos and found a pathway ringing the bay that was dotted with well-shaded park benches. He settled into one and began to pore through the contents of the envelope.

The first thing he pulled out was the picture of Richard—the one that had so arrested him the day before. He looked at the picture again, and realized that the setting—the white sands and the upturned Mirror dinghy sailboat—was the St. Lucia Yacht Club, a place seared so perfectly in his memory that for an instant he could smell the fiberglass resin they used to fix the old tubs. He ached to be back there. The Yacht Club was the place Nate learned to sail, the place he won his first trophy in anything (a third place finish crewing for one of the best sailors in the club—a local kid named Charles), and it was the place he had first kissed a girl.

In fairness, it was really the place he was first kissed *by* a girl, but time and boyhood bravado had spun things round so that he was the one doing the kissing. Her name was Rachael Stanton, and she was the most beautiful thing Nate had ever seen.

It had been the night of the big regatta, where the Commodore came out and thanked the club members for a great season of sailing with a barbecue and fete—a party that spilled out onto the beach and the dark open spaces around the club. Back then there were no hotels on Reduit Beach, save one at the very far end, and the only thing next to the Yacht Club was a huge white concrete slab running hundreds of meters inland. It was being slowly split and reclaimed by the sea grapes and tropical grasses, but the old abandoned World War II landing strip still served as an ideal beachside retreat for anyone looking for a quiet place to park or stroll.

For Nate, as he walked with Rachael along the beach and sat on the seaward edge of the great concrete runway, it was all he could do to take deep breaths and try to stop his hands from shaking. Everything about Rachael was amazing: her smell, the awkward way she smiled and tilted her head forward when she looked at him and, most amazing of all, how soft her hands were. That night, when she had reached out and taken his hand he had flinched, and then spent the next few moments trying desperately to reassure her that no, he didn't mean for her to stop, he just thought, well, a big bug had landed on him. Then he realized that he had just equated her touch with the landing of some giant creepy crawly, and so he backpedaled again. Eventually she laughed, and Nate was released from the terror of screwing up the most incredible moment of his life.

And then she leaned forward and kissed him. It was awkward, and impossibly soft. It lasted barely an instant, and once it was over, they both retreated in embarrassment, and sat rigidly straight staring out at the water.

Eventually, with Nate showing no signs of life at all, Rachael said she had better get back, and all Nate could utter was, *oh, okay, sure.* And that was it. They caught glances of each other at school after that, and occasionally Nate thought he saw a reserved smile, but he never had the guts to do anything about it. And so, in its own due time, Rachael's interest faded.

Nate slipped his hand back into the manila envelope and pulled out a bundle of newspaper clippings, all carefully held together with a large black paperclip. He flipped through them, and realized they were all in chronological order, starting from the day after Richard was reported missing. It was an exercise in time travel, and as Nate moved from one day to the next, he saw parts of 1976 unfold that were invisible to him all those years ago. It was like discovering a parallel universe that ran unseen beside his own, dotted with familiar places and names, filled with corollary events that swirled at arm's length but never touched him. He had been barely thirteen, and although he knew his mother and father had likely wrapped him in a protective buffer, he also knew, without the benefit of evidence of any sort, that there was probably insulation he had put there himself.

As he looked at the pages it occurred to him that even in hindsight, even after decades had passed, he had not considered any of it—not the De Villiers family's anguish, not Richard's mother's unravelling, not the police inquiry, and not the effect it had had on his own family. It was a chilling moment—in that terror of grown-ups yelling, shouting, demanding answers and imploring him to tell, tell, tell—Nate had most likely learned to gather it all up, for the first of many times in his life, and simply put it all away for safekeeping.

A picture of his mother brought him back to the present. There was more there than just his mother, but she was caught clearest in the photograph, looking back over her shoulder on the front page of the paper. She was walking briskly, one hand linked through Nate's father's arm, the other placed protectively on the shoulders of a small boy in shorts whose face was turned from the camera.

He read the caption and the story, which was largely about an inquiry that followed Richard's disappearance. The boys and their parents were all summoned to the police station where presumably they were each questioned. Again Nate was astonished by the newness of the information—information that he had been directly involved in making, and of which he had almost no recollection. On his bench at Rodney Bay, Nate laid the papers in his lap and wrestled with his mind, forcing it to cast backwards, back to the cusp of thirteen, back to the moment that photograph was snapped in Castries and the hours that would have followed it. He searched for moments, fragments, anything that might open the gates and let the memories come flooding back in. He primed his thoughts with visions of stark rooms, bright interrogation lights, weeping mothers and frightened glances between boys separated by heavy panes of glass—anything and everything that Hollywood might have supplied him over the years that could jar loose an actual and valid memory. But there was almost nothing there.

Nate pushed on through the clippings. Most of the coverage was about the De Villiers, about the discovery of the body, about the staggering loss to the family, the funeral, the investigation and the many lingering questions about what really happened. And fascinating as it was there was another area of inquiry that received a quiet but consistent level of coverage. It was a line of reporting that popped up four times in all, but never for more than two or three column inches. It was buried deep in the paper's interior, after the front page and well before the sports, and over the four insertions it told its story with almost no fanfare at all.

Nate read each of them, and then looked out over the water of Rodney Bay. He thought of his mother, and he thought about the many puzzles she loved to do. There was always one on a board that sat on the dining room table. It was moved in and out for the few occasions they ate there, but mostly it sat on the dining room table, slowly being completed, piece by piece as his mother gave it five minutes here and five minutes there. As he thought about her, he remembered that his father, who was always the one who bought her the puzzles, would always produce them in only the box's bottom—with no lid and no image of the puzzle itself. Nate had never questioned this, and for many years assumed that all puzzles were images that revealed themselves as you built them—until the day he found a small stack of puzzle boxes, tops included, in a closet up high. The uppermost one was a meadow scene with flowers in purple tones and a large white horse, and Nate knew immediately that this was the image his mother was blindly compiling on the board on the dining room table. It was a moment of elation, a rare slice of purity where everything coalesced and his understanding of the world moved a complete notch upward with an almost audible click. The puzzle was still unsolved, but he knew what the goal was.

Nate looked down again at the four articles, and as he sat on his bench at Rodney Bay in the warm wash of a gentle Caribbean breeze, he understood that he was looking at the top of a puzzle box that had been there all along. The picture was crafted in 1976, but the puzzle, like the lives it depicted, still lay in many pieces.

. . .

The four boys and Vincent, Tristan's dad, sat in the bedroom at the front of the house, eating dinner at a large wooden table set against a long set of windows. The windows lined the entire wall of the room, and overlooked the area in front of the house where they had parked the old Land Rover. The windowsill sat two feet off the room's floor and extended almost all the way up to the ceiling. But on the outside of the building, the same sill sat almost twelve feet off the ground, thanks to the concrete arches that served as the structure's foundation. The room they ate in had originally been a sitting room, but being among the largest of the rooms with a serviceable door, Vincent had adopted it as the bedroom. The door itself had two locks: a deadbolt and a sliding latch, both of which were securable only from the inside.

Through the window they could watch the day fading quickly, see the laborers strolling unhurriedly down the track toward their rickety houses, see the insects rousing from their slumber as the day's heat faded. And they could see the bats. There were hundreds of them, maybe thousands. As dusk fell, they swarmed from the house, from the high reaches and dark corners of its great rafters, peeling out through the yawning windows. Most of the house was uninhabited and open to the night air, with only the kitchen and the bedroom locked and secured with closable wooden shutters and mosquito netting. Before dinner, the boys had gathered in the main hall of the house, running back and forth and squealing with terrified laughter as the house swarmed with bats exiting into the night. The boys ran to and fro, stooped and bent, their arms held protectively aloft. They giggled and screamed as the small velvety creatures swirled around their heads before streaming out. But once the bats had cleared the house and set off for a night of feeding, the house seemed to darken at a pace that outstripped the night itself, and the boys quickly retreated to the bedroom and the only electric lights on the estate.

Directly below the bedroom sat a small Honda generator that supplied enough power to run a few lights and a portable radio/cassette deck. A length of blue nylon string ran up from the generator's on/off switch, through a hole that was bored in the floor of the bedroom, and tied to a small wooden dowel that stopped it falling back through. At the end of the evening, Vincent would simply pull the string, flicking the switch off and quieting the engine's gentle purr. And with the generator silent, the sounds of the forest and its millions of tiny, vocal inhabitants came through in an unstoppable insect clamour. Apart from that single lockable, temporarily powered room, the rest of the house was open to the night. No front door. No windows. No power. Just room after room of gaping blackness.

They dined on sausages cooked almost black, great torn hunks of fresh bread slathered with butter, and heaps of steaming sweet potatoes. They washed it down with mugs of strong, sweet tea and ate till their bellies could take no more—except, of course, for dessert: golden sticky buns so impossibly fresh that they stuck insistently to the roofs of their mouths with every bite.

As was the norm this far into the rainforest, dusk rolled toward darkness with a speed that had to be seen to be believed; Nate stood looking through the windows and down the track, and swore he could see the night coming on like a steadily turned dimmer switch. "That's why we have the curfew," said Vincent, clearing away the last of the sausages and bread. "You get caught out there when the day dies, and you're spending the night in the bush. It all looks the same in the darkness."

"It's creepy out there," said Nate to no one in particular. And as his eyes wandered to the darkness of the encroaching jungle, he felt the first pangs of what he guessed was homesickness. He was having a great time at Ti Fenwe, especially with those Wrist Rockets, but some part of him would have been happier tucked snugly in his single bed at home with his dad wedged tightly beside him reading a chapter of *The Hardy Boys*. There was something about the remoteness of the estate, about the blackness all around them that made Nate feel especially far from home.

"Nate," said Richard. "Check this out." He moved over to the far end of the bay window, and threw it open wide. There was no mosquito netting there, and the large pane folded easily outwards and against its neighbor. "You see that?" said Richard, pointing across the track that ran along the front of the house. "That pole there?"

Nate squinted into the darkness. To his left and below sat the Land Rover, but directly across from the open window he could just make out a thick pole standing upright with a platform about the size of a pizza box secured to the top. The small platform was at the same height as the window, and, sitting on the opposite side of the track, was only about fifteen feet away.

Nate pointed at the dark rectangular shape on the platform. "What's that thing sitting on top?"

Richard turned briefly and pulled something from his backpack next to his unrolled sleeping bag. He pointed it across the track and flicked it on, casting a bright beam into the night. The flashlight illuminated the pole, the platform, and the car battery sitting on top. With the new light Nate could also see that the pole was braced on three sides by smaller poles, each leaning in like the struts of a tepee, and it was clear the whole affair was designed to be dismantled and reassembled regularly. "What is it?" he asked, his face twisted in question. He was glad for the distraction; thoughts of home scatted. At least for now.

Richard smiled knowingly, brushed a blonde lock from his face and turned to the others in the room. Vincent was holding court with Tristan and Pip, sitting at the now cleared table showing them how to tie some knot or other in a thick length of rope. "Uncle Vince," Richard called out to him. "Nate wants to know what the pole's for. The one outside the window." Richard was smiling.

Vince didn't even look up from his knot. "No," he said firmly. "No way. Not you *lightees.*"

But clearly there was something exciting at hand here, and in an instant Tristan was standing beside his father and smiling, too.

"I said no," repeated Vincent, still not looking up from the length of old rope in his hands.

"*S'il te plait, papa!*" begged Tristan. "Please!"

His father shook his head lightly and muttered no again, this time with much less vigor. He was going to cave—he just needed another small push. "Tristan, you know I can't. These boys are just puppies. What are you?" he said gesturing with the rope toward Nate, "Eight? Nine?"

An indignant shadow skated briefly across Nate's face. "I'm thirteen in two weeks!" he declared.

Vincent backpedaled. "All right, all right, twelve, almost thirteen. But what about Richard—the poor lad's only…what? Seven?"

"Try almost eleven," Richard replied.

"And what would your mother say if she heard about this?" said Vincent.

"My mother knows *everything* already."

Vincent laughed and rose from the table with his hands raised in defeat. "Fine, fine. But don't complain to me if your parents ban you all from ever coming here again!" He walked over to Richard and buried the boy in a hug, and from somewhere in those coils Richard giggled in delight.

On the other side of the room, Tristan folded his arms and set his lips to a thin hard line. It wasn't the first time Nate had seen that hard edge in Tristan, particularly where his father's obvious affection for the youngest De Villiers was concerned.

"All right then," said Vincent, crossing the floor with all the drama and showmanship he could muster. He walked in a slow and deliberate fashion, like a man buying time and stoking his courage before some mighty task. He rubbed his hands together, fixed the cabinet on the other side of the room with an overly serious stare, and then cocked his head from side to side like a prize fighter readying for the ring.

"Oh puh-leeez!" said Richard, rolling his eyes and collapsing on the one bed in the room. The boys all laughed, and Vincent lost his composure and laughed, too.

"Okay, fine," he said, reaching for the cabinet and fumbling with a set of keys. "But we need to be serious here for a moment, okay?" The timbre in his voice brought all the boys to attention, and they gathered around him without needing to be asked.

Vincent swung the cabinet's double doors open and exposed two shotguns propped up against the inside wall. On the lower shelf were a few small boxes, and a bundle of rags. "These are not toys, understand?"

The boys all nodded.

"You only hold and fire when I give it to you, and the barrel never points anywhere except out of the window."

Nodding all round.

"Where does the barrel point?"

"Only out of the window," the boys repeated.

"Fine." Vincent reached down and lifted a small bundle of rags. Slowly he unwrapped the bundle, and at its center sat a small black pistol. The boys collectively gasped.

"This, my boys," said Vincent, pushing the black cylinder out of the housing, "is a snub nose Airweights .38 Special." He tilted the little black gun toward the boys, careful to keep the barrel pointing away from everyone, and let them lean in to look. Pip reached his hand out instinctively to touch it, and Vincent recoiled lightly. "No, no, Pip. No one touches this until we are at the window, ready to fire, and you've had some basic instruction."

Nate looked on at the gun in something akin to awe. He had never seen one before, not for real, and the little black chunk of metal with its wooden handle seemed to ooze a sense of threat. To Nate the gun was ugly, stunted looking, as if it had never completely finished growing into a real gun—at least not like the ones Dirty Harry carried. Still, the gun captivated him, and as he stared at it with the others he realized that its simplicity, its tiny size, its matte black color and its dull, worn wooden handle all seemed to be so unimpressive. Sure it was a real gun, but it didn't speak to him the way the Wrist Rocket did.

Vincent led them over to the open window, and placed a small carton on the sill from which he extracted a number of brass-cased bullets. He slid them into the cylinder one by one, and the boys all followed his actions with wide eyes and loose jaws—all of them but Tristan whose face was carefully pinned with an expression of impatient disinterest. His attitude said he'd seen it all before, but the effort was wasted. The others were studying Vincent's actions with rare intensity.

With all the chambers filled, Vincent snapped the cylinder closed and pointed the pistol through the window. "All right, boys. When it's your turn, hold it like this," he said showing them how to use both hands to cradle the weight of the gun. "Once you're holding it, I will pull the hammer back for you, because it's very hard to do just with the trigger. After that, just squeeze gently. Like this." As he said *this*, the gun let out a pop, and it flicked slightly in Vincent's hand.

The boys ooh'd and aah'd.

"Right, who's first?" he said, and everyone's hand went up. Vincent put a meaty hand behind Richard's head and gently brought him to the front. "Youngest first," he said, holding the gun out the window and guiding Richard's hand toward it. "Okay, it's cocked. Line up the sights on the battery over there, and just squeeze."

Again the gun popped and again the boys paid homage.

Next it was Pip's turn, and he too fired the little gun at the battery across the track. "Another miss!" cried Vincent, taking the gun safely back from Pip. "Now you, Mr. Almost-Thirteen." Vince winked at Nate and then set the little gun in his hand. *Pop!* Another miss. Nate let Vincent take the gun and in truth he felt better just watching; the gun felt awkward in his hand, dangerous, without boundary.

"All right, my boy," said Vincent, ushering Tristan to the front. "Here's your chance to show them how it's done. Three shots, three misses."

"Ha," said Tristan. "Watch this." The little gun popped again, and the battery across the track shuddered, gently rocking the pole. "How's that!" he crowed, instinctively turning to the other boys with his hands outstretched in victory.

In his hand still sat the pistol, his finger still curled around the trigger. He had fired the gun many times before, and he had heard his father's safety talk on every occasion. But Tristan was thirteen, and victorious in front of his friends. He forgot everything and turned to fully face the boys. As he turned, the barrel of the small black gun tracked across the chests of the little group in the bedroom.

And as his father barked in alarm, Tristan flinched, causing a quick tightening of all the muscles in his legs, his back, and in his hands.

15

By the time Nate's mind came back to the moment, the sun had moved and chased the shade a few feet away from his little bench by the water. He flicked his thumb softly through the pile of papers, lingering in what they had to say. Then he slid all the newspaper clippings, the photographs, and the assorted documents back into the manila envelope.

He thought of his father again, about the last time he had spoken to him and the promise he'd made himself to simply leave the old man to dissolve in his pathetic puddle of gin. The guilt was there, as it always was, but after reading the contents of the envelope, the old sensation was suddenly overwhelming, like a crushing wave driving him down into the hard sand. As Nate stared out over the shimmering water his mind knit together a thousand pieces of information gathered from family members and friends over the years. Everything suddenly fit together: the envelope was the Rosetta Stone, a key piece that made the puzzle entirely apparent once you had it, but left it unsolvable in its absence. Like the child he had once been, Nate looked down at the envelope with the same sense of wonder that had gripped him the day he found those long absent puzzle box tops sitting high up in the hall closet.

The envelope contained so much information, so many details, but it was those four little articles from *The Voice* that connected so much for Nate—four fairly unremarkable blurbs that helped close out the story that had gripped the island back in the summer of '76. Together they formed something of an epilogue, a chronicling of the demise of a diplomat whose son was somehow linked to the death of the De Villiers boy. It told of the sudden departure of the diplomat and his family, whisked away from the island and the unfolding investigation under the protection of diplomatic immunity. It picked up months later with the diplomat's dismissal from the Foreign Service, and then on the second anniversary of the boy's death, there was one final entry. In it, Nate's father was little more than a closing fact. It told of a series of arrests for DUI and domestic assault, and gently implied something of a karmic balance. That the former diplomat's life had ultimately disassembled entirely in the wake of Richard De Villiers's death was somehow fitting, according to the writer, given the privileged and untouchable exit their diplomatic status had provided them. It was a rather pathetic end to the whole story.

It connected things for Nate like a jolt of electricity, and the words hummed through his mind with a clarity that pained him: *I goddamn well shut the doors tight on those bastards. I protected you! I protected your mother, this whole family. I protected you. And then the bastards pull the floor out from under me.* He could practically see his father standing there, weaving unsteadily, accusing finger in place. Nate had never really understood the rant—or perhaps more accurately, he'd chosen never to listen to it that closely—but now, in the wake of the manila envelope and the four simple articles, it all made perfect, guilt-ridden sense.

His memory opened wide and was flushed with another version of his father, a version where the man was tall and powerful and imbued with the unassailability that all fathers have in the eyes of their sons. He saw him in the days after Richard's death, standing in the corner of the brightly lit room, watching as the questions kept coming and coming from lawyers, policemen and social workers. Finally, his father waded through the suits and uniforms, put up his hand and said, *Enough.* He remembered his father's hands about his shoulders, pushing him firmly past them all and walking straight out of the station. He was magnificent. He just took Nate and his mother right to the car, straight to the airport. True to his word, he shut the doors tight on those bastards.

But the fleeting sense of awe was quickly overshadowed by a

stark realization: that simple walk had come at a terrible cost. In that moment on the island, being ushered from the room with his Dad's hands wrapped protectively about him, it had, for Nate, just been his father making *everything all right*. He'd even said it as they moved past the people and out through the police station doors: *don't worry, Nate, everything's going to be okay*. But now, Nate realized his father's simple act had cost so much more.

Over Rodney Bay, the light was changing. The sky was still a perfect blue, the island breeze still moved the humidity along in warm ebbs and flows, but the afternoon was surely laying claim to the day. On any other occasion—any other occasion where Nate might have found himself on some tropical island paradise—the waning of another perfect day would be like a long, calming exhale. But today, here among sun-kissed tourists, the ageing day was daubed with foreboding. For a moment Nate let himself flounder helplessly; he had nowhere to go, nowhere to *be* tonight, and it struck him that he was, at least temporarily, homeless.

With his father unreachable—some things were the same in life as in death—thoughts of his mother crept in. Should he try to reach her? He knew he wouldn't—he wasn't even sure if he had a current number for her back home. But something in him softened for her, too. There was so much new information in that single manila envelope, so many new avenues of thought that would take years to fully explore. He thought of her up at the house in Vigie; it was the best image he had of her, and one he tried to keep as the go-to mental snapshot. But soon it was shoved rudely out of the way by another, less flattering memory.

In it her face was hard and expressionless. She looked down at Nate, an awkward, pimply-faced sixteen-year-old, and it was clear there was something she had wanted to say. But instead she looked away, at his father, who stood with his back turned staring out of the window. She stood that way for a long time, watching him, waiting for something to happen. When it was finally clear that nothing would, she picked up her suitcase and walked out the door.

He glanced down at his watch and was happy for the distraction.

He would need to find a place to stay, perhaps a little food to eat. He looked up and down the boulevard and there were plenty of options, plenty of air-conditioned restaurants boasting cuisines from around the world.

Perhaps it was the cliché of the newspaper held to obscure his face, or the fact that virtually everyone else around him was so clearly a tourist that made the man stand out.

He stood leaning against a wall about forty paces away, halfway between Nate and Smiley's car. He was facing Nate's direction and apparently reading a newspaper. He was well dressed in white pants, a blue T-shirt and sunglasses, but something about him drew Nate's full attention.

Had Nate seen him before? Nate stared at him plainly, and the man abruptly folded the newspaper under his arm and slipped around the corner of the building. *Was he watching me?* Nate wondered. *Was someone following me?* It was an absurd idea. A ridiculous notion. And so why, Nate wondered, was he now hustling down the sidewalk to see where the man with the newspaper had gone?

At the corner he saw nothing, just a pathway leading down to a boardwalk that followed the edge of the manmade lagoon. Nate hurried down the path, looked left and right at the bottom, but there was no one, save an old couple walking hand in hand toward a flotilla of moored sailboats.

Jesus, get a grip, Nate, he scorned himself. He bombarded his thoughts with logic. No one was following him; no one knew he was even there. Why would anyone follow him? It was ridiculous. But his mind wouldn't be so easily discouraged, and soon he was thinking of the man he had seen through the window of the Breadfruit Tree Inn at breakfast barely a day ago, the one who had held his stare just a little too long. Could it have been the same man? Nate rationalized that it was impossible to tell—between the newspaper and the sunglasses the man's face was largely covered, and in truth Nate could hardly recollect what the man at the inn looked like.

Stop it, he said to himself aloud, then turned back up the path to the boulevard and the car.

The man with the blue T-shirt and sunglasses was standing at the top of the pathway, newspaper held loosely at his side, watching Nate. The sight fully stopped Nate, and the two men stared at each other until at last the man in the sunglasses casually dropped the newspaper, turned, and walked out of view. A car door slammed, an engine revved, and somewhere around the corner a vehicle moved off down the street.

Finally Nate moved. He trotted up to the boulevard, and saw that whatever car had been there was now gone, as was the man in the sunglasses. By his feet, the newspaper fluttered on the ground. Despite the breeze it remained anchored to its spot on the carefully mown and perfectly green grass. It had been weighed down by a black chicken. It was clearly dead, and its feet were bound tightly with course string in coils like a hangman's noose. Its feathers seemed slick and oily, and as Nate stooped to look closer he could tell it was blood. He nudged the carcass with an outstretched foot, rolled it over on one side and then kneeled down beside it. The dead bird had apparently been gutted, and something had been stuffed into the cavity. It looked like a small bottle wrapped in leaves and shoots of some kind, and from what he could see there appeared to be more blood inside the small vial.

With his eyes locked on the bird, Nate stood and became suddenly aware that he was grimacing unabashedly at the thing on the ground. He looked around and realized he was drawing curious glances, so he dropped his head and walked quickly to the car. Whatever this was, whatever it meant, whatever it was somehow supposed to convey, Nate was convinced of one thing without reservation: the message was for him.

It was as if a door in a long-sealed and airless room had been forced open—and Nate knew without question where that door could be found. It was part of an old and decaying house on the far side of the island, where its rusting tin roof and dark archways were slowly being suffocated by a tangle of vines and wild thickets. He couldn't leave the island without doing what he'd come to do, even if it killed him. The thought calmed him some and as he focused on it, he realized that this momentary weakness was just a small matter of a failure to remember. He cast his mind back, immersed himself in the memory, in the horror of his past. Moments later, the courage—or at least a sense of grim determination—came flooding back. He was here for a reason, and with that focus once more set, Nate was able to pull himself together and get moving.

Back in Smiley's car, he reached over the seat to his hastily packed case, unzipped it and slipped his hand inside. It felt rigid and latently powerful in his hand, as it always had, even through the folds of the worn brown paper bag. And with that sensation came others—a swell of emotions so complex that Nate had to pull his hand from the bag to calm himself. He took an even, steady breath. He was here to fix it all. He would make it right.

Nate started the car and looked in the rearview mirror. Across the street, a police Jeep sat in the deep shade of a broad almond tree. He couldn't see for sure, but it looked like there was someone in it, and if he let himself, he could quickly be convinced they were watching him, too. Nate shook his head, refused to be drawn into the conspiracy.

His path was clear. He would drive away, find a place to spend the night, and in the morning he would make his way back into the past, back to Ti Fenwe Estate, back to the hollow in the forest where his life had been so clearly and regrettably defined.

16

"Tristan!" shouted Vincent, his eyes flashing wildly as he watched the gun track across the little group of boys. At the same moment, he lunged and snatched at the gun, and Tristan instinctively recoiled like a meek dog that had known many a beating. His arms automatically retracted, and his father's grab missed wildly.

"What the fuck you doing, boy?" cried Vincent, lashing out for the gun. This time he seized it firmly with both hands and wrenched it from the youngster. The others cringed at the reaction, and as they watched Vincent's anger gather in the space of a fractured second, they all felt a sharp and dangerous shift in the room. Vincent's face pleated like an unruly blanket, and the veins in his neck rose. Tristan had folded inside himself, retreating in every way that he could. His eyes were cast downward, covered by his thick and disobedient hair, and his arms were raised in a slight defensive posture across his chest and held nervously at the ready.

And in the very next instant the boys saw why.

Without another word, Vincent's hand sliced through the air like a tennis player driving through a backhand, and it caught Tristan cleanly on the side of the head. The boy never saw it coming; his hair exploded at the impact and he was sent reeling back against the windowsill. A second later Vincent's finger jabbed in his face. "Don't you ever, *ever,* point a gun at someone else unless you damn well mean to kill them, boy!" he shouted, and a fine spittle crossed the narrow divide between them. He reached down and lifted his son's chin with a sharp jerk. "You don't see your little cousin behaving like this, do you?" he spat, and something in Tristan shrank further still, twitching inward to a place from which part of him would never return.

Richard, too, reacted, and like an automated response, he reached out and took the other two boys by the elbows and quickly began walking to the door. The two didn't resist, and walked trance-like down the hall to the kitchen. Richard left them there for a moment with a gesture, and then returned to the room and closed the door on Tristan and his father.

In the kitchen, Nate and Pip looked at each other in total astonishment. Above them, the second of only two lights in the house burned starkly against the darkness, and neither was able to speak. What they had just seen was their first real glimpse of violence, actual violence—not the choreographed haymakers on *The Six Million Dollar Man*—but the real deal. They stood looking at each other, unable to process what had just happened, stripped down to the core of their boyishness. They were children. Alone, unprepared and incapable of understanding what they had just seen.

In the other room they could hear Vincent's voice raised and shouting, although the words were entirely lost. Pip finally lifted his hands and covered his ears, and Nate could see the wetness gathering in his eyes. "I wanna go home," said Pip in barely more than a whisper. "I wanna go home now. Right now."

Pip flinched when Richard's hand came to rest briefly on his shoulder.

Finally Nate spoke. "Rich, is Tristan okay?"

Richard busied himself in a cardboard box of food on the table. "Sure," he said without looking up. "There's some cookies in here somewhere."

Pip dropped his hands from his ears. "But he hit him. I mean, he hit him *hard*."

"Ah ha. Here they are." Richard, produced a bag of ginger snaps. He offered Nate a cookie.

Nate took one, sat down on an old kitchen chair and bit the cookie mechanically. "What should we do?" he asked hollowly. In the distance they could hear Vincent's voice, still raised and taut with anger.

Richard chomped at one of the hard cookies and offered the bag to Pip, who shook his head silently. Outside, through the open windows, the darkness was complete. There was no ambient light from towns or villages this far inland, and the thick tangle of the rainforest crowded around the house claustrophobically as if to cut them off and isolate them. Nate looked at the naked bulb above them, and at the cluster of moths that swirled about it.

The three boys sat in silence, listening to the muted shouting, the occasional sound of what sounded like a slap, and the thud of someone hitting the floor or a being driven against the wall. It went on for almost five minutes, and when it finally quieted, Richard collected a flashlight from the cardboard box and stood. "Come on," he said. "Let's go."

"It's pitch black out there, and we can't go in *there…*" said Nate, gesturing back to the bedroom.

"Follow me."

Richard led the boys out of the stark light of the kitchen and into the main hall of the house. It was even darker than the outside, and from the main hall the windows seemed to offer some sense of light, or at least something less black. They moved quickly through the hall, floorboards creaking, always following Richard's little pool of light, and out through the open front door and down the steps. They turned right, along the front of the house and the dark arches that supported it, and passed between the bay window of the bedroom and the pole with the car battery on it. They stayed on the track and walked in a tight cluster toward the workers huts, and as they made their way further from the house, the purr of the generator under the bedroom gradually faded and was finally lost to the night sounds of the estate. Nate looked back at the plantation house, at the glow from the upper window, and at the long line of impossibly dark archways that made up its base. Something about the place made him shudder, and he moved a little quicker to keep up with the others.

On their right the boys passed the square building they had seen earlier—the copra oven—and Nate noticed that a new pile had been made beside it, although what was piled there was impossible to say in the darkness. It was dark and lumpy, and Nate gave it all a wide berth.

"Come on," said Richard, sensing the unease in the group. "We're almost there."

Finally the boys reached the workers huts: a collection of rickety, ageing wooden shacks that seemed unchanged and unimproved in fifty years. They were scarcely larger than tool sheds, and without electricity, the only glow that came from their windows and through the many gaps in the twisted planks of wood that formed their walls, was from flickering candles. The dancing of their flames cast eerie, shifting shadows on the grass verge, and the boys were all washed in soft golden tones. Around them, behind the tiny huts and swallowing the track they had just walked down, was a carnivorous blackness. Nate looked back toward the plantation house again and could just make out the shape of the roofline and the bank of windows in the bedroom. The light was still burning, and it still cast sinister shadows on the bush-line on the opposite side of the track.

The boys stopped just short of the shacks and Richard stepped forward alone. Nate and Pip watched as he stole silently forward, his face an expression of nervous anticipation. As he moved into the doorway, his expression changed and then a voice inside spoke his name with mild but happy surprise. Richard went in briefly and before the others could get concerned about being abandoned, he was out again, motioning them forward and smiling happily.

Inside there were three large women, each a dark ebony with faces punctuated by brilliantly white teeth. They were dressed in simple colorful clothes, worn at the seams with a tear here and a fray there, but they were relaxed and happy in their home. On the walls were a series of simple shelves lined with a few blackened cooking pots, a row of plastic cups and an assortment of bags and cartons. Above the door was a framed and faded print of Jesus, eyes closed and hands pressed together in prayer.

The women sat at an old wooden table that had at some point been painted bright blue, but was now chipped and faded and worn through in most places to the natural wood. They shuffled along the benches to make space for the boys, and patted the vacant spots beside them, cooing and giggling like schoolgirls despite the fact that none of them was less than sixty. Richard sat, and motioned for the others to do the same. He said something to the women in patois, and the three of them roared with laughter and one of them folded Richard into her bosom. Before long there were loaves of bread and jars of homemade guava jelly on the table, and the boys were heaping spoonfuls of the sticky amber jelly onto pieces of fibrous brown bread and feasting upon it through bouts of laughter focused on nothing.

Then, from somewhere far off in the bush to the north of the house, came the sound.

It was half-shriek, half-howl, and it stopped the conversation cold. Everyone in the room turned to the yawning maw of the open doorway, frozen, listening, straining to hear the sound again. Moments later it obliged, this time shorter and more guttural, far away and muffled by the forest and the darkness, and as it ceased one of the women muttered something in frightened tones and brought her hand crisply to her mouth.

To her left one of the other women reached out and touched her arm reassuringly, then spoke calmly in clear and plain English. "Der gwan be much trouble now," she said, shaking her head woefully. "Much trouble."

17

The pain started not long after the drive began. It was an itch at first, but it soon grew in intensity and began to throb. Within the hour, the flesh around the cut seemed to take on a new weight and with every bump in the road, it tugged at the stitches. Halfway to Castries, Nate pulled over to the side of the road and turned the rear view mirror to his face. He gently peeled back the tape, and then tugged at the gauze that had fused into a hard mat of dried blood. It eventually came free, and Nate was able to have a good look at the wound and the five stitches that held it together.

The cut was just below his left eye and off to the side, tracing an inch-long arc like a smile on the point of his cheekbone. It was an angry red hue, and the meeting point of the smile's lips was crusting over with dots of yellow. When Nate touched it, he was lanced with a sharp pain for his efforts, but still he was compelled to probe it. It pulsed in time with his heartbeat, which he was suddenly and strangely aware of, and the bruising around the cut was creeping toward his left eye.

He put the car in gear and pulled back into traffic, through the potholes in the shoulder and onto the paved surface. Each jolt of the vehicle was magnified in his face, and he wondered if the pronounced pain he was feeling was normal, or if the yellow dots were the telltale sign of an infection setting in. He was in the tropics. He had been treated by someone who was allegedly a doctor, or an archivist, or perhaps something else. Was it all done in a sanitary fashion? He tried to think back to the kitchen table he was treated on. Was the guy wearing gloves? Was there sterile packaging?

Another jolt from a pothole brought the pain to his cheek

again, sharp and hot, and focused him on the present. He probed at the wound with his fingers, testing it, even squeezing it gently to see if there was any real pus inside. And within a half mile Nate was convinced there was a tropical infection setting into his face that would rampantly consume him.

Calm the fuck down, he said aloud to himself. And for a moment he did, but the doubts crept back in. Soon thoughts of the dead chicken entered the fray: What was in that vial? Did anything come out? Did it get on him? And from there it was a short leap to Smiley and Ma Joop, the hocus-pocus behind her hysterical reaction, the banishment to Smiley's car, all of it, and soon he was speaking to himself again: *Stop it!*

He was sweating now, too, even though the windows were down and a steady breeze whipped through the car. And that ache behind his eyes was back. Was he getting sick? Did he feel okay? Was this all just psychosomatic? Of course it was. Probably. Most likely. There was only the slimmest of chances that there was anything sinister going on. He thought on that for a moment. *Only the slimmest of chances.* And soon, that was enough. He needed to get to the hospital, and he knew just where it was.

Victoria Hospital wasn't far, just on the other side of Castries near the mouth of the harbor on the south side, and he was pretty sure he could still find it even thirty years later. He would go into the emergency room and have it looked at. They would know if there was something wrong. A doctor—one in a white smock with a stethoscope draped neatly around his neck—would take one look at it and declare it nothing, and then Nate would move on. He just needed that reassurance. That's all. After that it would all be fine.

But as he drove, the questions kept creeping in. What was it about this that had him so jumpy? Was it the heat? The tropics? No, it was none of them. He knew exactly what it was but didn't want to admit it—to do so meant it was a possibility, preposterous as it was. But his mind, full of its own sense of will, wandered over and landed squarely on what he was trying so hard to ignore. Hocus-pocus. Magic potions. Dark figures, cow's feet, and sacrificed chickens.

Local lore that works because people believe in it. They've grown up with it. They've been told stories by their mothers and their grandmothers. And they've been told it's real, and so for them it is.

Nate thrust it aside as best he could, pushed his head out of the window and took the full force of the wind in his face and hair. He breathed deeply and looked at the modern buildings around him, the construction equipment, the cranes, the trucks, the cargo ships looming over the rooftops as they sat at the quay waiting to be loaded. This was not a backwater part of the world anymore. This was no remote, forgotten island run by tribesmen with feathers and boned noses—no, this was a vibrant and modern commercial center and hocus-pocus had no place here—or in his head.

He would drop these thoughts here and now, but just before he could, his mind played one last highlight reel, one last soundtrack: the sound of dried nutmegs in their thousands rolling, rolling, rolling over wooden floorboards, rattling away as those heavy, short footfalls pounded across the ceiling in the loft above. Even in the heat and brightness of a full blown tropical day, the thought made a cold shudder run through him.

He moved cautiously through Castries, not for fear of being seen by one of the phantoms he had conjured up in his head or from thoughts of Smiley's warning (stay out of town), but more to make sure he didn't smash up the car through some North American expectation that the lines in the road—where there were some—were supposed to divide the oncoming traffic. He wound his way through the streets, past landmarks that he recognised from his youth—M&Cs where his father had bought him his first cricket bat, and past the building that had housed Geity Cinema, now a warehouse, where he'd karate-chopped and kicked his way through a hundred Saturday morning kung fu matinees.

He stuck to the water's edge, along the harbor, and only went wrong once before making it onto a stretch of road now called the Millennium Highway. It wrapped around the last section of the harbor and brought him up to the front gates of Victoria Hospital. He paused as he reached it, looking at the buildings, at the parking lot and the trees, and the clusters of structures that made up the hospital compound. He took it all in, waiting for the thunderclap, bracing for the jolt of memories that would wash over him and swamp his every sense.

But there was nothing. The place had changed almost entirely. He drove the car in, parked it, wiped the sweat from his forehead with a sleeve and went through the double doors marked "Emergency."

He shouldn't have been surprised, but he was: like every hospital, medical clinic or infirmary in every part of the world, there was a lineup. Nate took a deep breath and went to the back of what looked like a two-hour queue, crossed his arms and settled in for the wait.

He gazed around the waiting room and saw her almost immediately. She didn't fit in. The room was full of people from almost every walk of St. Lucian life—young kids coughing into their mothers' laps, old-timers staring blankly ahead, construction workers with bloodied hands. There were school kids, pregnant women, and a few business types sitting with heads in hands or closed eyes awaiting their turn. All colors and types were represented, and Nate didn't stand out in his dishevelled shirt and creased pants, or even with his tan-less white skin. Everyone in the waiting room was bonded by the one common element of poor health, and each of them wore a largely similar expression on their face that was a mix of discomfort, boredom and angst.

Everyone except her.

She was dressed casually enough, in jeans and a simple white blouse, but it seemed she worked hard at looking casual. She was a striking woman, probably in her forties, with sun-kissed sandy blonde hair that fell in a graceful arc across her left eye.

She looked up at almost the same instant that Nate saw her, and for a moment, their eyes locked. There was something immediately familiar about her—the soft pout of her lips, the dark, almost Egyptian eyes. As Nate looked at her, she rose to her feet and walked directly toward him. She stopped a foot in front of him. "Hello, Nate."

• • •

"What is that?" asked Pip in a quivering voice. The howl from deep in the forest was nearly more than he could bear. "I wanna go home!" To his right, one of the big women wrapped her ample arm around him. The small boy sank immediately into her embrace, and shuffled quickly and unabashedly along the bench and into her protective girth.

Nate was scared, too, but his reaction was all about flight. He stood from the table, his eyes riveted on the doorway. Everything in his being was on red alert; he was as tense as a drawn bow, ready to tear off in whatever direction the moment might call for. "Richard, was that a person?" Nate tore his eyes away from the doorway just long enough to glance at Richard, and immediately wished he hadn't.

This was Richard's world. Richard knew everything about it, he'd been here dozens of times before, hell it was part of his family's heritage, and he was the one who was supposed to tell them it was nothing, just the wind, just some drunk playing a prank—anything to diffuse the terror that gripped them all. But as Nate glanced over he saw that Richard's eyes were pinned open, his mouth formed a tight 'O' and he watched the doorway intently.

The woman with Pip tucked under her arm finally spoke. "De Bolom. He runnin' 'bout tonight. You all mus' stay here, yes? You stay here 'til de sun dun rise."

"But what *was* that?" asked Nate again insistently. "And what's a *Bolom*?"

Richard regained some of his composure and prodded at the piece of bread before him on the table. He looked at Nate but didn't answer.

"Seriously, Rich." His throat was dry and he swallowed hard. "What's out there?"

The young blonde boy looked back at his bread. "Bolom," he said in a whisper, and the darkness outside seemed to plumb a new depth of black.

"What's a Bolom?" Pip erupted, and everyone at the table

flinched. They watched as one of the women stood from the table and retrieved another candle and a worn rosary. She settled back into her spot, lit the candle from another burning on the table, and began running the beads through her fingers while her lips moved silently.

"The Bolom is something very old," began Richard. "It's something that lives here, always has—and not just here, but at all the great plantations on the island." He stopped for a moment and rubbed at his eye. "The Bolom is a kind of protector, a guardian of the estate that keeps watch over the land. It's connected to the master of the estate."

"The master?" asked Nate.

"The person who owns the plantation. At the moment that's Uncle Vince. And one day it'll probably be Tristan. But for now it's Uncle Vince's."

"But what *is* it?" said Pip, still lingering under the safety of the old woman's arm.

"I'm trying to tell you…"

"Sorry."

Richard tossed the lump of bread aside and leaned deeper into the table. "The Bolom is kind of like a little man. It's about this high," he said, holding his hand about three feet off the floor, "and it's supposed to look like a baby and an old man all at the same time."

"You haven't seen one then?" asked Nate.

"No, only the owner of the estate can see him."

"So just your Uncle Vince?"

"Yeah."

Pip piped up again. "What about Tristan?"

"He's not the master," replied Richard, slightly annoyed at having to explain it again, "so he can't see the Bolom—until he's the master."

Pip pressed on. "You mean *can't see him* as in he shouldn't, or *can't see him* as in he can't because the Bolom's invisible?"

"Invisible."

Nate's face twisted in question. "Come on, Richard. What are you talking about? That's a load of crap."

"No it isn't. It's real. Ask Augustine," he said, gesturing to the woman running the rosary through her hands.

Augustine nodded slowly and began to speak. Her accent was thick with an island melody, and her voice crackled and rasped as she told her tale. "Richard nah tell no lie," she began. "De Bolom, he a little fellow dat was once a chyle, but never had de chance to grow. But he been Bolom so very long, he now old, old. And dis little fellow, he very bored. Very mischievous. Run 'round all de time making trouble. Causing 'ardship everywhere."

Augustine paused, and looked at the doorway. She seemed far away to the boys, as if reliving some time long passed. "Dat sound way out dere in de bush—dat was de Bolom up to no good. He take some poor beast. He kill 'im. Eat 'im. Him behave like a troublesome, ill-tempered dog. Dat Bolom run round dis place, watching the estate, but hating him lot in life. Him forced to protect the land, for sure, but him have no love for de landowners. He must obey the landowner, and he hate dat, for sure. Him spend eternity hating one master after the other, forced to serve, but waiting de whole time for this one to die and the next one to come along— hoping de next one will treat him well, maybe even set him free. But it never happen. It a thorny dance between Bolom and master, for sure, with plenty trouble as a result."

Nate was now more worried than ever. "You mean the Bolom's not a real person? Not, like, you know, a human?"

"No, no, my sweet chyle. Dis creature want so badly to be a human. But him can't. Him made by a dark Obeah man, and de Bolom bound into service for de plantation for all eternity."

"Made him?"

"For true. De Obeah man take a chicken egg, him put it under de arm of a woman who push out a dead chyle first time."

"I don't understand…"

Richard cut in. "He takes the egg and puts it in the armpit of a woman who had a baby that was born dead. Her first baby. It has to stay there for a week or something, and then he buries it with the baby. I don't know what else they do, but that's basically what makes the Bolom."

Nate was frightened and repulsed. "The Bolom's a dead baby?"

"No. De baby is just de way into dis worl'," said Augustine. "De Bolom is a Devil ting for sure. A Devil ting trapped 'ere by some powerful Obeah."

Pip leaned into the table with the others. "But why would any woman let that happen to her dead baby? Why would she let some guy do the egg thing and have it do that…that…stuff—to her baby?"

"Some people terrible poor, chyle. Terrible poor. Not everyone live like a queen de way we do here!" she said, raising her hands palms up to the bare walls around her. The other two women chuckled lightly. "And besides," she continued, "if de Obeah man tell you he want make Bolom, den you let him make Bolom—otherwise he gone curse you." The other women became serious again and nodded their heads in agreement.

Pip looked at each of the women and realized they were deadly serious. It unnerved him even more. "Curse you? What is this Obeah man thing? What is he?"

The woman with the rosary and the sandpaper voice drew a breath in reflection. "Obeah man? Well, him—and his like—dey are a most powerful force on dis island. Dey keep de rhythm, keep de balance in place 'tween good and evil. Dem can capture love for you, or cause you neck to break—jus' like that," she said, and punctuated it with a crisp snap of her fingers. "Him wield terrible, terrible powers."

Nate was spellbound by what the woman was saying. Could this all be true? He had to know more, had to ask more. "This Bolom, is it around all the time? I mean, how do you know where it is if you can't see it?"

Pip eyed the room nervously.

"My dad told me that once when he was a boy," said Richard, "he took a banana from the cart the laborers use to load them up, and something slapped him really hard on his butt when he peeled it—but there was nothing around. He said you could see a welt on his butt in the shape of a small hand when he pulled his pants down."

"No way," said Pip wide-eyed and anxious.

Augustine tut-tutted. "Das true, you know. De Bolom watch over every-ting. He catch you tiefing, he gone pay you some attention. Your Papa lucky him jus' get a slap. Many fare worse, you know. Much worse."

"Tiefing?" asked Nate.

"Stealing," said Richard, swinging his gaze suddenly back to the doorway.

Everyone followed Richard's lead and turned their heads to the black opening. "Quiet," he said in a voice that was eerily calm. "There's something out there."

18

"You don't remember me, do you?" she said, filling in the uncomfortable silence that had gathered between them the very instant she had said hello.

Nate's brain was in full stall. He blinked, then blinked some more, and finally managed to speak. "Hello," was all he could come up with, and then immediately realized he was one response behind in the conversation. He quickly blurted out a catch-up. "I mean...I don't. Do I know you?" His mind raced as he tried to find her in his memory, but despite something vaguely familiar about her—perhaps a hazy similarity to someone he had once seen but couldn't bring to mind—there was nothing.

"Well, you *did* know me," she said, smiling a guarded smile. "Back when we were kids."

Nate's mind took a hard left for a blistering ride down memory lane. It took a few heartbeats, a wrinkled face and a bitten lower lip, but then he found her. She was standing on the beach at the foot of the abandoned airstrip by the Yacht Club, feet planted in white sand, a pink T-shirt flapping in the wind, lips pursed and eyes closed in that visceral moment right before the kiss. It was Rachael Stanton.

Nate smiled his first real smile in what felt like years. "Rachael?"

"So you *do* remember!"

"Oh my God," he said. "Rachael Stanton!" He wasn't sure if hugging someone you hadn't seen in more than thirty years was socially appropriate, but it was too late. He was already committed and had his arms around her before the thought finished. Thankfully Rachael hugged him back warmly. He pushed her gently away so that he could look at her again. "You look absolutely fabulous, only bigger."

Rachael patted her hips and smiled awkwardly. "Well, that's age for you."

"No! No…that's not what I mean!—You're not the kid I have in my memory. And take it from me—you've got nothing to worry about in the age department. I'm not kidding, Rachael, you look great. Really great."

Rachael smiled modestly and waved her hand. "You're going to make a girl blush." Her accent was a unique island blend—not hard-core local, but definitely island—and liberally mixed with British stylings.

Nate's mind was still spinning. "What are you doing here? Well, I mean, you live here—you still live here, on the island, right?"

"Yes, up in Cap." For a brief second a shadow seemed to skate across her face, as if the answer had cost her something. But she shook it quickly. "I should be asking you what you're doing here, but by the look of your eye, I'm guessing you're here to get it looked at."

Nate involuntarily lifted his hand to his eye. "Yeah, this." he said, scrambling for an explanation and finding none. "I hit it."

"And stitched it up yourself?" Rachael smiled disarmingly. "Let's get that looked at. Come with me," she said, taking him by the arm and leading him through a set of doors at one end of the waiting room. As they walked she asked a million questions—where had he been? What did he do now? What was his life all about? And by the time they reached the nurse's station Nate had not been given the chance to answer even one.

Rachael spoke politely but firmly to one of the nurses in white. "Sister, can you clear a curtain for this gentleman, please."

The nurse quickly complied, and Nate was ushered into a small curtained-off bed where Rachael sat him down. "So, you're a doctor?" asked Nate.

"Not really," she said, smiling. The shadow was there again—as fleeting as a blink. Again she brushed it aside. "Let's have a look at this." She probed the wound and Nate winced, and then she dabbed it with a cotton swab soaked in something that smelled like rubbing alcohol. "Looks a bit angry, but nothing to worry about. We'll start you on a course of antibiotics just in case." She dabbed at the cut again and dried it with gauze. "So who stitched you up? They did a decent job."

Nate wasn't sure why, but he lied without thinking. "The doctor at my local clinic. I got the cut just before I left home—fender bender. Face versus steering wheel."

"Face loses."

"Yup. I got the stitches just a few hours before I left. There was no way I was missing my flight."

"So you're here on holiday?"

"Yeah, for the most part. Just wanted to come back and see the old place. I've been driving around, but the face started to hurt so I thought I'd come get it checked out."

"I think you'll be fine. Give me a minute and I'll speak to the sister about the antibiotics. Are you allergic to anything?"

"No, nothing," he said. "You sure you're not a doctor?"

Rachael smiled and walked through the curtain. When she returned she handed him a plastic pill bottle filled with capsules. "So where are you staying?" she asked.

"Well, funny enough, nowhere as of right now. I was at the Breadfruit Inn downtown, but I checked out and now I'm just kind of wandering, going with the flow. That kind of thing." He tried to make it sound romantic, self-directed, but he wasn't sure he'd pulled it off.

Rachael sensed it immediately. "Then come up to the house and stay for a few days. I've got lots of room."

"No, no, I don't want to be a bother…"

"Don't be silly, Nate. Come up to Cap. I insist."

Nate was tempted. It would be good to have a base, somewhere familiar, somewhere that felt safe. But just before acquiescing he mustered his courage and threw up his hands. "No, really, I can't. I'll tell you what. You give me your phone number, and I'll call you and we'll connect for dinner or lunch. But for now I really just want to explore the whole place. It's been thirty-odd years and I kind of just want to buzz around and check out all the old places. You know, the Yacht Club, the Morne where we lived when I first came here—the old house on Vigie. I also want to go check out the marina where my dad moored that disaster of a boat he bought—*Symbols* it was called. There was a little restaurant there, on the point, more like a cafe really—the Wikki Up. They made the best burgers."

"Oh, Nate! You can cross that one off your list. The Wikki Up hasn't been there for twenty years. It burned down."

"Really? Shit, that's too bad. I have some great memories. Anyway, that's the kind of thing I want to rediscover, you know?"

Rachael looked genuinely disappointed. "Are you sure? It'd be great to have you over…"

"Really, I'm sure. But I do appreciate the offer, and we will connect for dinner or something. I promise."

Rachael scribbled her number on a pad at the nurse's station and pressed it into his palm. "Well how about tonight?" she asked.

"How about tomorrow night?" he countered, wincing slightly, as if the question pained him to ask it. "I need to get settled, and I have some more exploring to do before the day's out—and I might not end up back in Castries tonight. I'd hate to be late and keep you waiting."

"All right then. Tomorrow it is. Call me in the afternoon and we'll set up a place." She took his hands and smiled a far off smile. "It really is so good to see you, Nate," she said. And then she swirled around and disappeared through the curtain like a spectre.

Wow, Nate thought to himself. *Rachael Stanton!* As he marveled at his luck in running into her, he looked down at his hands and the bottle of pills. He would need to pay for those, he thought. He came out of the curtained area and leaned over the nurse's station. "Excuse me," he said. "Where do I pay for these?"

The nurse, the one who had cleared the curtain area for him, looked up with mild surprise. "It's taken care of, sir. Have a nice day." And then she turned back to the notes she was making.

Nate walked out of the hospital somewhat bemused. Rachael had never actually admitted to being a doctor, but she must have been one: she had authority over the nurses, and the ability to prescribe drugs, and the whole visit was covered. There wasn't a better person to put his mind at ease where the cut under his eye was concerned. No more jungle fever, no rampant infections, no dead chicken juju to worry about.

In the car he swallowed two of the capsules, then sat for a moment to gather his thoughts and plan his next move. He needed to get back to Ti Fenwe Estate. That was the goal. That was the key to the trip and the only thing that really mattered. Smiley, Ma Joop, and their voodoo bullshit would have to wait. What was it Smiley had said? Be back at the shabeen by 5:00 pm tomorrow? That wasn't going to happen.

Nate had a car, he had a few hours of daylight left, and a clean bill of health. He turned back onto the Millennium highway, which was nothing like a highway at all, but more a fairly serviceable road that ran along the harbor at the industrial end of Castries. He followed it out of town running south, relying on nothing more than instinct to guide him. The buildings soon fell away, and he drove through lush green stretches of nothing but sea grape and windswept bushes. The sea peeked through constantly on his right, until he swung eastward and inland, and started the climb into the interior. He was heading for Dennery, a small town on the east coast, and the only solid landmark he had in his memory of where Ti Fenwe Estate actually lay.

His plan was simple, unfettered with complexities and cunning. He would go to Dennery, find a place to spend the night, and ask the locals how to get to Ti Fenwe.

And then, in the morning, he would go there and give the damn thing back.

19

The three boys and the women in the tiny hut stared intently at the doorway. The candles in the room cast a nervous fluttering of light into the darkness outside

"Something's out there," said Richard in a voice that was eerily calm.

On the other side of the table, the old woman with the crackling voice and a fistful of rosary solemnly agreed. "Mm hmm. Me hear it, too. Sometin' outside. Sometin' waitin'."

Nate was standing again, legs bent and at the ready, hands hovering lightly above the table. His every sense was on full alert. And like the others, Richard, too, watched the doorway intently.

With no one speaking, the sounds of the night took on a palpable, throbbing beat, as if the insects were goading something on, jeering, willing it forward. And then, as if on cue, the sounds stopped all at once.

They saw the cutlass blade first: it came slowly around the corner of the door frame, slicing steadily into the light from the darkness. It was the color of dark honey, flecked along the sharpened edge with orange and black rust. Holding it was a large and gnarled hand, thick with calluses and weathered knuckles. Finally the whole form of a man came into the soft candlelight, and as he stood in the doorway he easily filled it.

He wore a beaten palm-frond hat, a scowl to match, and nothing else but a pair of old cut-off jeans pulled tight at the top with a thick and worn leather belt. In the light of the naked flame, his black torso was licked with blacker shadows, and the sinewy muscles beneath his skin were lean to the point of wasting. It was the man the boys had seen earlier at the copra oven.

The relief in the room was practically audible, like a kettle being taken off the boil, and the shoulders of everyone around the table loosened, if only a fraction. The man spoke quickly and in a deep baritone, and while the Creole was unintelligible to Pip and Nate, they could tell that what he was saying was grim, and the reaction in the faces of the three women confirmed it.

The woman holding Pip asked a question, and the man answered it sharply as if reprimanding a disobedient child. He spat out a parting comment, turned and plunged back into the darkness. The boys could see now that there were other forms outside, moving past the doorway like shadows, heading up the hill toward the forest. Among them there were undulating pools of soft yellow light cast by hurricane lanterns, rocking gently as they walked up the hill, leaving the scent of burnt kerosene behind them. The light was diffused and tentative, and cast long, dancing shadows about the legs of the men. The blackness swirled quickly behind them, jealously filling the spots the light had brightened only moments before.

The boys silently moved to the doorway, watching as a group of about seven men and their pools of yellow light moved up the hill and into the forest. Soon the glow of their lights turned into twinkles, strangled by the bows and branches, and then it was gone, snuffed out by the forest night. They watched the spot where the men had been swallowed by the darkness.

"What's going on, Rich?" Nate finally asked in a whisper. "What did he say?"

"He said he was going up to the north ridge with a group of laborers. They say the Bolom took a…" He turned to one of the women at the table. "*Kabwit?*" he asked.

"Goat," she said in English.

Richard turned back to Nate. "A goat—they said the Bolom took a goat."

"What do you mean, *took a goat?*"

"Well, we don't farm any animals here, but the laborers have them for food. They think the Bolom killed one to eat it. Tristan's really in trouble now."

"Tristan? Why's Tristan in trouble?" said Pip.

Richard turned back from the doorway and sat again at the table. The others followed suit. "Do you guys remember when that man—the one who was just here—when he was speaking to Tristan by the copra oven?"

The boys both nodded.

"Well, he was mad at Tristan because Tristan hadn't put the food out. It's Tristan's job. Whenever Tristan is at the Estate, he's supposed to do the feeding." He shook his head slowly. "Uncle Vince is gonna kill him. He's supposed to have it up there before the sun goes down. So that it can get smelly. It's really hot up there and it makes the thing stink, but that's how the Bolom likes it."

"What do you feed it?"

"Chicken. A dead, plucked chicken. You take it into the attic and leave it in the corner in this big tin bowl, and by the time the Bolom shows up, the thing is good and ripe."

"And Tristan forgot?" asked Nate.

"Maybe. Or maybe he just decided not to do it. Either way Uncle Vince is gonna kill him. Someone's going to have to pay for the goat—it's worth a lot of money to the laborers."

"So why was that guy so pissed at Tristan?" asked Pip. "Why should he care if Tristan doesn't do his chores?"

"'Cause he cares about Tristan. When it doesn't get fed, the Bolom does bad things—like killing the goat. So now because of Tristan, Uncle Vince will have to pay for the goat."

Nate could feel a knot of anxiety twisting tighter and tighter in his gut. He took a long, deep breath, but he couldn't shake it. "This is fucked up."

Even Pip was surprised to hear Nate swear, but if there was ever an appropriate time, this was it.

After a silence long enough to let the word soak in, Pip wrinkled his face in question. "How come only the family can feed the Bolom?"

"It's something to do with the smell," said Richard. "The

Bolom needs to know who's feeding it. I think that's how it knows who the master is. Tristan's supposed to prepare it with his hands, his bare hands, so that his smell is on it when the Bolom eats. And if Tristan's not here, it has to be Uncle Vince. No one else's smell is allowed on the chicken."

"And if your uncle's not around?"

"Nobody's happy when my Uncle's not around. A lot of bad stuff happens."

And then, without having made a single sound, Tristan stepped into the hut from the darkness. All three boys let out a yell, the women shrieked and jerked in their seats and their combined weight rippled through the floor like an earthquake. The table shuddered, glasses spilled, hands flew to mouths and Pip began to cry.

Tristan stood in the doorway, barefoot and clad only in a dirty T-shirt and shorts, and began to laugh.

Nate, who had cleared the room and was already against the back wall of the shack, was momentarily furious. "Tristan! You…"

It made Tristan laugh all the more, and soon everyone was infected with a highly contagious, if at first nervous, laughter. Everyone but Pip.

"Aw, you need your mommy?" said Tristan, immediately picking on Pip.

"Leave him alone, Tristan!" barked Nate, a little surprised himself at fierceness in his voice, and how quickly he had gone from nervous laughter to hackled anger.

"Oh yeah? Or what?" Tristan knew the program. *Or what* would be followed with, *Just keep going and you'll see*, to which he would reply, *Oh yeah? You and what army?* And so Tristan was caught completely off-guard when Nate launched himself forward, smashing headlong into him and driving the pair into the night.

The two boys tumbled backwards through the door, howling and swearing as they went. Behind them a string of bodies followed, led by Richard and then Augustine, who was surprisingly nimble for such a large, old woman. *Stop it!* yelled Richard, but the two boys were locked in a tangle of thrashing arms and legs. Before Richard could shout again, Augustine was upon them like a dark cloud. She reached into the fray and extracted the boys, one in each hand, and pulled them roughly apart. "Stop dis nonsense now or you backsides gwan feel my hand! *Now* I say!"

The two ceased their struggling and glared at each other through bruised expressions and wildly mussed hair. "What's your problem?" screamed Tristan at Nate.

"No more, you hear?" said Augustine sternly, releasing Tristan and putting her finger on his nose. "And dat go fuh you, too, boy!" she said, switching her attention to Nate. Both boys folded their arms and brooded. They dared not anger Augustine, who was simmering just below something ugly. "Back inside," she ordered.

At the table Pip had stopped crying, and was once again wide-eyed in amazement—this time at the sudden eruption between the boys. They took their seats again and everyone settled, this time with Nate and Tristan staring sullenly at the floor.

"What was that all about?" asked Richard, smiling wryly. He was stifling a laugh, but doing a poor job of it. "He really got you there, Tristan…"

"Pé la!" shouted Tristan. *Shut up!*

But it was too late, Richard had begun to giggle.

Tristan went on, "I wasn't looking!" Tristan was getting upset again, and Augustine was about to intervene.

Nate beat her to it. "Tristan, look, I'm sorry," he said softly. "I just wanted you to lay off Pip."

The room fell once again into silence, and Richard's giggles sunk away. Tristan sat awkwardly looking at Richard and then Nate, and finally draped something smile-like across his face and bobbed his head side to side. "If I'd seen you coming you'd still be out there—black eye and knocked out…"

"Whatever," said Richard, rolling his eyes.

And, quick as a mongoose, Tristan reached out and smacked him on the back of his head. "Remember you're still just a *lightee*…" he said to his younger cousin.

Richard held his head and glowered at Tristan. An instant later,

Augustine reacted. In a blur of speed she reached across the table, administered a sizeable smack to the back of Tristan's head, then brought her hand crisply around to his face. Before Tristan could even react to the pain he had Augustine's finger on his nose for the second time that night.

"I can reach all of you from 'ere," she said in an icy calm voice. "I dun warn you."

Pip asked a question about a small statue on the wooden shelf, and Augustine was glad of the normality it brought back to the room. She answered it calmly, which started a murmur of conversation among the women, Nate and Pip. Richard, however, was not part of it, nor was his cousin.

Richard's gaze had fallen to Tristan's hand, and to something shiny he saw held there. Tristan seemed to feel the weight of that gaze, and when he slowly opened his hand he appeared almost surprised to see the metal tube sitting there. It was a brand new flashlight, small enough to almost disappear in his hand, still marked with the orange price tag from M&C's. Tristan looked up at Richard, and a small knowing passed between them. It lasted only a second, and then Tristan thrust the flashlight deep into his pocket, and turned physically away from Richard.

But the blonde boy had already sunk back into his chair. It was a flashlight this time, but in the past it had been a knife, a small balsa wood glider, and even a Daisy pellet gun among other things. But today it was a flashlight. And Richard knew where the flashlight had come from, and worse, he knew why.

He heard the words in his head, and he heard them in Vincent's voice. There were at least three occasions where he'd been close enough to hear them spoken himself—always at the completion of one of Vincent's violent outbursts at Tristan. It was always the same: after the beating, the gift. And the words ran through his head again: *Learn the lesson, earn the reward*—spoken, as always, in that softened paternal voice Uncle Vince only used with Tristan, and only once his anger had burned itself fully through.

Outside in the darkness, shapes were moving again, and the

soft pools of swaying yellow lights were making their way past. Instinctively, the group rose from the table, relieved to be out from under the watchful eye of Augustine, and filed out into the darkness. With men moving from the forest down past the shack, the darkness outside lost its menace and the boys watched as the figures filed by. They spoke in hushed tones, some with glowing red embers at their lips, others with swaying pools of yellow light cast by their hurricane lanterns.

The last two men in the group walked single file with a long bamboo pole between them supported on their shoulders, and from the pole hung the carcass of a large white goat bound by its feet. As they approached Augustine spoke to them in Creole, and the men stopped and lay their load on the grass outside the shack as they spoke with her. The boys crowded around the still, white shape, and as one of the other men approached, the lantern he was carrying exposed the scene.

The goat had died horribly. Its throat had been torn out, and there was a gaping cavity starting just under its chin, extending down to the middle of its chest. Its white coat was spattered with a pink hue all around the wound, and a length of blue entrails lay in a tangled heap that had been dragging along the ground since the goat had been trussed up on the pole.

The boys were transfixed. Richard turned and spoke quietly to Tristan; neither Nate nor Pip could hear what was said.

"I know!" shouted Tristan venomously at Richard. "Do you think I'm stupid?" He shoved Richard hard, and then swore so viciously in Creole that the three women, including Augustine, all inhaled sharply.

And then, from the perfect darkness of the track toward the plantation house, came a stern voice. "Hey, what's all this? What the hell happened to it?"

Tristan's head dropped and his arms folded tightly around his body.

It was Vincent.

20

Dennery was simple to find. On an island fifteen or twenty kilometers wide, Nate couldn't go *too* wrong, and by the afternoon he was standing in a small room at the back of a restaurant called Diana's. He wasn't even sure if it was an actual inn, a hotel, or just someone's quick thinking, entrepreneurial answer to his question: *Is there a place to rent a room for the night around here?* Still, the room was clean and had a working lock on the door. He didn't need much more.

He left his bag unpacked beside the bed and set out into the town. It didn't take long to find someone who could tell him where Ti Fenwe Estate was, and before the first beer was gone, he was armed with a hastily sketched map. It would take him to a turnoff the main road, a turn into the bush that would lead him to the old plantation. The man who drew the map for him was bent and curled with age, and laughed when Nate asked if he could make the drive in a car or if he'd need a four-wheel drive. *Dat place have a bitumen road nowadays. Many touris' go deh now.* And then he put a gnarled hand out and smiled as he waited for Nate to pay him.

The idea that the road was now paved surprised Nate, although as he thought about it he supposed that in thirty years there was bound to be a few changes. In his mind, the old place was still as it had been, waiting silently in the depths of the rainforest, slowly succumbing to the ravages of climate and time. But if the road had been improved, what of the plantation house itself? Would it even be there? And what about all the secret places they had crawled, jumped and run through as kids…What about the clearing? The thought that it all might be changed—perhaps even gone, like Tristan—left a hollow feeling inside him.

He ordered dinner at Diana's—fresh red snapper, sweet potato and plantain chips—but he had no real appetite and just pushed the food around the plate until finally leaving it alone. He returned to his room and checked out the cut beneath his eye. It still looked angry and red around the edges. The antibiotics got him thinking about Rachael, and wondering how she had recognized him after so many years. He must not have changed much, he reasoned. He must still have all the same features he did as a kid. People had told him before that he had a boyish face, or was it a young face? Either way, perhaps he simply still looked like the kid he had once been. Rachael had known it was him, and she was sure of it, too.

He sat on the bed wearing only his underwear and a white T-shirt. It was hot in the room. There was no air conditioning, not even a ceiling fan, and there was no TV or radio to distract him. Just as well, he thought.

He collected the envelope Smiley had given him and spread the papers on the bed, searching through them, looking for one in particular—the image of Richard by the sailboat. The aftermath of Richard's death had been a grim one. That afternoon by the river had torn the De Villiers family apart, and like echoes in an empty canyon it had returned again and again across great spans of distance and time. Those closest paid the highest price, and as he thought it, Nate reached into the pile and picked up the photocopied headline that screamed, *I will take a life in payment.*

He looked at the image of Richard's mother, Collette De Villiers, and he understood the torment that had driven her to take her own life. With her son gone, her life would have simply collapsed.

In the warm room in Dennery, his mind wandered back to that afternoon, back to what had become mere shards of sharp memories. They were still sharp, still able to cut as keenly as the first time. They came back to him as snatches, bursts of icy cold moments.

Officers at the door: *Mr. Mason?*

Yes...?

A large, uniformed man with a moustache. *I'm Sergeant Cole...I need you to come with me...drunk driver...to the hospital quickly...*

Doctors in blue scrubs with sleeves that seemed too short. *Her injuries…too severe…the boy…conscious but critical…*

He remembered the light. It was too bright, too stark and clinical, without comfort. He found his six-year-old son crying but alive, shivering on a gurney, terrified and bloodied in ways no child ever should be. He tried to calm him by stroking his hair and telling him over and over again that he loved him.

And when Cody died four hours later, Nate became entirely hollow.

And three months after the accident, after Nate had drifted as far from himself as he could, Sergeant Cole had shown up again like some blue-clad angel of death. It had marked the beginning of the odyssey that had brought him to this little room on this little island.

He shook his head, trying to physically dislodge the thoughts. The room in Dennery was hot, and he knew sleep would not come easily. Thoughts of Sergeant Cole stayed with him. He could hear the sadness in the man's voice even now. *Ain't this a goddamn son of a bitch.* And he could see the gray slippers, the perfect 'V' they made. What was the last thing he had said to his father? Had it been a harsh word? God knew there was enough bullshit between them to stack the odds in favor of that.

He thought hard but couldn't bring the conversation to mind, couldn't place any specifics. It was probably while he was drunk, though, thought Nate. Probably the same old rants. The same old derision.

In his mind's eye, he watched his father raise another glass to his lips. And then another. He watched as his father's face aged and drooped, as his hair fell out and his clothes hung limply off him. The old man's face took on a red swollen tinge and his skin became papery and dry. His father raised the glass again, and Nate saw that his father's hand was not alone raising that glass. His own hand was there, too.

Soon Nate was asleep. His sleep was deep and fitful, and his comatose body flinched and twitched as he lay there. In the archways, there were eyes watching. He couldn't see them, but he knew they were there. There were dark rooms and low-slung rafters, blackened roofing joists and airless spaces, and finally that sound that reached through his chest and wrapped tightly about his spine and began gently shaking it, like a loose skeletal hand about a baby rattle. It was the sound of nutmegs.

They rolled and rolled, their hard dry seeds bouncing along the wooden floor of the loft, rattling and chattering away. It was a sound that held terror for Nate, and the dream always culminated the same way. The footfalls in that dark garret space would get heavier and faster, hammering along as the nutmegs rolled and rolled, until Nate's whole head filled with their crescendo and he was ejected back to a waking state.

But tonight the rattling of the nutmeg and the stutter of small feet above him didn't work their way to a climax. Instead they rapidly fell off, as if the being had stopped suddenly to listen, and the thousands of nutmegs chattered slowly into silence.

And then, in the seamless and unquestionable way that only dreams can transmogrify, he was in the audience at a play. The cast just stood there, high up on the stage, motionless, watching Nate from behind their makeup and masks. As he looked up at the players on the stage he recognized many of them. He saw Smiley dressed as a colorful parrot, and he saw Ma Joop clad in white robes and heaped with talismans and charms. His father was there, too, drinking of course, and among the many others on the stage was a small wet boy with a tuft of blonde hair. He was standing at center of the group, sopping wet and dripping into a puddle that grew around him. The water crept across the floor, steadily expanding, and eventually included everyone in its cold wet circumference. Nate knew it was Richard.

Nate jumped up from his seat, and watched as all the people on the stage stared back in silence. And then, as if controlled by a single impulse, the entire cast took one step backwards. They were moving away from Nate, that single step seeming to put an unfathomable distance between him and them. One small figure was left standing alone at center stage. He was wearing pajamas, his face was bloodied, and Nate knew it was Cody.

His own crying woke him, and as he swung his feet onto a floor bathed in the cobalt blue of 4:00 am moonlight, he was startled by what he saw lying there.

. . .

How long had Vincent been standing there in the darkness? Had he seen the fight with Tristan? The memory of Vincent pummelling Tristan was still fresh in Nate's mind, and he was suddenly terrified that he was about to get some of the same. He looked up hesitantly toward Vincent, half expecting to see the man's weathered face inches from his own, a scowl carved deeply into it and a hand raised and ready for the first blow. But instead he saw Vincent tussling his son's hair, and then throwing an arm around his shoulder and cinching him in affectionately. It was the picture of a father and the son he adored.

Nate flicked his eyes to Tristan. Oddly, the boy was not reserved or sulky. No crossed arms, no half turn away, no sullen fixed expression. Instead Tristan was looking up at his father and smiling, if perhaps a little too much, Nate thought. Tristan seemed to be reveling in the attention, and for the moment it seemed there was no one else in Tristan's world—just his father.

With an outstretched foot, Vincent pushed the goat's chin to one side and further exposed the cavern that was once its chest. He grimaced. "Whose animal is this?"

"Joseph's," answered one of the pole-bearers.

Vincent nodded. "Tell Joseph I'll buy it from him. We'll roast it up for everyone tomorrow night."

The pole-bearers looked at each other with raised eyebrows, then nodded quickly and hustled the dead animal onto their shoulders again. As they joined the rest of the group moving back down toward the other shacks the boys could hear them talking in excited tones.

"That should make everyone happy," said Vincent, watching

them go. "Not so, Augustine?"

Nate looked over and the large, old woman seemed to have shrunk to half her size. She was now meek and obedient, not the towering force that had descended upon him and Tristan in the heat of their earlier brawl. "Yes, Mr. Vincent. Very happy." But her tone was conciliatory, required. Nate noticed her eyes were cast downward.

Vincent tussled Tristan's hair again. "It must be fed, son. And you are the man for the job. Come. Let's all get back to the house. Tristan has some chores, and the copra oven needs a spark."

Richard's eyes lit up. "Oh, Uncle Vince! Can I light it!? Can I please, please?"

"What, a *lightee* like you?" said Vincent, toying with his nephew.

"Aw, please!"

"All right. Fine. You can throw the embers."

Richard pumped his fist in the air. "Yes!"

The group marched off with Nate last in line. As they trooped down the path toward the glow of the bedroom window and the growing hum of the generator, Nate looked back toward Augustine. The other two women had already gone back inside and Augustine stood alone, silhouetted in the doorway by the glow of the candles inside.

"Come on, catch up!" called out Vincent, and Nate trotted back into the group.

Once inside, the boys gathered in the kitchen. Vincent busied himself in another room, and the boys formed a loose circle around the small wooden table that sat beneath the only bulb in the room. The bulb itself hung at the end of six feet of wire hanging nakedly from the ceiling, and it swayed gently with the breeze that came in through the glassless windows.

On the table sat a battered tin bowl—probably a large mixing bowl at one point in its life, but now just a battered tin vessel about as wide as a hubcap. In the bowl was a chicken, headless and dead, and swimming in a shallow sea of blood and other fluids.

"That's just nasty," said Pip recoiling, then bobbing his head back in for another look. He was at once horrified and fascinated.

"Do they actually run? I mean, when you cut their heads off? Does that really happen?"

Tristan was delighted to answer and laid it on thick. "They sure do. Wings flapping, running into walls and trees, spattering blood as they go…"

Again, Nate felt the urge to defend Pip, but the night's earlier encounter tempered his approach. "No way. That's crap—they do *not*."

"No, Tristan's right. They really do," offered Richard.

"Seriously?"

"Seriously."

"That's friggin' gruesome."

Richard and Tristan laughed. Pip joined in and then so did Nate. Richard put his hand on Nate's arm as the group continued giggling. "Nate. You go with Tristan. Go help him leave the food."

Nate felt the laughter evaporate. "Why me?"

"Don't look so horrified! I'm going to light the copra oven with Uncle Vince, and there's no way Pip'll go up into the attic. Plus, Tristan would just torture him."

"What if I don't wanna?"

"Because you're too scared?" It was a taunt, for sure, but somehow because it was Richard doing the taunting, it came off as good spirited.

"Whatever."

Richard picked up the bowl and pushed it into Nate's less than willing hands. Inside, the chicken and its grim basting sloshed sideways, and some of the bloody fluid splashed onto Nate's shirt.

"Come on," said Tristan, already turning away. "I carry the light, you carry the chicken. Let's go."

The stairway to the attic came off the lightless main hall of the house, and consisted of a series of steps that doubled back on themselves halfway up the climb. Tristan and Nate stood before it as Tristan shone the flashlight up toward the first landing. The darkness seemed to gobble the yellow wash of light, and despite the murkiness of the stairs, Nate felt an urge to get moving: rather the relative safety of the light pooling on the stairs than the inky blackness of the main hall.

He looked over his shoulder and could just make out the glow of the kitchen and the bedroom down a corridor off the opposite side. The safety of those rooms seemed so far away now, and only the bobbing light of Tristan's flashlight offered any hope at all. "Let's get going," he muttered.

The stairs creaked as they took the boys' weight, and in Nate's mind something in the attic—something evil with long teeth and hooked claws—suddenly pricked up its ears at the sound, and turned murderously to see what tasty morsel would emerge at the top of the stairs. They made the first turn, and Tristan angled the light upward, toward the top of the stairs, and the beam disappeared through the door-less frame. It seemed to be devoured by the blackness of the attic proper.

"Point it back here. I can't see the steps," said Nate. The darkness was so complete it seemed to suffocate him.

Tristan complied, and finally the two boys stepped through the doorway and into the attic. Again Tristan flashed the light upward, and this time the lonely column of light caught the ceiling and the wooden planks that sat atop joists and beams to form the outer roofing. It was more spacious than Nate had imagined, and the two boys were able to stand fully if they kept to the center where the roof was pitched highest. Tristan panned the light around the ceiling, then across the walls and the inside of the gables that gave shape to the many steeples at the roofline's edge. As his light crossed the small windows in the gables, the boys' reflections were momentarily cast back at them; two small faces outside in the blackness looking in.

It was dark and riddled with clichés; cobwebs, looming shadows, and creaky floorboards, but it was the smell that caught Nate off guard the most. The attic air was rich with a distinctive and almost overpowering aroma—something like cinnamon, only softer, and perhaps edged with a sweetness that hinted at candy coated nuts. To Nate it was a new smell, but one that was so close to another that he knew so well. It wouldn't come to him at first, but he breathed deeply and there it was. It was the smell of Christmas back home. "What *is* that smell?" he asked.

"Look, here," said Tristan, flashing the light to the floor.

The broad boards that made up the attic floor were littered with small orbs the size of misshapen ping-pong balls. They were irregular, mostly oval shaped, and dark brown with raised swirls of red wrapped around them like string. Tristan panned the light slowly along the floor and over to the furthest reaches of the attic, and Nate could see that the entire floor—the ceiling of the house below—was covered with thousands upon thousands of these small brown and red spheres.

"Nutmeg," said Tristan simply. "We dry them up here."

Nate was awed by the sight, and it felt suddenly as if he were intruding on the peaceful slumber of some vast community of seed creatures. He didn't want to move, because moving surely meant stepping on them. Would they squish? Or were they hard? Nate's question was answered as Tristan bent down and picked up one. He took the tin bowl from Nate and offered him the nutmeg. "Here. Check it out."

It was harder than Nate had imagined. Its center was solid, like the seed in an avocado, but the red web-like structure that encased it unevenly, the mace, was the consistency of pliable plastic. He put it to his nose and smelled the Christmas in it, then dropped it back to the floor. It landed hard against the wooden floorboards, then rattled awkwardly as the mace casing and the hard inner nut worked to find a resting place.

"Come on," said Tristan again. He pointed the light at his feet. "Walk like this. You have to slide your feet or you'll trip," he said, showing Nate how to shuffle forward through the field of drying nutmeg. And as he did so the nutmeg began to roll. They bounced and clattered against the hard wooden floor, and with each step they let out a collective grumble, then settled until the next step.

The boys shuffled forward through the drying nutmeg, and the community at their feet grumbled at the intrusion, rattling out their displeasure as they jostled with their neighbors to find a new space. At the far corner of the room there was a clearing just below a window, and as Nate looked through it, he could see it was the window he had noticed from outside the morning they arrived, the one that was cocked open and felt like someone, something, was watching him through it. The thought of it made him shiver, and he reflexively looked back into the expanse of the attic. Tristan had put the flashlight down and was fussing with the chicken in the bowl, and so no light was cast into the center of the loft. The darkness was so complete it seemed to draw the very breath from Nate's chest, and as his eyes struggled to find something to focus on, he became quickly alarmed that there might be something out there, in the black expanse, watching them and waiting its turn.

"I can't see anything over there, Tristan," he said, and his voice gave away his concern. "I think there's something there. Shine the light. Shine the light over there."

Tristan lit the room and the shadows retreated. There was nothing there, and the return of light to the darkness felt like a thick and suffocating blanket ripped from about his head at just the last minute. "All right, the chicken's all set," said Tristan. "Let's get out of here."

"I'm good with that," whispered Nate, shuffling his feet forward and giving life to the nutmeg chorus once more.

21

Nate blinked again and tried to focus on the object. It sat in the penumbra of the blue moonlight, veiled in navy tones that wouldn't give up its shape. He hadn't left anything there when he went to sleep, had he? No. His clothes and shoes were on the chair at the foot of the bed. Nate leaned in and caught what looked like something shiny, perhaps a reflection. And as he came closer he saw that it was indeed a reflection, a chance moonbeam bouncing off the surface of a small glass vile—a small glass vile pressed into the hollowed-out abdomen of a bloodied bird.

Nate recoiled like a hand from a hot stove, and then, gaining his wits, lunged for the bedside table light. In the stark light of the lamp the shades of blue in the room retreated, and the thing on the floor called out in reds, while the open window became a maw in flat black. Nate's eyes flicked back and forth between the open window and the dead bird. Both registered as threats, both urging him to react. But somehow their opposing forces paralyzed him into inactivity and only served to get his heart racing wildly. Finally Nate's mind committed. He lunged again, this time for the window to slam it shut. He could see nothing out there. The window resisted closing, and the more he struggled with the latch the more defiant the glass pane became. *Shit!* he exclaimed, and the sound of his own voice in the stillness of the night made his fear real, and his heart raced again. At last the latch came free and he swung the window closed. Then, as an afterthought, he drew the curtains tightly against whatever—whoever—might be watching outside.

Nate then turned to the thing on his floor.

It looked to be much the same as the one from Rodney Bay:

black feathers matted with crimson, limp-necked and bulging at the gut with a protruding glassy vile. The small bottle was wrapped, much like the last one, with leaves and something stringy and vine-like, and inside there was a dark red liquid that clung to the inside and coated the glass with a red hue.

Jesus Christ, muttered Nate squatting in front of it. *What should I do?* he thought. What do you do when a dead bird—some kind of black magic, voodoo, dead bird—shows up on your floor in the middle of the night? What's the protocol? He'd have to tell someone. Yes, he'd go wake the manager, or the owner, or whatever the title was of the woman who had rented him this room. He'd go find her and tell her, and she'd call the police. No. The police could not be trusted—he'd learned that lesson already. And whoever was out there—was that what they wanted him to do? Unlock the door and come out into the 4:00 am darkness where they could lash out at him from the shadows, truss him up like a pig for the slaughter and drag him off to God knows where?

In the stall before a decision could be made, he realized he needed a weapon. He needed something in his hands that was hard and had a bit of heft to it. What could he use? There wasn't much, nothing in fact, nothing except the old wooden chair at the foot of his bed where his clothes lay. It was old and heavy, and the two uprights that formed the rear legs and extended up to make the chair-back supports were thick as truncheons.

Without so much as a thought to the owner, Nate seized the chair, hoisted it above his head and brought it crashing down onto the floor. It held together, but he felt it flex. The second blow did it, and a few kicks saw the structure collapse entirely, yielding two solid pieces of heavy mahogany that made a menacing pair of clubs. Nate hefted them both, felt their weight, then put one aside in favor of a single weapon.

Moving quickly, he checked the door to his room, made sure it was locked, and then darted over to the window to look out. As he swept back the curtain his heart lurched; he was confronted by a man with a club staring back at him, and Nate instinctively yelped and leapt backwards into the room.

With the light on, it was impossible to see out through the window, and at the same time anyone outside would have a perfect view of Nate. He scrambled for the bedside lamp. With a click, the room was plunged into darkness, and Nate froze by the bed, waiting, watching for anything to move. After a few moments his hand began to cramp. He loosened his grip on the makeshift club, changed hands and moved stealthily over to the edge of the window. This time he moved the curtain slowly, from the side, and with darkness cloaked around him, he had a clear view of the scene outside.

The small courtyard was quiet. It was finished in flagstone with seams of white concrete. To the right was the back of the restaurant, and the area to the left and straight ahead was bound by a small track, and then gave way to bush. A lone and stark security light burned above the back door of the restaurant, pointing away from the structure and down the two ruts of the track. And above it all a bright and waxing gibbous moon drenched the scene in blue.

Nate scanned the area. Everything seemed quiet, but his mind ran wildly around trying to figure out what to do next. No one would be awake right now, he rationalized. The smartest thing to do would be to just sit tight and wait it out. Wait until the sun was up and the threatening darkness was pushed well back. He would make better decisions then, he thought. Nate wiped his forehead. It was warm in the room, so warm. And now with the window closed there was no breeze. Was it just heat, or was it a fever?

Using pieces from the broken chair, Nate picked up the carcass of the chicken and put it in the small trash can by the door. It was lined with a white plastic bag, so Nate tied it up securely, and put the bag and the small bin in the furthest corner of the room. It would have to do for now. Nate then checked the door one more time to make sure it was locked, propped the pillows up and crawled onto the bed. He would wait it out in the warm little room. He would sweat some, but he would be safe. He sat silently with his knees up, the club lying across his thighs, and tried to listen for the sound of someone approaching.

• • •

It occurred to Nate that perhaps it was all staged, an elaborate trick to scare the crap out of him and Pip. He thought about it hard: the dead chicken in the attic where all the nutmeg was drying, the dead goat, the stories Richard and the old woman in the hut had told them. Maybe it was all just quality theatre. But the goat thing bothered him. Goats were currency this far off the beaten track, and killing one was an expensive prop to impress a thirteen-year-old.

"Keep watching," said Tristan, and Nate was snapped back to the present. "You'll see the whole upper part start to glow."

The two boys were standing in the bedroom at the bay windows that sat up over the track. They had shuffled down to the right end, where the windows angled in and afforded a view back toward the workers' huts. Halfway down the track sat the small square form of the copra oven, and Nate could make out a series of flashlights bobbing around and occasionally lighting up the three figures out there—Vincent, Pip, and Richard. Nate felt good about standing in the relative safety of the bedroom. After his adventure into the attic with Tristan, he was happy to be a bystander for now, watching as others floundered about in the darkness.

"It's cool when you throw the spark in—it all lights up at once, and you get these wild flames from the burning husks," said Tristan excitedly, and as he said it the small square building suddenly surged with an orange glow, with most of the light emanating from the six-inch gap between the top of the walls and the raised tin roof.

"There it goes!" squealed Tristan, patting the windowsill in excitement. "I love that!"

Nate saw that he was smiling, but as Richard came hopping excitedly around the structure with his uncle's arm about his shoulders, Tristan's smile quickly vanished.

"We'll all be going to sleep now," Tristan said, turning away from the window and flopping down on the bed at the center of the room.

Nate watched as the two boys and Vincent stood basking in the glow of the copra oven. He could see that the flames were settling, and that the orange glow was calming to a modest blush. He turned and looked at Tristan. "That bowl we left upstairs. You believe in that stuff? I mean, for real?" He tried to sound tough, dismissive, but it came out with an edge of concern.

"What do you think?" asked Tristan derisively. "You think I like going up there? Of course it's real."

"But you've never seen it, right? The Bolom. You've never actually seen it yourself." It was a statement.

Tristan propped himself up on his elbows and looked at Nate with something akin to pity. "You *vwayajes* are all the same, tourists with no understanding of this place. No appreciation. No consideration for anything outside your narrow North American experience."

The lecture struck Nate as hollow. It was a recycled invective, probably something his father was fond of saying. It rang entirely false in Tristan's delivery, but Nate stood quietly and let him go on. "Of course I haven't seen it—yet. But I've felt it. I've felt it close to me, I've heard it and I've seen the things it does. It's real, Nate."

Nate turned back to the window and stared down at the group of three figures watching the coconut husks settle into their glow for the night. It was smoking much more now, billowing up through the gap at the top of the structure, muting the glow to snatches of orange brightness peeking through the haze. Vincent motioned to the boys and they began to move away from the structure. They moved slowly, backwards, hanging on to the moment and lingering as much as they could. Finally Vincent clapped his hands and the boys fell in behind him.

It took another hour to settle the boys, but by the time Vincent pulled on the blue nylon string in the floor and silenced the generator—and the single light in the room—they were all ready to sleep. Vincent lay in the only bed, pushed up against the wall near the bedroom door. The boys lay in their sleeping bags on one-inch thick foam rectangles by the bay window. They giggled and swatted each other for a while, but stopped when Vincent mumbled at them from a state of near sleep: *Boys, come now, time for bed.*

Soon the old room was silent, and all five slipped speedily into a deep sleep. The house settled into its rhythm for the night. The winds crept through the open windows, blew through the empty, lightless corridors, and chased stray leaves along their way. The bats, filled from a night of gorging on fruit from plantations all across the island, fluttered back in and found their roosts, squeaking lightly and wrapping their wings about them like shrouds in the blackness. Spiders set to work on new webs, mice patrolled the dark corners and edges for new scraps, and ants trouped through the kitchen, unseen and in single file, liberating spilled sugar they found on the floor.

And, in the black hours before dawn, Nate woke in the darkness to the sound of something else—something much larger than spiders and bats—and the sound of it sat him up on his mattress. It came through the open front doorway of the plantation house at Ti Fenwe, hesitantly at first, stepping cautiously, and then, after a moment of silence that threatened to coil Nate's ears, it thundered up the stairs and into the blackness of the attic.

22

Nate was sweating hard in the little room in Dennery. He had fallen asleep much easier than he might have imagined, perhaps in part because of the heat, or because of his exhaustion after the unsettling business with the dead bird. He had settled back into the pillows on the bed, and the sweat coming off him as he slept had pooled in the notch at the base of his neck. It ran down his chest as he sat bolt upright, torn from sleep by the thunderous sound at his door.

Nate lurched from the bed, wide-eyed and confused by the rough awakening, and was startled again as the club he had set across his legs tumbled to the floor and clattered around his feet.

"Nate!" came the cry at the door, followed by more banging. "Nate, man, you in dere?" Nate steadied himself and tried to focus. His head hurt, and the flesh behind his eyes felt thick and spongy.

"Nate! It me, man. Smiley!" The voice was more insistent now.

"Just a sec," he replied. And he was surprised again, this time by the meekness in his own voice. As he crossed the room to the door, Nate realized he felt awful. He twisted the deadbolt and Smiley came through like a stocky brown bull, arms spread wide and at the ready, eyes flitting quickly about the room. "Nate, are you okay? Is everytin' okay?" He finally looked at Nate and recoiled physically at the sight. "*Bondie!* My God!" He called out. "What has happened to you?"

Nate's mind struggled through a sticky bog. "What do you mean what's happened to me?" Something in Nate slipped and he found himself getting angry.

"Are you not well, my friend? You seem ill."

"Yes, yes," said Nate scaling an unreasonably steep ridge of irritation. "I feel like shit. I don't know what's wrong."

"Sometin' happen?" asked Smiley, and then, awkwardly, "you sick in de night?"

"No, no, I wasn't. But there was this thing…" Nate's mind was clearing quickly. His head still hurt and pounded like a marching band drum, but he was putting things together more cleanly now. The complete disconnect of Smiley's presence dawned on him. "Smiley, how the fuck did you know I was here?"

Smiley was sweating, too, Nate could see, and a little crop of sweat beads had risen like dew drops on his nose. He ran his thumbs around the radius of his belt and administered a three-point hike to his navy trousers. "Nate, man. Dis room will cook you to death. Come, le' we get outside and out of dis heat. It terrible in here." He reached a hand out to Nate and flicked his chin at the closed window. "You should have propped dat open. Get yourself a nice evenin' sea breeze."

"It was open, until that showed up," said Nate, pointing at the garbage can in the corner.

Smiley wiped the sweat away from his nose and forehead with a handkerchief produced from his pocket. "What's in there?" he asked cautiously, edging up to the container like man approaching a spitting cobra.

"Some voodoo shit. A dead bird with a bottle stuffed in it. A chicken I think." Nate's voice was calm, almost detached. "It's my second one in as many days." The sense of urgency and panic that had gripped him so tightly the night before had been all but burned away with the daylight.

Smiley looked into the garbage can from as far away as he could, but all he was able to see was a dense shape wrapped in white plastic. "Dis bird. Dis chicken. It black?"

"Yeah, black."

"And it have glass inside? Glass with sometin' red?"

"Blood I'm guessing."

"Mm hmm. Blood for sure. Come," he said again. "Le' we get you outside."

He helped Nate from the bed and the two men walked into the brilliance of another idyllic tropical day. Outside in the courtyard behind the restaurant sat an old blue Gallant Sigma, a refugee from the mid '70s, rusting some but still fighting the good fight. Nate looked at its boxy sheet metal and chrome, and he couldn't help but be drawn into the nostalgia of the thing. He remembered them being a staple in his youth, and anyone pulling up to the Yacht Club in a new Gallant was guaranteed nods of approval from the veranda, and perhaps even a decent semicircle of beer-swilling auto enthusiasts. Smiley gently ushered him over to the back door of the restaurant.

Inside, they sat at one of four little tables on rattan chairs woven from local palms. The restaurant was really a bar, and Nate got the feeling it rarely saw people during the day. No one came to serve them, and Smiley walked through the open doorway into another part of the structure and came back with a tall glass bottle of water and a pair of plastic cups. Nate realized he was thirsty on a scale he couldn't remember ever feeling before. His whole mouth was dry to the point of being tacky, and any two parts that touched were momentarily fused together.

He snatched at the cup and found himself trembling as he raised it to his mouth, and much of the water spilled as he shakily tipped it to his lips. He swallowed deeply, and Smiley was ready with the refill. "Go slowly, Nate," he said in an oddly paternal way. "You t'row all dat back up if don't slow down."

And on cue, Nate turned quickly and stumbled for the door. He retched twice, steadied himself, then returned and sat heavily at the table. "Jesus, what's happened to me?" he asked, cupping his face in his hands. "I feel like shit."

Smiley exhaled slowly. "I'm surprised it has taken dis long," he said.

"What—you're surprised what's taken this long?"

Smiley pursed his lips. He leaned forward and became solemn, like a man delivering news of the death of a loved one. "The Obeah, Nate. You have been touched. You have been set upon by some fearful darkness, my friend."

Nate held his gaze for a moment, and then shook his head dismissively. "Darkness…? What the fuck, Smiley." Nate knew about Obeah. As a kid, he remembered people talking about it—the Caribbean version of African black magic. Island voodoo. Nate's parents had seen its power firsthand, when the gardener they employed got sick, lost forty pounds and died in a matter of two weeks—all because he believed in the power of Obeah, and in the power of the Obeah man who had put the curse, the spell—whatever it was—upon him. *The incredible power of suggestion,* his father had called it. "Come on, I don't believe in that shit," said Nate.

"No matter. You don't have to believe."

Nate took another tentative sip of water and felt a curdling in his stomach. "I don't think the antibiotics are kicking in yet," he said, partly to himself and partly to Smiley. "I think I'm running a bit of a fever, too."

"Nate, it inside you, man. Dis sickness you feel, it—"

Nate cut him off in a burst of agitation. "Give it a rest, Smiley! This nice cut I got from the Thompson Twins is a little infected—that's all. Enough with the hocus-pocus."

Smiley understood people. He understood when to push someone who was about to tell him what he wanted to know, and he knew when to leave it well enough alone. The large black man sat back in his seat and folded his arms. "All right, all right, Nate," he said, and blew out a stream of air to punctuate the subject change. "So, what are you doing out here in Dennery?"

Nate was about to answer when his mind began reshuffling his thoughts. He furrowed his brow deeply. "What am I doing here? What are *you* doing here, Smiley? You told me to get lost for twenty-four hours, and that's what I've been doing. So how is it that you're here, on the other side of the island? How did you know I was here?"

Smiley laughed glibly. "Nate, you forget I am a reporter. Nothing happens that I—"

"Oh cut the bullshit, Smiley. Don't give me that *nothing happens on my island without me knowing* crap." Nate's head was throbbing with a new ferocity now; it made him nauseous and supremely agitated.

"How did you know where to find me? And why the fuck are you here pounding on my door wondering if I'm okay? You know, Smiley, it occurs to me that all this black magic shit started right after meeting you. Some asshole waves a bloody cow foot in my face, some other asshole throws a dead chicken into my room and, lo and behold, you're there. Do you see the connection I'm making here? Do you? Explain that to me, Smiley. I'd really like to hear your thoughts."

The round man with the kind face just sat and absorbed the ire like an understanding parent waiting out a tantrum. Nate finished his tirade and dropped his head back into waiting hands.

"You dun now? You finish?" asked Smiley patiently.

Nate answered with his head still in his hands. "Yeah, I'm finished."

"Aright, then. For now, don't worry 'bout how I know what I know. Jus' believe me when I say I be your friend, and as your friend you must listen to me. Fair?"

"How'd you find me?" It was a demand, not a question.

"De car. Someone called the paper to report it."

"What the fu—?"

Smiley lifted his hand as if to silence a child. "Let me finish. The car I loaned you—dats a company car. It belong to the paper and it have a sticker on the bumper with the phone number and it says *The Word: Call us when news happens.* The people see it outside here and they call de paper. De paper call me."

Nate was still bristling. "Why would they call? It's a car…"

"De car has been vandalized. Considerably. You'll see when we leave, all right?"

Nate took a deep breath and clenched his jaw. His head was pounding and his gut was churning an evil brew. He tried to trim himself, get back to an even keel. Finally, he nodded once. "Okay."

"Good, fine," he said. "Now it be my turn. Firs' off: Why you here, man?"

"You know why."

"I know what you tell me, but I don't think dat's de truth, at least not de *whole* truth."

"Like I said before, because you wanted me to come back."

"Dat's partly true, for sure. But not de whole 'ting. Right?"

"Smiley, my head is about to split in two. What are you getting at?"

"You here on de island, and here in Dennery because you on your way to Ti Fenwe."

Nate lifted his head and looked at Smiley. "Yes. That's right. But it's just—"

Now it was Smiley's time to get angry. "*Bloodclat* man!" he cursed. "You don't have time for dis kind of childishness! You headed to de damn grave, man!"

"Smiley, the Obeah stuff doesn't…"

"Dat only part of you problem!" Smiley took a breath and regained his calm. "We need to get you back to Castries, back to Ma Joop, and then back to your worl'. Off de island. You hear me? You need to go home."

Nate tried to resist. "It's just some assholes trying to scare me," he said, but it didn't sound convincing—even to himself. In his gut, a warm stew brewed and his head felt stuffed with feathers.

Smiley leaned in and put his face mere inches from Nate's. "There is more I need to tell you, man. Le' we get in de car and go—I will tell you on de way and you can decide what you want do. Please, Nate. Trust me on dis…"

In the short time Nate had known Smiley, he'd never seen him so compelling. "Okay," he said meekly, and the resignation seemed to steal away any last trace of strength that he had. Nate slumped in his chair, and would have slid under the table had Smiley not reached out and seized him.

Working his way around to the other side of the table without letting go of his grip, Smiley easily hoisted the man and walked him out to the blue Sigma.

Nate roused himself as they crossed the courtyard. "What about your car?" he asked weakly. "It's out front."

"Don't worry 'bout de car—I'll fetch it another time."

Smiley helped Nate into the back seat. He immediately laid back and closed his eyes. Smiley quickly collected Nate's things from the room and tossed them into the trunk of the Sigma. He started the car and rounded the restaurant, stopping briefly, just long enough to see the group of people that had gathered around the white Honda Nate had been driving. They were careful not to get too close, but it was clear they were drawn inescapably to the scene. Smiley turned the blue Sigma onto the main road, moving slowly to navigate the impressive collection of potholes, and passed directly alongside the white Honda.

The car's windshield had been drenched with a red paste. It wasn't blood, but something thicker, something that allowed words to be scrawled in it. On the roof was a pair of dead birds, much like the one Nate had found in his room, and more of the red paste had been sloshed liberally around the bodywork. The net effect was that the car looked like it was bleeding, and where the paste had run thinner it had streaked down the sides and pooled on the ground.

"What does it mean," Nate asked quietly from the back seat. "What does it mean, those words on the windshield?" His voice was hollow, far off.

"It says, *Fè défini*. It means *to put to death*."

23

It ran through the blackness with the gait of a very short and stocky man, *thump, thump, thumping* over the hardwood planking of the main hall at Ti Fenwe. In Nate's mind he could see the dark shape: unshod, menacing, and hunched over. The bedroom itself was dark and silent, broken only by the sound of Vincent snoring lightly across the room and the other boys' heavy breaths of sleep. Nate's ears were so focused on listening for the footsteps they hurt, and if it weren't for the terror that seized him like a gnarled old claw about his throat, he would have screamed out to the others.

Instead he stared wide-eyed at the ceiling, and listened as the short staccato of footfalls pounded their way up the stairs to the landing, paused, then climbed the next set to the attic. Nate remembered the inky, lightless staircase, and his having been there only hours before made the horror that much more intense. The thing that wandered through the dark passages of Ti Fenwe stopped for a moment, and Nate's ears strained harder still to hear it. Then it stepped into the attic and Nate heard just two footfalls on the hardwood. It paused again, presumably looking around, weighing its options, perhaps smelling the stale air around it. Nate was sick with fear, and looked around again to see if anyone else had woken.

To his left, he could see Pip. He was awake, Nate was sure of it, but the young Dutch boy had not stirred. He lay stiffly in his bed staring wildly at the ceiling above. Seeing Pip's eyes open was enough to give him the courage to speak. "Pip," he whispered frantically. "Pip! Did you hear that?"

Pip, however, was in a state of near shock and unable to answer. All he could do was move his eyes. He flicked them at Nate and then back at the ceiling, knowing that the inch of wood in the ceiling was all that separated them from the beast roaming in the attic above.

And then the footfalls began again, this time shuffling more, sliding across the wooden floorboards and displacing the nutmegs that had been laid there to dry. They let out a rattle by their thousands, a hollow forlorn sound that ebbed and flowed as the mace-wrapped orbs turned over and over again, slowly rolling to a stop. The sound came in waves with each footfall, and the two boys moved their eyes along the ceiling, tracking the sound, convinced that they could see the woodwork bowing downward slightly with every step. It began to move with more purpose, as if it had decided where it was going, and it broke out into something close to a run, sending the nutmegs into a rattling, cackling chorus. It passed directly over the boys, and they instinctively pressed themselves deeper into their mattresses, putting as much distance between themselves and the thing above them as they could. Pip could contain himself no more, and let out a short, high pitched squeak: the thing above them abruptly stopped.

The nutmegs rolled and rolled, jockeying for position in the wake of the footfalls, slowly subsiding to a chatter, then trailing off to nothing like a fall into a dark well. Above him, Nate could practically see the thing looking down, edging toward a crack in the woodwork, kneeling awkwardly and placing one filthy, yellowing eye against the boards and peering gleefully down at the boys so terrified in the room below.

Both Nate and Pip held their breath, and eventually the footfalls began again, hesitantly at first, and then picking up speed as it crossed the room toward the gabled window. "What do we do?" Pip whispered through vocal chords tight as piano wire.

"Tristan!" Nate called out lightly, and was about to call again when a clatter arose above them. It sounded like a baking tray tossed violently down a bowling alley, and was attended by a light clicking and clattering of nutmegs disturbed along the way. Pip squeaked again, but this time it was muffled by the blanket he had drawn tightly about his face.

Nate looked over and could make out the form of Tristan

sitting up, his face also tilted toward the ceiling. "Tristan! Is that the…?" He couldn't bring himself to say it.

"Shh," said Tristan, a rigid finger across his lips. And as Nate peered through the darkness he could see that the boy was smiling. Nate watched as Tristan pushed the covers back, rolled onto his knees and reached down beside him; it was enough to give Nate the courage to move as well, and he suddenly realized that since the sound had started he had moved no part of himself except to swivel his head. He sat up and narrowed his eyes as Tristan flicked on the beam of a small flashlight.

"Watch this," whispered Tristan. He raised the beam to the ceiling, and to the spot where the boys all knew the thing was standing in that attic above. Then Tristan moved the beam slowly away, and the footfalls began again, seeming to cautiously follow the path of the beam.

"What are you doing?" whispered Nate in a tone that was more accusation than question, a warning for Tristan not to screw around.

"It follows the light, see?" And as he swung the beam back across the ceiling the footfalls followed, raising a protest once again from the drying nutmegs.

To Tristan's left Richard was now awake, too, and he reached out a hand to Tristan's wrist and gently pushed the flashlight beam downward. "Tristan, you're scaring them."

But Tristan would have none of it. He pulled the flashlight away and swatted at Richard with his other hand, catching the youngster on his shoulder with a loud smack. "*Bay wipo!*" he hissed. *Leave me alone!*

Richard simply moved back onto his own mattress and away from Tristan, who was again flashing the light at the ceiling. Nate watched as Richard unfolded himself from the blankets, and moved silently over to Pip's bed and sat beside him. He could see Richard whispering something to Pip, but could not hear the words. Soon Pip moved for the first time since the sounds had begun, and he wiped at his eyes with the stretched out body of his T-shirt.

The room suddenly plunged back into complete darkness as

Tristan flicked the flashlight off. A moment later he turned it back on, but this time it was pointed at a different part of the ceiling some five feet away from the last spot he had lit. Above them the creature dashed forward to the new source of light, and then Tristan promptly turned it off again. The footfalls stopped cold. A second later Tristan flicked it on again, again at a new spot, and once more the thing in the attic dashed forward, only to stop once more when Tristan extinguished the light. He did it twice more before Pip spoke up half in anger, half in fear. "Stop it!" he shouted. "You'll make it angry!"

Pip's objection was delivered forcefully enough to make Tristan stop and turn, this time with the light off. And as their eyes adapted to the dark room Nate could see that Pip and Tristan were locked in a staring war. It didn't last long before Pip looked down, but it was a glimmer of resolve Nate had never seen before in Pip.

"What the hell are you boys playing at?" came a gruff, sleep-sandy voice from the other side of the room. But before Vincent could give the boys the bellowing they all knew was coming, the attic erupted in a storm of clattering and crashing as the tin bowl left by the boys was seized by rough, leathery hands and beaten into scrap on the wooden floor, blow after furious blow. Then there was a pause, just for a second, as the metal form apparently flew through the dark attic air, then clanged against the rafters. The boys collectively cringed at the sound, and every eye—Vincent's included—watched the space above them with lids peeled back well past their limits.

And then, silence.

All five in the room sat motionless, watching the ceiling, waiting for something to happen. It stretched for almost a full minute, a minute cloaked in shadow and a stillness so complete it seemed the whole forest had stopped to witness the outcome.

The sound, when it came, was something Nate and Pip would never forget. It started in a tone close to hopelessness, and *aww*, like a child lamenting the loss of a favorite toy. Then, in the same note, it changed. It transitioned to frustration and then to outright rage, and ended as more a growl than anything else. It stopped abruptly, and was replaced by an equally ferocious burst of footfalls: heavy, anger-laden stomps that were running hard for the attic door. And with every landing of a foot, the nutmegs rolled. They rattled away in clear disapproval, sending up a hollow drone that was full of dread and warning.

Nate instinctively looked over to Tristan, and to Vincent, looking for the comfort of a smile or a knowing wink—anything that would reassure them this was just part of the scene, part of the program up here at Ti Fenwe. Instead he saw fear on Tristan's face for the first time, and a glance over to Vincent showed a grown-up momentarily caught without all the answers.

"Papa!" shouted Tristan in a tone so packed with panic that it popped Nate to his feet without thinking. "It's coming!"

Vincent lunged from the bed in a swirl of sheets and legs, and stumbled to catch his balance. "Quickly, check the door!"

24

Nate woke coughing and spitting, and the knitted white blanket that covered him was spattered with yellow fluid. He tried to push the sheets aside but couldn't, and another wave of nausea coursed through him and made him retch again. Behind him, his pillow and sheets were damp and cold, and he felt rivulets of sweat trickling through his temples and down toward the back of his skull. He wanted to cry out for help but it was already there. An unseen hand whipped the sheets away and a clean-smelling towel firmly wiped the vile spittle from his face.

A moment later he saw her—a slender black woman in a white dress with a silver watch hanging from her lapel. She dabbed at his face again and spoke in soothing tones, but Nate could not make out the words. He looked around frantically, confused by a sudden awareness that he recognized nothing at all. Who was this woman? What was this place? And why was he in this bed? The questions were about to tumble from his lips when the woman in the white dress cupped his face in both hands and calmed him.

"Come now. It's all right. Calm yourself," she said with a comforting smile. "Dat quite some way to wake up."

Nate's eyes said everything and the woman spoke again. "You be here at Dennery hospital. I'm guessing you no remember 'riving las' night?" she asked, and her voice was as melodic as a softly played steel pan drum.

It was calming Nate quickly. "Um, no…" He scouted around in his mind for memories but came up with nothing.

"You have a good friend d'ere in Terrance," she continued. "Him bring you in las' night, full of fever and mumbling away somethin' fearful."

"Terrance?"

"Terrance Edwin," she said plainly, "Him go by Smiley," she said.

"Oh, right. Smiley." Nate's mind managed to reach out and snag a lightly floating recollection, and then pull it in tight. The evening came back to him—to a point. He remembered the room in Dennery, the conversation with Smiley, the incredible thirst. And he remembered the car, the old Sigma, and seeing the Honda bleeding among a group of onlookers. What was it Smiley had said about death? He mumbled the word as the thought lingered. *Death*, he said in a dreamy, far away manner.

The nurse raised her eyebrows sharply. "No such nonsense," she commanded, folding her arms sharply. "You gwan be fine. You jus' need some res'."

Nate looked up at her and realized she thought he was talking about his condition. "No, I didn't mean…"

But she cut him off with a towel wiped firmly about his face again. "You gwan need a sponge bath. Or you can take de shower if you t'ink you able."

"I think I can manage with the shower," he said, as much to himself as to the nurse. He took a moment perched on the side of the bed to assess his condition. His head hurt—dried out like a world class hangover—and he felt as frail as a reed. He was damp from sweating, and the motion of his body moving through the air—just the simple act of shifting to a seated position—was enough to start him shivering.

Finally he stood, meekly waving away the assistance of the nurse, and made his way across the room to the bathroom. He paused and looked down at himself. He was completely naked—and mildly surprised that he didn't care, even with the nurse still puttering around the room.

In the bathroom mirror, he could see that his body was under attack. His face was drawn and hollow, and his eyes seemed to have receded into dark, bruised cavities beneath his brow. His lips were white and cracked, and in places it appeared they had bled during the night. The skin on his body was pale and seemed papery and tight, and he felt sure he was five or ten pounds lighter. He tried to remember his last decent meal but couldn't place it; he couldn't even remember the last time he had had an appetite.

Nate showered off the sweat and spittle and settled back into the clean sheets of his freshly made bed, and slept again. When he awoke, he found Smiley beside him reading the paper.

"*Terrance* Edwin?" asked Nate sarcastically.

Smiley's face dropped. He flopped the broadsheet in his lap. "Woman!" he yelled at the nurse. "What you been tellin' dis man?"

The nurse erupted in laughter and wobbled out of the room.

"It's Smiley. Don't no one call me Terrance—not since I was a little one."

"Thanks for bringing me here," said Nate. "And sorry about the car. And for being a dick."

"No problem, no problem. How you feelin'?"

"Like shit, to be honest. My head hurts and it feels like my heart has been kicked around inside my chest."

"You think you all right for a drive?"

"Now?"

Smiley nodded like it was the most natural thing in the world.

Nate shrugged. "Well, I guess, but the nurse…"

"Don't worry 'bout dat one," he said, but at the same time cast a nervous eye toward the nurse's station through the door.

"Did they say what's wrong with me? Is it the infection in my eye here?"

Smiley looked at him solemnly. "Nate, man. I don't think even you believe dat for true now."

He knew what Smiley was talking about. The conversation from the other night ran clear through his mind. The Obeah, Ma Joop, the car covered in red. "So why did you bring me here instead of right to Ma Joop, who I'm guessing you think can help me?"

"I brought you here as a favor."

"To me?"

"No, to an ol' friend. I promised I would let de hospital doctors tend to you before anyt'ing else."

Nate was confused. "What old friend?"

"Come—le' we get out of dis place and into my car. We'll talk den."

They dressed Nate in his clothes, which had been laundered while he slept, and the two slipped easily out of the small hospital and into the parking lot. In a few minutes, they were on the road again, heading out of town, up into the hills through stands of wild sugar cane, tangles of yellow hibiscus, and broad swathes of brilliant green Tanya the size of elephants ears. Nate recognized some of it from his days as a boy—a peak here, a bend in the road there—but much had changed. They were headed north to Gros Islet, back to the small roadside bar and, Nate suspected, to Ma Joop.

Nate watched the land flit by. "Okay—so who is this *old friend?*"

Smiley nodded slightly as he drove, and glanced over at Nate. He took a deep breath and spoke in even measured tones. "You remember when you firs' contacted me at *The Word?* When you send de email tellin' me you were finally ready to sit and speak wit me but that you needed…what did you call it now?"

"A professional courtesy."

"Das it," he said, smiling and raising a finger in punctuation. "A professional courtesy—you wanted to see everthin' I had collected 'bout de mess at Ti Fenwe. Do you remember I asked you not to use my email address at de paper after that, but to use my personal one instead?"

"Yeah, sure. I think you said something about it being a more reliable address."

"Right, man. I did, but dat was a fabrication. In truth it was because I needed to keep our communications very, very quiet and away from the paper. You see, there is some history here dat you don't know 'bout. About three and a half years ago there was another email that came through the general mailbox in the editorial department. It was a reques' asking for details 'bout de incident at the De Villiers estate in 1976, 'bout Richard's death. I had no idea dat email came in at de time. It was picked up by a colleague of mine, Desmond Bailey.

"Now, Desmond and I were friends, colleagues for sure, but we also competing, you know, for good stories. We had been talking 'bout the De Villiers incident for years and years, both of us coming up with theories and suppositions, but gettin' nowhere. As I said, I had no idea 'bout de email dat come in to de editorial department, or dat Desmond had since started seriously working on dis story. It still hard to believe." For a moment Smiley drifted off in thought.

"And?" said Nate impatiently.

"Well, man. Dis mystery at Ti Fenwe had always fascinated me even back when I was a young reporter, back in my twenties. I had been collecting pieces of information over the years, here and there, trying to get people to tell me their stories, but I had nothing serious. Nothing concrete. I was pretty sure the truth, the *real* story, had left the island in '76. Desmond, on the other hand, had been workin' hard to put everything together since the email he collected. But him do it all on his own, in secret, gatherin' information, photographs— everything he could. In fact, most of what I gave you at Vigie Beach came from the stuff Des gathered over the years.

"Of course, I knew nuttin' 'bout dis at de time. Des kept everything real quiet—maybe so he could trump me and claim braggin' rights—it was like dat between us—or maybe because he knew he was in something dangerous. Plenty dangerous. Back den I was not even workin' de crime beat, just de city scene. You know, local happenings, celebrity sightings on de island. Lot a parties, man, I could tell you."

Nate couldn't help himself. "Sorry Smiley—the story—the information Desmond collected."

"Right man, right. So Des apparently collected all dis information, and then I get a call from his mother one night. She all upset. Crying and carryin' on. Tellin' me to come down to de police station because dey won't let her see Desmond. So down to the police station I go. But in my mind I'm thinking *why she want me to go to the police station? After all, Desmond workin' de crime beat and knows every constable on de island by name. If anyone has sway down there, it's Desmond.*

"Anyhow, I go on down to de Bridge Street station an' I find his mother. She inconsolable. Weepin'. Cryin'. Head in hands. And I'm not understanding what's going on. Finally she blurt it out: Desmond is dead. Jesus. Let me tell you. Here I am thinking my friend Desmond is drunk an' locked up for de night and that because of dis his mother is *joliman* upset. Very much upset with him. Then I find out he dead! Jesus, man. Anyway, I ask de sergeant what's going on, what happen to Desmond an' he tell me him drown.

"Desmond drowning—dis struck me as odd. I know Desmond, an' him nevah like de water. Nevah."

"And yet he lived on an island."

"Not so unusual. Many island people stay clear of de water, man. Maybe couple splashes 'round de ankles. But swimmin'? Desmond? Nevah. Anyway, then de policeman tell me Desmond fell out of a boat and drowned. A boat! Man, something inside me just freeze up. Just like that. Desmond in a boat? Nevah," he said, chopping the air sideways with his free hand.

"So you think…"

"Mm hmm. Me think. I say nuttin' to de policeman. I jus' ask if there was any personal effects dat his mother should have—he say dey have nuttin'—an' I take his mother home."

Nate looked back out of the window as the island rushed past. "Wow," he said quietly, as much to Smiley's story as to the scenery around them. They were winding their way up through the hills now, on a narrow road that followed the contours of what was probably better described as a small mountain. St. Lucia was a volcanic island, thrust up violently from the ocean floor eons ago and made of jagged steep shapes all dressed in brilliant green. To their left, the terrain rose sharply, and water from the undergrowth leached out and ran across the road in broad shimmering sheets. And to their right the land fell away steeply, disappearing into a lush emerald valley lined with trees that clung to the cliff-side at impossible angles. There were no people on this stretch, and no other cars, save a battered blue Honda a few hundred yards behind them.

"So what did you do?" asked Nate.

"Man, at first, nuttin'. The whole t'ing seemed wrong to me. So I just lef' it be. But it trouble me. Trouble, trouble, trouble. I can't let it go, you know? I find myself thinkin' 'bout it all de time. But me a little worried because of how de police handle this. All a little strange, man. But still it trouble me. Finally, I can't take it no more. I go to my editor an' tell him something not right here. He say have a look. So I have a look.

"I collect everything Des had at his desk, on his computer, in his car. Everything. And I start readin'. That's when I find everything Des had collected—all de information 'bout de whole t'ing in '76, 'bout the De Villiers boy. Dat's when I realize what he been secretly workin' on."

"Richard's death."

"Mm hmm. Richard's death. And as I read all de research an' notes Desmond made, I start to see two mysteries—not jus' de one. Firs', what happened to Desmond and de others on dat boat—I mean, what *really* happened?"

Nate interrupted. "Others…?"

Smiley put up a hand; Nate would have to let him tell it his way. "Second: what happened to Richard De Villiers in 1976? No one was charged back den, and no one gave evidence. All very strange, no?" he said, glancing over at Nate again, who was now suddenly very uncomfortable.

Smiley went on. "Now, I made some headway with what happened to Desmond specifically—nuttin' I could prove, mind you, but I pretty damn sure I know what happened. And now you here, and I pretty damn sure *you* know what happened at Ti Fenwe in 1976. You were there. But your father invoked *diplomatic immunity* an' had you out of de police station an' off de island before anyone could get any answers." Finally he said, "I nah placing any judgement, Nate. I would do the same for my son if I had one. You mus' protect your own. I understand that. But there is a connection between de deaths three years ago, Richard's death in 1976, an' events transpiring around you today."

Nate looked at Smiley with a face like a man who had just bitten a lemon. He took a deep breath and steadied himself. "You said *deaths*, not death."

"Hmm?"

"You said the *deaths three years ago*. Plural. One was your reporter friend, Desmond, but who else? Who else died?"

The car hit them hard from behind and to the right, violently forcing the front of Smiley's Gallant around and pointing it toward the edge of the road where it dropped away into the endless green. The impact jerked Smiley's hands from the wheel, and both he and Nate were driven momentarily back into their seats, and then pitched instantly forward again hard against the seat belts. The wind was forced from their lungs and they simultaneously grunted like prize-fighters eating body shots.

Smiley grabbed wildly at the air trying to regain his grip on the wheel, desperate to spin the car back toward the road. But it was too late. The engine raced, the wheels bit in and the small blue Gallant roared off the road and into the yawning green.

• • •

To Nate, things seemed to be going downhill quickly.

He stood on top of his foam mattress, watching Tristan and Vincent bound across the darkened bedroom toward the door, unable to move at all. All he could do was hover in a state of quivering hyper-readiness. It was coming.

There was one door to the room and Tristan and Vincent were jamming their meaty hands against the locks to make sure they were secured. "Tristan, the gun case! Quickly!" Vincent pointed at the cupboard. The thing in the attic was now thundering down the stairs, and the nutmeg in the loft above was still howling and rattling in murderous anticipation. The footfalls hit the main hall in a single floor-shuddering thump, as if the thing had cleared the last few steps in a single leap. In an instant it was running again, and while the nutmeg chatter slowed and died, the sound of its approach intensified, the darkness around them making it somehow more awful. The boys could feel each step now, and each one seemed loaded with malice and bile. It thundered through the main hall, down the corridor, past the kitchen until it was right outside the door.

And then it stopped.

All four of the boys were now standing, every muscle and sinew humming, every hair raised. Pip was the worst off. His hands were curled into tight fists, and then pressed into his lips so tightly he was close to drawing blood. His cheeks were wet with tears, and the only thing stopping him from screaming was the intensity of the silence. The nutmeg had stopped rolling. The creature outside the door was still. The boys strained to hear something, anything, but apart from the trembling breaths being drawn inside the room, there was nothing.

All four of the boys flicked their heads suddenly toward the door, toward the metallic snicker of the hammer being drawn back on the pistol. It was Vincent. He was holding the pistol close to the door, making sure the sound of the hammer being drawn back was clearly audible in the corridor outside. Something on the other side of the door shifted at the sound, like a half step back, and Vincent smiled.

"Yes," he said in a long drawn out breath. "You know what that is, don't you." He seemed to be talking to himself, or perhaps to whatever was outside in the hall. Then Vincent fell quiet, and pressed his ear against the door. The silence became so complete that Nate was sure he could hear the heartbeats of everyone in the room, and his own loudest of all. A moment later came a soft padding sound from outside the door. It retreated hesitantly through the house and when it left, the whole structure seemed to exhale.

Vincent seated the hammer again and placed the pistol on the chair beside his bed. "At ease," he said to the boys, who were all as rigid as soldiers on parade. "One of these days, my boy," he began, speaking to Tristan in inclusive, fatherly tones. "One of these days you're going to piss that thing off with all your teasing and he'll get in here while he's all hot and bothered. He can be a mean son of a bitch when he's upset." He slapped his son on the back in that *chip-off-the-old-block* kind of way, and then noticed Pip. "Hey, Pip. Come on, toughen up."

Pip turned away and sat heavily on his mattress.

But Vincent wouldn't let it go. "You know you can't go through life crying about—"

"He's okay," interjected Nate in a tone more bold than he had intended. "He's just tired. We all are." And with that Nate turned away and sat on his own mattress, trying not to let any of the others see the trembling in his hands and legs.

"Right, well," said Vincent awkwardly. And then, shrugging it all off, "Look boys, it's after four. We normally check the copra oven at five, but it's close enough. Then we can all have a bit of a sleep-in once we come back."

Nate looked at each of the others and could see none of them wanted to leave the room just now. None of them moved.

Finally Richard spoke up. "Are you sure that's such a good idea, Uncle Vince? I mean, it's pretty upset, no?"

"Ah, come now boys. Don't worry about all that," he said, waving one hand casually around in the air. "We've been living with that little bugger for generations. He cools off quickly. Probably over at the Kinnock estate by now. Long gone."

"I don't want to go out there," said Pip bluntly without looking up.

Vincent's face pinched with annoyance. "Pip, son, it's just an animal…"

Again that fine seam of defiance rose up in Pip. "That's not what Augustine said."

Vincent shook his head in exaggerated frustration. "Don't listen to that old witch. She's just very old and very bored. And probably senile. Now everyone get your shoes on. We're going to check the copra." It was an order, and the boys quietly complied.

The walk through the darkened house was unnerving, and not just because of the long shadows cast by the flashlights: the fact that

Vince put the pistol in his pocket rather than back in the gun cabinet was not lost on any of the boys.

They made their way through the corridor, past the kitchen and into the empty main hall. Vincent, at the front, paused for a moment and panned the beam of his flashlight around the room.

"What's wrong?" said Richard from the back of the line.

"Nothing," replied Vincent casually. "Just checking."

Tristan put a hefty elbow into Richard. "Chicken shit," he said snidely.

The line moved off again, across the hall and out of the house through the open doorway, and then down the worn concrete steps. The night was much louder outside; the wind stole through the forest all around them, and the chorus of crickets and other night insects chirped and clicked incessantly. It was a short walk to the brick copra oven, but Nate spent it with his head swivelling all around, trying to catch a glimpse of whatever had been running through the house. *Invisible my ass*, he thought. Whatever it was, if it was running around in the house and he could hear it, he could damn well see it too. It was probably just one of the laborers. Paid a little extra to scare the crap out of a bunch of kids. He'd have to get paid pretty damn well though, thought Nate. That attic was seriously dark and scary.

At the oven, Vincent began working the copra with a long steel rake, and the boys instinctively kept a watch on the bush-line around them. They didn't talk, but instead cut nervous glances at the forest, searching intently for dark foreboding shapes. They bit nervously at lips and nails, impatiently willing time on so they could scurry back to the sanctity of the bedroom. As Nate looked around, he saw the black sky was softening. The dawn was coming on, and before long the coconut trees would frame another perfectly blue Caribbean sky. That would be good, he thought, and perhaps there might be a way to convince the others to go home early. One night at Ti Fenwe was enough. He missed home, he missed his mom and dad, and he didn't want another night of unseen creatures running around above him and animals having their throats torn out in the woods.

But when Nate looked back down, the thoughts all evaporated. Vincent was standing beside him, deadly still, with the pistol held out in front of him in the firing position. He was facing the bush-line. He looked left to see where the others were and the motion made Vincent speak. "Don't move, Nate my boy. Don't move a bloody muscle."

"What is it?" whispered Nate, suddenly more scared than he had been all night. Behind him he could hear Pip begin to whimper, and a flash of anger sparkled through him for an instant and then was gone.

"It's that little bastard again," said Vincent. His tone mostly conveyed a sense of wonder—a kind of grudging respect for a wily opponent—but there was an edge of fear in there, too. It was that sharp little edge that had Nate worried. "He's right there. Right next to the mango tree." Vincent stepped a little closer to Nate to open the angle and presumably expose more of his target. "That's it," he whispered. "I've got you now *bata*, you little bastard."

In one fluid motion, Vincent pulled the hammer back to fire.

Beside him, Nate was watching the drama unfold with increasing horror. He couldn't see anything near the tree—hell, he couldn't be sure he was even looking at the right damn tree. In the space of a fractured second Nate's mind ran through a quick checklist of the night's eventualities. There was the brutal business of Vincent doing God knew what to Tristan, there was the goat, torn apart from chin to chest, the scuffle at Augustine's, the dead chicken, plucked and left in the attic, and there was the thing itself, the Bolom, running through the house. It was all enough already. Enough scares, enough cruelty, enough everything. Whatever—or whoever—was hiding by the tree was about to get shot and something in Nate had had its fill.

Without thinking Nate yelled, *No!*, then flicked out his hand and swatted down on Vincent's wrist just as the gun discharged. It let out a pop like a champagne cork, and the dirt a few feet from where they stood spat up from the ground.

A second later, something in the bush-line moved. There was a rustling sound, and Nate swore he saw something—perhaps just a branch or a bundle of leaves shifting—but something, and right beside the mango tree, too. He looked up at Vincent and saw the man was furious. The gravity of what he had just done settled quickly on Nate, and he looked to the others for a way out, a helping hand, anything. Their faces were blank, unbelieving. All except Tristan's. The heir to the estate was smiling a cruel smile.

Nate looked back at Vincent who was now struggling to contain himself and fidgeting with the gun in his hands. Finally he looked directly at Nate and spoke aloud to the whole group. "All of you. Back to the room," he said coolly. "Now."

25

To Nate, it sounded like someone shushing in a movie theatre, only in a more regular, consistent fashion. One followed the next, then a pause about the length of a breath, and then it would repeat. He listened for a moment longer and thought about opening his eyes. His lids felt impossibly heavy, as if his lashes had been dipped in lead while he slept. He also felt uncomfortable, as if he had been somehow sleeping in an awkward position, thrust up against the headboard with the pillows and blankets wrapped and heaped about him.

But when he did finally open his eyes, he found that he was not in his bed at all, but crammed tightly into the foot-well of the front seat of a car. On his chest he could feel the seat belt, but it held no real tension, and as he followed the blue fabric strap, he could see that it had ripped itself clear of the anchor point below the seat. He twisted up and backwards, and couldn't understand why he was pitched forward so. His feet and knees were in the foot-well and his arm was resting on the part of the dash normally facing the passenger. Finally his head cleared, and he understood that the car was somehow sitting vertically, nose down, surrounded by a world of green.

And there was that sound again, the shushing, regular and off to his right. In the driver's seat beside him sat Smiley. He was still in his seat, belt cinched in place, but because the car was standing on its front end his arms were hanging forward and down through the frame of the now glassless front windshield. As Nate's faculties fully returned, he realized that the car was suspended nose-down in a tree, and around them was an impossibly dense tangle of vegetation of every type. The car rocked gently as he moved, and one look down through the front windshield showed him they were stopped hard in the 'Y' of a sizeable, dark wooded tree. The car was suspended in place by a web of thick vines the size of climbing ropes massed together in every direction. The car was a crumpled wreck of blue, and steam gently rose from somewhere down at the front.

Smiley was struggling to breathe, and in considerable pain. Nate pulled himself from the foot-well, and was relieved to find that all of his parts were working. He was bruised for certain, but no breaks, no gaping wounds. Smiley, he saw, was less lucky. Nate pushed himself up and straddled the dash, sitting on it with one foot inside and the other hanging out over the hood of the car.

The tree that had caught their vehicle and saved them from tumbling into the valley had done so at a price. A broken branch, about the size of a baseball bat, had come through the opening where the windshield had once sat, and was now jammed firmly into Smiley's shoulder, pinning him to the seat. A red stain spread from the spot and worked its way down the branch. Nate stared for a moment in horror. Had the branch gone *through* Smiley? Or was it broken off and simply pressed firmly against him. Smiley wheezed again, the shushing sound, and he became aware of Nate looking on.

"Nate," he said weakly. "Help me."

The voice broke Nate from his stupor. "Don't move. Don't move. Let me see." He stood almost upright in the wheel-well, and peered into the back seat. If the branch had gone through the man he was not sure what he would do, and he found himself wondering what he would say to Smiley. *Gee, it appears you've been run through by this here tree. You'll probably bleed to death if I pull you off it.*

Smiley wheezed again. "What is it? Tell me!" he said insistently.

"It's okay—it's not through you. I think you're just wedged in." He looked at the angle of the seat-back, and could see that the left side—the side where Smiley was pinned tight—was twisted back by the force of the branch.

Nate looked around for a solution, then again at Smiley's

predicament. "Okay, I think I can get you out. Can you reach down beside you? Between the seat and the door—there should be a seat-back adjustment." Nate looked at the assembly on his own seat. Yes, there was a simple lever there. One pull should free the seat and allow it to move to a new angle. "You should be able to feel a lever. Go ahead and pull that and it should let the seat-back go free. It should release the pressure on your shoulder."

Nate listened as Smiley grunted in pain, fumbling blindly for the lever beside his seat. He wondered if releasing the pressure would cause more pain, or if there would be some new bleeding he should prepare for. Or—God help them—if the whole car was being held from shifting by that one branch wedged against Smiley. And as he thought it, Smiley pulled the lever.

The seat-back released like a gallows trap door and snapped Smiley backward and into a near standing position. The car shifted violently, dropped another foot, and the branch that held him rode up and over his shoulder. Nate threw out his hands and braced himself for the fall, but with a jerk hard enough to wind him, the car groaned and wedged tightly into its new spot.

"You okay?" he asked Smiley.

The big man blinked and looked around before he answered. "Better," he said finally, and Nate could hear him drawing lungfuls of air. The shushing has ceased.

"Are you bleeding?"

Smiley looked down and under his shirt. "Some. But nah too bad."

The two men looked at each other and after a moment the relief at being alive showed on their faces.

"Honestly," said Nate. "This might be my worst vacation ever."

Smiley laughed, and then coughed, and then laughed some more.

They found Smiley's cell phone sitting in pieces near the accelerator, and decided climbing down seemed a better option than trying to scramble up through the trees. It took the two men nearly an hour to sufficiently bind Smiley's wound, then extricate themselves from the car and the tree. They worked their way through the mass of green and finally reached a road lower down the slope. When they emerged they were just yards from a small collection of houses.

Smiley knocked on the door and asked to use the phone, and Nate sat heavily on a pile of building stone by the roadside. A boy came out of the house with lime juice for him and a green towel soaked in warm water. Nate smiled, drank deeply, and wiped the grime from his face. With the adrenaline rush over, he was beginning to feel as he did before the accident—feverish, weak, and tired. All he wanted was a warm bed and some sleep. Maybe a handful of antibiotics to get things back on track.

Smiley dispatched the boy into the bush and he returned twenty minutes later with Nate's small case, as well as a small backpack that belonged to Smiley. He paid the boy with a handful of change, which sent him squealing away in delight.

Smiley sat beside Nate on the building stone and watched the boy skip away. "You remember when life was dat simple, man? When you get a few shillings in your hand and dat's all it take to be happy?"

Nate wiped his face again with the towel. "Ah," Smiley said, lifting himself awkwardly from the stone pile and cupping his hand over his shoulder. He flicked his chin out in the direction of the road. "Here we go."

A liquid-silver Seven Series BMW floated gently to a halt in front of them, and the sun glinted off the chrome with an intensity that forced both men to shield their eyes.

She was dressed in khaki shorts, a simple white T-shirt and flip-flops, each adorned with a single bejewelled starfish.

Nate had never seen Rachael look so lovely.

26

Morning, with its brilliant sunshine, had the power to dissolve all manner of horrors. The incident of the night before was swept away, not spoken of or addressed in any way. But Nate knew this visit would likely be his last. Still, the prospect of the day ahead was so bright, so light and filled with promise that thoughts of unseen creatures in bushes, pistols and offended grown-ups were easily cast away.

The boys ate quickly, before Vincent woke, stuffing their faces with bowls of Muesli flooded with warm Carnation Evaporated Milk straight from the tin. They skipped through the main hall, now bright and airy with fuzzy shafts of sunlight streaming in through unshuttered windows. It held no sense of malice, no bleak pall. It was just a large, empty room. Only the stairwell entrance to the attic seemed at all unsettling, and even that was a minor condition. Still, the boys all gave it a wide berth just the same.

The track leading from the house was bathed in warm light, that unique daybreak radiance—lasting only an hour or so—that is somehow buoyant and touches everything with gold. It had a hopeful quality to it that wrapped around all of them. Even Tristan was affected.

"What do you guys want to do?" he said in a tone close to enthusiasm.

"Explore…" suggested Pip.

"Yeah," said Nate. "Or maybe we could go back to that place, you know, and shoot more ball bearings?"

"Yeah, lets!" Richard chimed in.

The boys ran wildly through the forest, ducking through natural corridors of cascading lianas, over fallen trees wrapped jealously with vines and creepers, and down winding paths still damp and slick with morning dew. They ran through curtains of tumbling leafy thickets, whipping the branches behind them across the path to swat the next kid in line, laughing, finding sticks, throwing stones, being eleven, twelve, and thirteen.

At the clearing, Tristan went straight to the box on the old industrial-wire spool that served as the main table, and retrieved the two Wrist Rockets. Nate smiled at the sight of them, and couldn't wait to send a ball bearing crashing through the polystyrene blocks. He looked up at the natural cathedral above him, scooped out as it was like a secret dome within the forest. It seemed almost sacrilegious to have all this discarded furniture dragged into its midst.

"Okay—ten-minute ball bearing search," cried Tristan. "Whoever finds most gets first try!"

The boys sprinted as a herd toward one end of the clearing, the target end, where the ground was dusted with tiny white beads from all the polystyrene blocks that had been destroyed over the years. They plunged through the green wall, crying out like warriors into battle, and scattered among the trees and bushes on hands and knees.

Ten minutes later and Nate was the clear winner. At the edge of the clearing, Richard set a few well beaten blocks of Styrofoam in the tree branches and retreated to safety beside the group.

Nate drew the yellow elastics back as far as his arm span would allow. He could feel the power humming in the rubber, and the tension in the slingshot pressing into his forearm through the wrist-brace. It was dizzying, intoxicating stuff, and he held onto the moment, stretching it out for as long as his muscles would hold. Finally, with a burning in his forearm, the moment had come to let fly.

Thwack! The silver bearing hurtled forward, struck the white block cleanly and punched a perfect hole straight through it. A small shower of white polystyrene beads floated down from behind it, and the boys collectively let out a cheer.

Nate smiled. It seemed this was something he was good at. Really good at. He was thrilled. Elated. Cracking that bearing through the white block on his first shot was like cocking a leg and marking his turf. He'd never felt so *connected*. He looked around and saw that the others recognized it too; his status had just ratcheted upward with an almost audible click. Richard stepped up to him and smiled with one hand splayed out wide. "Nice!" he said, but before the moment had fully unfolded Tristan shoved him hard out of the way. Richard caught his foot on the edge of the wooden spool table and went down hard.

Nate shook his head lightly. "Come on, Tristan…"

But the blonde boy smiled resiliently as he picked himself up. *It's okay, It's okay,* he mumbled.

Tristan had already lined up a shot with his own slingshot, and when he let the leather pouch go it sent the ball bearing hissing past the target and *pit-pat-pitting* through the leaves at the clearing's edge. No one said a thing.

The game continued, and when at last they'd had their fill it was Nate they had to convince to move on. "Just a few more shots," he pleaded. "Just these four that I have left."

Finally the Wrist Rockets were tucked back into the box on top of the spool. The boys went back to the Estate house, ate crudely made peanut butter and jam sandwiches, and then tore back down the trail, past the clearing and deeper into the forest. They followed Tristan, who was moving fast—trying to lose them, it felt like—but they managed to keep up for the most part. Only once they lost sight of him, but Richard knew the way and a few minutes later they emerged at the bank of a small river carving its way through the rainforest in search of the sea.

The bank pitched steeply to water's edge where the river moved like a lazy serpent through the trees. The water was cold and clear, and the bottom was gravel and coarse sand, dotted with patches of smooth and mossy bedrock. Tristan was splashing through it in moments, wading out to the middle where he stood in water up to his thighs. The others watched from the safety of the bank until Tristan raised his arms and goaded them. *"Poul!"* he chided them. *Chickens!*

And that was all it took. The other three charged headlong into the river, whooping and hollering like newly freed lunatics. The water was mountain pure and clear as a lens. Soon the boys were reaching down to the bottom, bringing up stones and waterlogged branches, and calling each other over to show off their finds.

And it was Tristan who started it. He dug a handful of coarse sand from the bottom and plopped it on Nate's back as he was talking to Richard. It was cold and slithery, and when Nate shrieked in surprise they all laughed. It grew quickly, and soon the boys had each claimed a spot in the river and were reaching down to the bottom in waist-deep water, retrieving handfuls of river sand and hurling it at each other. It would break up in the air and shower them with stinging pellets, and they would turn and cower, taking the sand on their backs, and then howl in protest. Countless handfuls were raised and thrown, complete with sound effects from bullets to bombs, and cries of anguished Hollywood deaths to boot.

Eventually Pip got something in his eye, a fleck of coarse gravel, and he retreated to the bank with Tristan still flinging handfuls of wet sand his way. *Stop it! Stop it!* he yelled, but Tristan was gripped by the moment. Like a jackal toying with its prey, he continued to pepper Pip as the boy made his way to the river's edge. Nate followed to see if he was all right and also got hit, while on the furthest edge of the river Richard stood waiting in the water, a handful of sand at the ready.

"Come on, Tristan, stop it," he said.

Tristan turned and let fly at Richard with a handful of river bottom. It splashed wildly around the little blonde boy, and only hit him lightly about his shorts. Richard laughed and retaliated, sending a handful that somehow held together in flight and hit Tristan clean in the chest. Nate and Pip (squinting with one eye closed), both saw the hit, and let out a collective *Oh!*

Tristan's lower lip disappeared into his mouth and he bit down hard. He was instantly enraged, and everyone could see it. Like a car engine revving out of control, Tristan started throwing handful after handful of gravel at Richard, with no respite from the withering fire. Richard covered his head, turned away and ducked low in the water, cringing as the sand and gravel lashed at his back.

Moments later the stony rain stopped, and Richard heard the splashing sound of someone approaching fast.

Something in the way Tristan moved brought Nate to rigid attention on the bank. "Tristan! No!" he cried out with growing alarm.

Richard raised his head and looked: Tristan was only six feet away. His hand was already raised, his fist locked tightly around a rock the size of a brick.

• • •

Nate hadn't left his apartment since the death of his father two days earlier. Instead he watched TV. He watched the glossy screen for hours at a stretch, letting the sounds and images wash over him. Occasionally a comment or a scene snagged his attention, just for a moment or two, but soon he would slide back into something softly catatonic, and the television would hum along in front of him.

The letters still sat in their two neat rows on the kitchen table, and he knew on some level that he was avoiding them. Still, every few hours his head would tilt just enough to see the table and the letters—just to make sure they were really there.

On third day the phone rang—a timeshare salesman that never made it to the second sentence before Nate hung up. But for a moment, a very brief moment as the first chirp sounded out from the phone, Nate had thought it was his father calling.

The call jarred a memory loose. It floated into view like a silk scarf caught in the wind. He hadn't been able to remember the very last conversation he had with his father, but it returned now, crisply and in full focus. It would have been an unremarkable conversation, really, if not for the fact that it was the last one.

"Hello?"

"Nate, it's your dad. I'm on my own tonight."

"Everything okay, Dad?"

"I miss him, you know. I really miss him."

"I miss him, too, Dad."

"Family, you know. It's the only thing…"

"Dad…"

"You seen your mother lately? How's she doin'? Is she…is she seeing anyone? When I took that big walk with you, with your mother, there was s'posed to be more, you know? That was s'posed to count for something. Let me tell you something, son, I gave everything up for you. My career, my wife, my house, all of it. Everything. For you. Both of you. I was on the fast track. I was going up, but when I had to close ranks around my family I did it—cons'quences be damned. 'Cause that's whacha do, goddamn it! That's what family's all about. And when they leaned on me to explain myself, I said no. No fuckin' way. 'Cause that's whacha do. That's what family's all about. And they're still askin' Nate. They're still askin'. I goddamn well shut the doors tight on those bastards. I protected you. I protected your mother, this whole family. I protected you! And then the bastards pull the floor out from under me. Abandonment of post, they said. Dereliction of I don't know what the fuck. And then your mother walks out. And then the fucking bank, the house, all that shit."

"Dad, I'm…"

"And what do I have now, huh? What's my legacy to the world? What has my sacrifice brought?"

"Dad?"

"What are you going to do now, Nate? I'd like to see you do one damn thing properly, you know? One damn thing that honors everything I did—everything I gave up. For you. What'll it be, Nate? How 'bout something solid, like I did for you back then. Something I can be proud of, something Cody, God rest his little soul, can be proud of—or how 'bout just something you can be proud of. Don't you get it, Nathan? It's about doing the right thing, and to hell with the goddamn consequences. That De Villiers boy. Jesus, there was nothing I could do for him. Nothing anyone could. But you. I could still do right by you. And I damn well did. That's my legacy, goddamn it."

"Dad, I love you. And I'm so sorry."

For the most part he always played it cool when his father got like that, just turned the proverbial cheek and went on his way, but it always hurt. His father had been a drunk since Nate was in his early teens, perhaps even earlier. And when his mother left a week after his sixteenth birthday, it seemed the world had really ended. The drinking got much worse, the blame much thicker.

But this call, this memory that had somehow eluded him since his father's death, it burned now with an intensity and panic he recalled from the early days, before the drinking and shouting had all became a numbing routine. The memory brought emotions he hadn't felt since then, since his teens when his father and mother fought wildly, or even worse, when they retreated to a deathly silence that lasted for days.

The memory of that call with his father—it seemed grotesquely bloated with importance now. Was it because it was the *last* conversation? Was it because Nate had hung up on the old man, silenced him just as he'd meant to, but this time forever? It settled on him thickly now—his father wouldn't be calling back. There would be no *next time* when Nate could decide to finally dig deep and listen, really listen to the old man. His father would never kick the habit, never sit down and have some candid twelve-step conversation about life and loss that Nate had somehow always secretly believed would come. There would be no chance to make up for anything.

In his mind Nate saw an image of Richard he hadn't conjured in years. The boy was bright and smiling, and in the space of a single heartbeat it brought him to Cody. His face crumpled as he fought the memories.

He rose from the chair and walked zombie-like to the bedroom, where he picked up the shoebox from behind the door and opened it. The pain came faster now, but it was important to feel it. It was all he had left, that burning, untouchable, un-soothable pain that had become his definition, his demonstration of how much he missed Cody.

He reached in and lifted a small plastic figurine, a well-muscled Spiderman, and he rolled it through his fingers the way some might handle the Hope Diamond. He set it back and dipped his hand again, this time a yellow fuzzy sleeper from when Cody was only a year old. He held it to his face and breathed deeply; it didn't hold the scent that it once had, but still he tried to take it in, to find some last trace of that once perfect boy. He sobbed quietly, and dropped the sleeper back into the box.

Finally he reached in and took out one last item. It slipped into his hand easily, and he sat looking at it for a long time before he pressed the power button. When he did, the little screen on the voice recorder brightened, and a red light flashed its readiness. On the small screen the message said "File 1: 6 minutes, 43 Seconds."

Nate held his breath, and pushed play.

Cody laughs. He is five, and his laughter is as light as angels' wings.

But instead of the wallowing that would normally follow, Nate felt something else. It seemed some threshold within him had finally been reached—perhaps from too many trips into that harrowing shoebox, or maybe thanks to his father's sudden and violent departure—but whatever the cause, the sensation rising inside him felt steely and unyielding. Where there was usually pain, there was a new sensation, like a hard and silvery ball bearing pinched in the leather pouch of a fully drawn slingshot, ready to let fly and tear off in new direction.

Nate walked purposefully to the kitchen table and collected the letters. In the hall closet he found the simple file folder—the one he had tucked away carefully out of sight and out of mind. He checked to see the contents were still there, then tucked it under his arm and returned to the bedroom.

Something was beginning to gel, to make sense. Nothing could be fixed. None of it. Nothing could be salvaged, repaired or propped up. It was completely and utterly fucked, and the blame was in the right place. The thought of it was suddenly energizing.

And in that instant, he finally understood where salvation lay.

Nate took the two letters from the file folder and placed them on the bed. Then he placed the others, the ones he had collected from his father's house, on the bed as well. It was clear they had all come from the same place. They bore the same handwriting, the same postmarks, and all had stamps from St. Lucia.

The two Nate had in his folder had been sent to him in the last four years—one in 2008, and the other just last year. He knew unequivocally that, like the others sent to his father, they were all from Smiley Edwin. And they all wanted the same thing.

As Nate looked at the postmarks he understood that over the years, both right after the events and in the decades that followed, Smiley Edwin had been quietly calling out for someone to set the record straight.

He resolved to go back to the root, to the beginning where he knew it had all gone wrong. Nate believed there was one event, one offense that might have echoed through time and set everything in motion. He would go back, way back, and fix the first one. The first sin. The first bad call.

It might not bring everything in line again—in truth he knew it would do nothing for the mess swirling around him now—but it would be a start. For Cody. For Richard.

And for right now, that would be enough.

27

The ride north was quiet, awkward, with no one really trying to keep the conversation alive. The car was cool with the air conditioning blowing hard, and Nate sat in the back seat reveling in the sensation of the icy jet of air against his feverish forehead and eyes.

The car slowed and turned off the road, then slipped through a security gate that hummed closed behind them. Nate looked around and saw they had entered a beautiful estate; they followed a sinuous driveway that carved like a river through perfectly manicured lawns of brilliant green, past ordered flower beds and soaring palm trees that wore their tin rat-bands like jewelry. They stopped in front of a low-set house designed to sit perfectly into the hillside it occupied. Its walls were alabaster set against dark wood trim with large, thick plantation shutters in the windows. There were huge sections of floor-to-ceiling glass panels that swept back and opened the place up like an endless veranda, and brilliant tropical flowers beaming from tastefully positioned pots and planters, some as large as oil drums. It was like a Frank Lloyd Wright design brought to its most contemporary, thought Nate—the kind of million-dollar property you'd find in a magazine dedicated to life at the platinum end of the scale.

Nate could see right through the house. Through the glass walls, through the main living room, and out to the intense azure blue of the expansive pool on the other side. And beyond that, to the Caribbean Sea.

They went inside and into the living room. It was dressed with wide, oversized rattan furniture appointed with rich, white fabrics and luxurious, chocolate throw pillows, and at one end there was a sweeping white bar with a soft blue glow that lit the bottles from behind. To the back of the house was another unobstructed view, this time to the pool, and when the floor-to-ceiling glass panels were drawn back the room spilled out almost seamlessly into the backyard space. The far edge of the pool was flush with the surface of the water, giving the illusion that the water ran right up to the horizon and merged with the sea in the background.

Rachael took Smiley into the kitchen, and Nate explored the deck and marvelled at the beauty of it all—and the cost. He could see a set of stairs winding down beside the pool and terminating at a small and very private beach with impossibly white sand. There were coconut trees at perfect intervals, flower beds that curved and undulated around the pool in architectural harmony with the house. Christ, even the retaining wall at the far end was a work of art.

With all the white and glass, Nate found it too bright to stay outside. His feverish head was already pulsing, and the brightness only made it worse. He turned back and noticed that from this angle the house revealed much more of itself than it had from the front entrance. It was actually comprised of two levels. It was luxurious, magnificent, but never over the top. A remarkable building, thought Nate, but he couldn't help guessing: Three million? Four?

"Nate, come inside," said Rachael from a gap in the glass. "You'll blind yourself out there without sunnies."

Inside, he found Smiley reclined on one of the lounge chairs in the living room. His shoulder had been cleaned and bound, and he wore a fresh shirt, unbuttoned, and with only one arm through the sleeve. He looked remarkably comfortable for a man nearly speared to death only hours before.

"How is he?" Nate asked Rachael.

Smiley answered for himself: "I am jus' fine, man. Just fine." His smile was back.

Rachael patted him on the shoulder gently as she brushed past him. "No real damage done, just some nasty lacerations and a bruise he won't soon forget."

"Shouldn't we get him checked out at the hospital?" Nate

asked hesitantly.

Smiley laughed. "Man, you haven't been in dat room she calls a kitchen. De size of my house an' better outfitted than de whole hospital," he said cheerfully.

Nate and Rachael sat down in chairs. "Okay," said Nate. "I'll go first." He turned and looked at Smiley. "What happened back there? In the car. Who was that? I know it was no accident, and it's high time you told me whatever you know." He let the moment hang, watching as Smiley processed it all.

"Well, let I lay it out for you," said Smiley. He rubbed his shoulder and shifted slightly. "Dis thing today, you right: it was no accident. It was intentional for true."

Nate leapt in. "The same person responsible for all the black magic bullshit, right?"

A flash of disapproval swept briefly over Smiley's face. "It not bullshit, Nate. And yes. Same people." He took a long breath. "Dis thing today—it an attempt to repeat what happen three years ago. It all tied together." He looked over at Rachael, whose face was buried except for her eyes. "Dat right, Rachael?"

Smiley continued. "Three years ago, when Des died, it was on de *Spice Rack*, a forty-foot pleasure craft owned by Tristan De Villiers. Dat day three men died, and two of those men were invited on board for a diving trip, as I understand it, by Rachael."

Nate looked toward her in mild surprise, but Rachael just continued to stare at a point somewhere far away on the horizon. "By Rachael?" he asked.

"The *Spice Rack* belongs to her family."

Rachael protested in a quiet voice, and one that was perhaps at the edge of uncertainty. "*Belonged*—past tense."

"Back den, Rachael here was married—and Rachael, please jump in if I dun get anyt'ing wrong here—to Tristan De Villiers."

Something in that news stung Nate, but it was irrational. He brushed it aside.

Smiley was about to continue but Nate cut him off. "I don't understand. You said three men died. Who else? I mean other than

Des, who else died? Who else was on the boat?" he asked.

"One of them was Pieter Prinsloo."

Nate's face was pleated with questions. "And he's related to all this how?"

Rachael lifted her head momentarily from behind folded arms. "Really? You don't know?"

"No. Who is he?"

"Pieter Prinsloo." said Rachael in a tone of mild disbelief.

Nate found himself getting mildly annoyed. "Still don't know."

"Everyone called him Pip as a kid."

The name struck Nate like a slap in the face. He blinked hard and his mind raced to assemble the pieces. "Pip?" he asked incredulously.

Smiley nodded. His face was solemn.

"You're fucking kidding me. It was Pip who called Des? Pip came here asking questions about what happened all those years ago. When we were kids?"

"Dat's right, man," said Smiley flatly.

"Did you send him letters, too? Like the ones you sent me and my Dad? Is that why he came?"

Smiley turned his palms upward. "No. I would have, but I was never able to find him. He worked overseas most of his life. But he came back here on his own. And of his own will."

Nate's mind was reeling. Again he went silent, forcing unwieldy pieces together. Finally: "And you say this was no accident—that Des would never go out on the water, let alone a diving trip?"

Smiley cut in. "I believe what happened to dem out on de water was no accident," and as he said it he looked over to Rachael and waited for a reaction. None came. "I believe those two were taken out on dat boat an' drowned because dey was digging up de past."

Suddenly Nate was angry. His mind began connecting thoughts, linking ideas and seeing plain logic where there had been none only seconds before. The accident on the boat was no accident, and it was Rachael who had invited them out on the boat. He began to bristle. "Rachael, did you know?"

Smiley cut in again, this time raising his hand. "Now hold on, man. Me never said Rachael knew what was going on dat day. I could never prove it, an' in fact I believe she knew nothing. She was not on de boat—she just make de invitations. If I am correct, she was a patsy in dis."

"But why invite them to the boat? Why?"

"My guess? Because she was told to," said Smiley, again looking to Rachael for a reaction. Nothing.

"What do you mean *told to?*"

Smiley shifted again and moved his shoulder to a new position. "Tristan De Villiers was a very powerful man on dis island. An' I believe dat de relationship he had with Rachael was a very controllin' one—if he tell her do sometin', I think she had to do it. Otherwise…" Smiley raised his hands and gazed around the beautiful room they sat in. "Where you think all dis dun come from? It just dat simple."

"You're saying Tristan forced her to invite Des and Pip out on the boat?"

Smiley nodded once. He could see Nate making the connections.

"So Tristan was on the boat, too?"

"Um hmm."

Nate's face lit up as in revelation. "Jesus Christ," he muttered. "Tristan was the other one, wasn't he? The other person who died on the boat that day." His mind ran instantly back to the envelope, to the obituary. The timing all made sense now.

Smiley confirmed what he was saying with a single nod.

"But what happened?" Nate continued. "What happened to Tristan on the boat?"

Smiley shook his head. "Some mysteries will always remain so. But if I guessin', I say at some point Des and Pip see what happenin' out dere on dat boat. Maybe dem fight back. I think something go wrong out dere with getting rid of de two of them. Something go wrong and no one come home dat day. Police find de the *Spice Rack* floatin' free, 'bout four kilometers off Ans Couchon beach down the coast. Dey find Des's body an hour later about a kilometer down current, and Pieter Prinsloo's shortly after dat. Tristan's body was never recovered—just one of his shoes floatin' 'round out dere."

Nate leaned back in the soft cushions and stared vacantly ahead of him. "Jesus Christ," he said again, shaking his head lightly. Finally, "What about Pip and Des's death? I didn't see anything about that in the clippings you gave me." Across from him, Rachael sniffled silently. Behind her folded limbs, she was weeping.

Smiley looked at her and then at Nate. "De Villiers family is a major force on de island: politically, economically, and physically. If dey decide sometin' not gettin' in de news, it not gettin' in de news. The family hush everything up. There was no public acknowledgement of the other two deaths. Des's mother had all her expenses quietly covered, and the coroner had Pip's body on a plane home in a matter of hours. Accidental drownin' listed as de cause of death.

"Influence, man. Power is all about influence. It goes back to the plantation days, but the family wealth and influence was cemented in the '70s, when Vincent De Villiers struck a land deal with Hersh Oil—now a major refinery on de island—and negotiated a piece of de action on every barrel of crude dat is refined here. You see, there was all kinds of protest 'bout an oil refinery here, on an island whose beauty was her real treasure. People worried 'bout spills, damage to de beaches, de reefs. Without tourism dis island would struggle. But Vincent De Villiers owned a large tract of land jus' south of Castries, an area with a natural deep-water harbor perfect for industrial development. And somehow—there were stories about payoffs and threats—somehow, it was all passed an' approved and then Hersh builds that huge refinery you see der today. It made the family wealthy at a scale…well," he said, raising his hands and eyes again to the ceiling, "look around you.

"And with de kind of finances dey have, Nate, comes influence. The influence dey have here is far, far reachin'. And before him disappear out der on the *Spice Rack*, Tristan was at de helm of the De Villiers fortune. He held no political office, but he made appointments at will. Barristers, judges, civil servants, de police—all were beholden to him in some way. If you listen to popular tales, you gwan hear he was dirty. Up to his neck in it. But no one dared touch 'im.

"Now with Rachael here, I believe he was reckless. I know some of de constables at de station and dey told me, unofficially of course, 'bout de calls, 'bout de beatings, de black eyes. But nuttin' ever get dun 'bout dat. Now, I jus' guessing here, but I think Rachael escaped for a while when she went to de US to do her medical degree. She was married still, but keeping a good distance from dis place." He looked again at Rachael, baiting her, hoping she would join the conversation. She stayed silent, save the occasional sniffle.

Smiley continued. "She was gone almost six years, and when she came back she worked at de hospital in Castries. But a few black eyes and few years later, I think she said *enough*, an' tried to divorce Tristan. And den, all of a sudden, her local medical license get revoked. No more hospital work. No more doctoring. Influence, you see?

"She got as far as a separation. The De Villiers influence made the divorce proceedings drag and drag—and I believe dat was more Vincent De Villiers's doing than Tristan's. Anyway, when everything happened out on the Spice Rack, court say Tristan must be gone seven years before he can be legally declared dead. In the meantime, she got dis house, some money, and some kind of ongoing maintenance. Alimony, stipend—sometin' like dat—but I fear she living something of a hollow existence. She still a De Villiers, but livin' outside of them. Das a special kind of hell, for sure."

Nate stared at Smiley in astonishment. "Jeez," was all he could say.

"And even after these years dun pass, with Tristan more than three years in de grave, she still can't get her license back. She dun try three times at least: denied, denied, denied. Even in death Tristan still controllin' her fate. Now, Rachael and I," he began, speaking gently as if addressing a child, "we have had many a conversation over de last three years. Well, maybe conversation is too strong a word. I have spoken an' she has listened to my theories. She has been very gracious with her time, never turning away de ramblings of dis sad little reporter from *The Word*. But so far, no confirmations."

Finally, it was Rachael's time to speak. She wiped her eyes and let down her wall of limbs. "I've made my share of mistakes, it's true," she said. "And I've always listened to you, Smiley. But I don't want either of you to mistake my silence as weakness." She stood and walked briskly to the bar, fetched three crystal tumblers and a bottle of Bowmore single malt Scotch. She poured three liberal belts and placed them on the table before the two men.

Rachael drank deeply, then fixed her eyes on Smiley. "I know exactly why you called me when you found out Nate was coming to the island. You thought I'd collapse, that I'd go all weak-kneed and woe-is-me, and come gushing to you with confessions. Well that's not me." She drank again, and curled around the tumbler like a cat in a basket. "But I am sorrowful. I didn't cause intentional harm to anyone. I didn't set out to lure those men into a trap. I just did what I had to do. I did what I was told."

"So you really had no idea anything was going to happen to those men when you invited them onto the boat?" asked Nate.

Rachael's eyes dipped and a shadow of sadness ran across her like a dark cloud. She drew a heavy breath, and then stifled the answer that was coming.

Nate pressed on. "And why the meeting on the boat, anyway? Why would Des and Pip get on the *Spice Rack*? What did you say to get them on board?"

Rachael sat silently and ran her finger around the shapes in the crystal. "Rachael," said Smiley in a tone sincere as a sharply honed blade, "dis thing, dis thing has been hanging over you for three long years. An' for sure you can run from it. And I do believe you had no understanding of what you were *really* doing when you asked those men onto de boat. But now Nate is here, and it all starting over again—plain to see for everyone. Including you. An' Rachael, if something happen to him, to me, as it happen to Des and Pip, well, dat blood will be on your hands for sure."

Another set of tears welled up and Rachael buried her head in her hands. Her shoulders were racked once, then twice, but she gave up little else.

"Dis thing on the road earlier today," continued Smiley. "You know who dat was, Rachael. You know dat was de De Villiers's people. Most surely Vincent."

Rachael's shoulders shook again, this time more deeply. She looked up at the two men and mouthed the words *I'm so sorry* through streaming tears. She cried silently, and then, as if to exorcise a demon, she began to speak. "I didn't know," she said almost pleading. "At least not really. I didn't know what would happen to them." And then, almost whispering, "maybe I should have."

Nate sipped at the scotch and pressed the cool glass against his forehead. The fever was boiling again. "You know, something happened here thirty-odd years ago that destroyed my father's life. And it was my decision that did it. When we left here I clammed up, kept my mouth shut tight, and you know what? My father never pressed me. He asked, I didn't tell, and he just hugged me and nodded. But after that there were consequences. I guess I never really realized they were all tied to me, to what I did back then, until this trip. He refused to explain what I'd done, what had happened, to his superiors, never explained why he left the island so abruptly, and his career as a diplomat flamed out. He took me off the island and away from all the craziness that was going on here. And if I had just made a different decision."

Nate stood and walked from the room and out onto the pool deck. The sun was setting now, and it reminded him of that daily ritual, all those years ago in his youth, in the house on Vigie. On the clearest days everyone gathered on the balcony as the sun slipped down below the horizon, watching and waiting for the *green flash*. As the last part of the orange ball dipped below the watery curve of the earth, a brilliant green flash would hang suspended for a fraction of a moment and then disappear. His dad would say it was the sun winking the promise of a new tomorrow. Had he ever really seen it? As a kid, Nate swore up and down that he did, but the debate between the believers and the nay-sayers would rage on and on.

As the sun set now on the postcard-perfect vista before him, he watched for it again. He watched for that redemptive flash, that promise of a new tomorrow. But the sun, burning orange with a waning blue sky overhead, simply sank uneventfully beneath the crisp line of the horizon so very far away.

"So what now?" asked a voice behind him. It was Rachael. Night was coming on, and the gloaming was bordered perfectly by the glow of the pool lights, the swaying palms and a softly backlit horizon in hues of gold and orange.

"Well, I can't fix all the disasters in my past, but I've been hanging on to something for too long now," Nate said plainly. "I need to go to Ti Fenwe. I have to set something straight."

Rachael was pensive, thoughtful. "There's just Vincent up there now in that damn plantation house all by himself. You know he won't see you. And Smiley's probably right anyway—what happened on the road, the Obeah, and what happened to Des and Pip, it has to be the De Villiers. It's Vincent. He's ruthless. And he's gotten worse over the last few years. The family's net worth is incredible, yet Vincent insists on living up in that old house in the bush. The place is rotting, falling apart, but he rarely leaves. It's like he's a shut-in, but still pulling the damn family strings." She drifted off for a moment, caught in some private, unpleasant memory. "I never liked that place. I never fitted into the family, and when I began the divorce proceedings Vincent was incensed. He blamed me for everything. I think he was even angrier about it all than Tristan."

Nate turned and looked into her eyes. He reached instinctively for her, gently taking her face in his hands, and she offered no resistance.

"Miss Rachael," came her housekeeper's voice from the glass doorway. "As you requested—Ma Joop is here."

In the living room, Smiley and Ma Joop were talking quietly and when she looked up and saw Nate, it seemed this time her expression was something closer to pity.

"Come," she said to Nate calmly. "Le' we do dis now." Nate looked toward Rachael and she nodded in approval, and so he followed Ma Joop down a hall and into what seemed to be a study. The large woman in the floral pattern dress pulled a chair from a beautiful roll-top desk in the corner, placed it at the center of the room and waved him to it, and then left. Nate sat and looked around the room, and concluded it was indeed a study, but one that was rarely used. The shelves were lined with books, many of them medical texts, and on the wall was a series of degrees and awards, one of which was Rachael's Doctor of Medicine degree from the University of Washington. Ma Joop returned holding a small tray. She smiled and set it down, and began lighting candles and placing them about the room.

Nate felt awkward, and in truth, a little apprehensive about questioning Ma Joop. But it had been an eventful few days already; why stop the excitement now? "So, what are we doing?" he asked hesitantly, trying to sound as polite as possible.

Ma Joop smiled and snorted like a parent amused by a child's naive question. "Mr. Nate," she said slowly as she lit another candle. "We jus' gwan try save your eternal soul, is all."

Nate wasn't sure how to react to this news. Having his eternal soul saved was new territory—even on this trip. "Oh. So you're a practitioner in... this?" he asked, turning his palms up.

Ma Joop took a deep breath and brought her substantial girth down to Nate's eye level. She leaned forward and put her face directly in front of his. "I know what you thinkin'. I know you look at us as foolish island folk and—"

"No, I—"

Ma Joop snapped bolt upright with an agility unexpected of a woman her size, and she jabbed a chubby fist toward him with an index finger extended threateningly. "I'll t'ank you *very* much for not interruptin' me!" she boomed, and Nate was sure everyone in the living room had heard. He dared not even say sorry.

Ma Joop raised a single eyebrow, waiting to see what Nate would do, and then snorted in satisfaction once it was clear he had been properly silenced. "As I was sayin'," she said, scolding him one more time with a sideways glance, "I know you look at us as foolish island folk, but let me tell you dat what is upon you is absolutely real. Obeah is a powerful, powerful force, and someone has put a dark shadow upon you. Now, I can help you. But you mus' not fight me on dis. You mus' accept my help, or you doomed for sure. You una'stand me, boy?"

Nate nodded. He was ready for whatever she would do next. Blood, dead chickens, eyes rolled back into heads, rhythmic dancing and chanted incantations. Bring it on. He just wanted to get it over with.

"Good," said Ma Joop, nodding once curtly. She then collected a string of beads from the tray, much like a rosary, Nate thought, and held them in her hands. She stood in front of Nate, closed her eyes and spoke silently as if to herself, her lips occasionally moving with the unspoken words. Finally she opened her eyes, put one hand on Nate's head and began speaking. It sounded like a prayer, it had a rhythm Nate seemed to recognize, and after a few moments he understood why. He knew it well, and once his ear had tuned to her island accent, he could follow along easily.

"The Lord's Prayer?" he asked hesitantly.

Ma Joop stopped and Nate realized he was about to be told off again. But she was calm this time. Her tone was sarcastic, just short of mocking. "You know something more powerful than Jesus Chris'?"

"No, no."

And Ma Joop continued.

Fifteen minutes later, she lowered her great frame to the candles, blowing them out one by one, muttering something in Creole that ended in *Amen* at each, and then walked out of the room. Nate sat for a moment wondering if he was done.

A few minutes later, Rachael appeared at the door. "Well, that's that," she said.

"Am I done?"

"Ma Joop seemed satisfied. She's gone home now so I guess it's safe to say she's finished. Are you okay?" she asked.

"Well, yeah. It's just not what I was expecting. No charms, no throwing of bones."

"That's because you don't know much about Obeah. It really is powerful stuff here, Nate. And it goes way back."

"But everything she was doing—it all seemed based pretty much in Christianity. You know, rosaries, the Lord's Prayer."

Rachael linked her arm through Nate's and walked him from the room. "You're at the conflux of many cultures, religions and practices here, Nate. Depending on who you listen to, Obeah has its roots in Egyptian times, and goes back to Moses parting the Red Sea—if you believe that sort of thing."

"And what about you? Do you believe in that sort of thing? In Obeah?"

Rachael guided Nate into the kitchen. "Let's just say that I respect its power here," she said, reaching into a cabinet.

"Even though you're a doctor? Someone based in science?"

"Especially because I'm a doctor. You have no idea how many people I've seen in Emergency whose major complaint is Obeah."

"And you treat them how?"

Rachael placed a container of pills in front of Nate. "Often like this," she said, smiling.

He read the label: amoxicillin—more of what she had prescribed at the hospital. He popped open the lid and swallowed one of the pills. "And what about Ma Joop? Do you prescribe her also?"

Rachael smiled in a way Nate had not seen since they were kids. "If need be."

Nate smiled in return, and the moment that had slipped away outside by the pool began to quietly reassemble itself. It swirled around them like a welcome breeze. They stood on opposite sides of the breakfast bar, watching each other, both secretly cursing the yard of polished marble between them. It provided a physical space that separated them, just enough distance to allow Nate's mind the time to swing inevitably back to why he was there. He knew his next comment would ruin the moment. "I have to go," he said quietly, but his eyes said otherwise. "I have to go back to Ti Fenwe."

28

Tristan stood motionless in water up to his thighs, his back to the boys at the river's edge. His arms hung loosely, the rock still held tightly in his right hand. After a moment he looked down, raised his hand slightly, as if somewhat surprised to see the stone set there, and then dropped it with a plop into the water. He turned slowly and began robotically sloshing his way back. Behind him, Richard's form bobbed in the water.

Pip was the first to call out. "Tristan, what did you do? Is he all right?"

"Oh shit," said Nate, suddenly terrified. He launched himself forward, and raced through the water with Pip right behind him. Richard was floating face down, and Nate seized him by the back of his T-shirt and hauled him upward, flipping him over at the same time. Pip grabbed his arm and the two immediately began dragging him to the shore, calling his name and shaking him as they went.

At the bank, they set him down in the shallows, with his head and shoulders clear of the water, and his hips and legs still submerged. Nate looked up and saw that Tristan had scrambled up the bank, and was now squatting on his haunches, arms wrapped around his shins, watching the boys with a blank, ashen expression.

Pip was shaking Richard, and shaking him harder with each call. "Richard, wake up!"

Nate reached out and firmly pushed him aside: "Pip, stop. You'll hurt him!" And for a moment all the boys stood motionlessly. Nate's word's carried hope.

"What do we do?" asked Pip on the verge of tears. "What do we do?"

Nate squatted down and turned Richard's face toward him. The boy's eyes were half closed, and his expression was slack, fully relaxed. "Richard?" he said, gently patting the boy's face. "Richard, you okay?" With no reaction whatsoever, Nate placed his ear against Richard's mouth and listened. Beside him Pip was moaning. Nate exploded. "Pip, shut up! I'm trying to listen!"

Pip stifled himself, and bobbed back and forth from one foot to the other in terror. Nate dropped over Richard once more and listened, but there was nothing. He didn't know what to do. He sat up, took his hands from the boy's face, and for the first time noticed something odd above Richard's left ear. It was the wrong shape. The arc of his face was somehow interrupted just over his left ear near the temple. Nate reached down and gently rolled Richard's head to one side. The boy's skull seemed dented, like an empty tin can that had been discarded and clipped by someone's heel. Nate looked closer and could see that there was some blood there, not much, but some, and that the blonde hair was dark and matted in the concave depression. It was about the size of a fist, and pushed into Richard's skull a full inch at its center.

Nate felt suddenly light and hollowed out, as if his insides had been abruptly snatched away. He stood and looked up the bank. "Tristan," he said emptily.

The boy at the top of the bank finally unfolded himself. He stood for a moment, watching the scene below him, and then slid down to the water's edge. His expression was still impassive, his face gray. Finally Tristan spoke, his voice trembling. "He's…he's…"

"He's dead," said Pip in a whisper.

To his left, Nate stood rooted to the spot, his eyes and face pleated, his chest heaving but finding no air in the tropical humidity.

Tristan stooped beside Richard and shoved his cousin's shoulder with a tentative, outstretched foot. "Richard, wake up Richard." But nothing happened, save the gentle lolling of the boy's head and the vacant expression that hung there. Tristan rose slowly, never moving his eyes from the boy at the water's edge. "Shit. He's really dead." And because Tristan said it, it was finally true.

• • •

"Please don't be offended, Rachael. I have to go. I have to get back to Ti Fenwe."

She stopped shuffling the contents of the cupboard and stood still, her back to Nate. "And at what cost?"

Nate scrubbed his face with both hands. He was tired. Between careening off roads and being exorcised, the day had been pretty full. "It's just something I have to do. I did something stupid here years ago, and I feel like it's followed me since then. Like my life has taken on a pattern—one I set the day Richard died."

Rachael turned and faced him at last. She looked tired, too. "Have you ever told anyone? Have you ever told anyone what happened that day out at Ti Fenwe?"

Nate shook his head and marvelled at the truth of it. He had carried that secret a long time. And for most of that time it had remained somewhere in the far, dark reaches of his mind, almost never venturing forward into the light of conscious thought. But it had always been there, he realized. Always informing his decisions. And it had taken years, a lifetime as it had turned out, for the weight of the consequences to slide home.

Rachael continued. "And what do you expect will happen if you do speak to him, to Vincent? What do you want him to say?"

"To say? Jeez, nothing. And there's nothing I need to say to him. I just have to go back to where it started. There's baggage I can't drop anywhere else but there—and I know that sounds stupid, but it's just what I have to do." That was it. Nate felt thoroughly exhausted. He needed to sleep, to just close down and fade to black. "I'm sorry Rachael, but I'm beat…"

"You can stay here tonight. Smiley as well. We have lots of room."

Rachael said goodnight to the two men and disappeared into her room at the other end of the house, leaving Nate and Smiley alone in the living room. They stood looking at each other for a moment, until Nate finally dipped his head forward. "Are you ready for payment?" he asked with a forced smile. "I don't know what'll happen tomorrow, but I promised you the exclusive—the full story on what happened to Richard De Villiers."

Smiley nodded, trying not to let the excitement show through. "Le' me grab a notepad," he said.

They spoke in quiet, reverent tones, Nate running unflinchingly through that day at Ti Fenwe, Smiley nodding, asking the odd clarification, and making notes in the pad resting on his knee. For Nate, it was the first real telling of what had happened that day, and breaking thirty years of silence came at a price he hadn't expected. By the time he was done, Nate was exhausted. The emotions had come thick and fast with the telling of the story, and the sheer effort of holding them in check—of fighting to stay in control in front of Smiley—had taken a heavy toll. But among those emotions, and perhaps tied somehow to each of them, he acknowledged a quiet sense of relief.

An hour later, Nate settled into the soft bed in one of the spare rooms, and buried himself deep beneath the extra blankets Rachael had provided to fight the fever. He fell asleep quickly and found the dream again. It was the same stage, the same theatre, but this time the players had all gone, all except the wet boy sitting with his legs hanging over the edge of the stage. The boy with the wet blonde hair looked over to where Nate sat in the front row, and mouthed words that Nate couldn't quite catch. He did it again, and again, but still Nate couldn't quite make it out.

And then someone or something sat heavily beside him. It, too, was wet, and while Nate wanted desperately to turn and see what or who it was, he found he was powerless, unable to move his neck. And so the thing beside him gradually moved into his view, encroaching slowly, very slowly, from the far extremes of his peripheral vision. It crept onward, and soon Nate could see the edge of a face, the hint of an eye, but everything was wrong. It was pallid, wrinkled like bath-time toes and sloughing skin in great sheets, and as it finally moved into view Nate was horrified to see its eyes had been nibbled and clawed away.

Finally, Nate was able to turn and look, and he knew without question it was Pip. And as he looked at the rotting, waterlogged face of the little boy from his youth, it opened its mouth and shouted the words Richard had been mouthing from the stage: *That's two of us!*

Nate sat bolt upright as hands seized upon him. It would pull him to some watery grave now, he knew it, and he flailed his arms and legs in a pathetic attempt at resistance.

Stop, Nate, it's okay! The voice was wrong and it confused him, it didn't match the voice from Pip. Sweat ran down his face in rivulets, and Rachael dried him with a thick and fresh smelling towel, running it around his forehead and down to his chin in gentle sweeping arcs. Outside, the night seemed to swallow the Caribbean in great swaths of black, while the lights from the pool glowed beneath the surface and cast wobbly, shifting shadows across Nate's ceiling.

When at last he was calm, she spoke. "What happened to you since you left the island, Nate?" she asked tenderly.

Nate shifted uncomfortably, but there was no dodging the question. "You really want to know?"

"If you're okay telling me."

"You're not going to like me much afterwards."

"Who says I like you now?"

Nate smiled briefly and with it decided that yes, if she wanted to hear his story, he would tell her.

And so, with a deep breath exhaled through puffed cheeks, he began.

He spoke of his marriage, the way it slowly spiralled downward, perhaps even from the beginning. He talked about his career, if that was what you could call it, about the dullness of it, the frustrating monotony of being entirely unremarkable. He told her about his writing, about his shelf full of unpublished, perhaps unpublishable manuscripts, and about the way his world seemed to come undone when his ex-wife took full custody of their son.

He admitted to being entirely bitter about the divorce, the custody hearings, and the whole damn process. "Losing custody of my son was probably a big part of all this," he began again. "My wife, well, my ex-wife…her lawyers shredded me at the custody hearing. It was humiliating to have my rights—or what I thought were my rights—systematically and legally stripped away from me. Losing custody of Cody was like having my arm amputated with a hammer. And the way I was painted—my limitations, my lack of progress, lack of success—it was like being whipped—and not because they were being mean spirited, but because it was, in part, true."

And then he told her about Cody, about his little boy who died. And for a brief and stinging moment, thoughts of Richard crept in like some bitter, distant harmony.

He told her how his life was completely disassembled, stripped bare by his son's death, and that when he walked into his father's house three months later to find him dead on the floor of his bedroom, he had almost nothing left inside to feel the pain. Instead he wanted only to sleep, to give in to the tiredness, to escape the effort it took to simply *be*.

And Rachael listened to it. All of it. And when he was done, when he was spent and empty, she simply lay down beside him, pulled him close and ran her hand around the curve of his face. He turned to her, and her hand moved to his chest. She began tracing a line along his body with her fingers; over his chest, his abdomen and finally to a spot deep between his legs.

29

In the morning, Nate slipped quietly from the bed, letting Rachael sleep. He took his clothes and dressed quickly in the hall, then went to the kitchen with the intention of rifling the cupboards until he found a can of instant coffee and maybe a slice of bread to toast.

What he found was Rachael's housekeeper waving him to the pool deck, where a white tablecloth topped with plump halved grapefruits, flaky croissants, and an urn of fresh coffee awaited. As he looked at the bounty, he realized he was starving. He also realized that he felt much better; the fever seemed to have ebbed, along with the lethargy, and the aches and pains. In his mind's eye, he saw himself swallowing the antibiotics Rachael had given him the night before, and in the same instant he saw Ma Joop, eyes closed and praying. He wondered whom he had to thank for this morning's relief.

"We should all live like dis, no?"

Nate turned and saw Smiley stretched out on one of the padded reclining chairs at the pool's edge. He was hoisting a cup of coffee in salutation.

"Be careful wit those pastries, man," he said. "If you eat one, you gone have to have more. Lot more!"

"How's your shoulder this morning?" Nate asked.

"A li'l stiff, but no big ting. And how 'bout you-self?" There was a knowing grin spread liberally on Smiley's face. "You get through de night aright?"

Nate stalled for time as he grappled with what to say when the glass doors in the house slid open.

"Good morning," said Rachael. She was dressed in white shorts and a soft blue sleeveless top, and walked toward them with crossed arms and a curt half-smile. Nate immediately regretted the evening before, and felt suddenly selfish and cloying, like some lecherous old man taking advantage of easy pickings. But as Rachael passed him on her way to the coffee urn, she placed her hand on the small of his back for the briefest of moments, and suddenly the mood inside him shifted. The day was perfect once again, like all the others on this tropical jewel, and it held promise.

They ate beneath the fabric of a large, white umbrella framed in the same dark wood tones that accented the rest of the house. Behind them, the sun was already arcing high into the sky, and the blue sea was awash with silver glints and little triangles of white sailcloth. They talked about nothing: the weather, the view, anything but what had brought them all together.

Smiley told a story about a smuggling operation the paper broke last year out on Pigeon Island—the dual-peaked little land mass that they could see just to the south west of Rachael's house. Once a pirate hideout, the island was connected to the mainland with a causeway, and with Rachael's binoculars he could see that a new hotel now stood there. "When I was a kid, we would sail to Pigeon Island as part of the Sunday regattas, from the Yacht Club down on Reduit beach. The causeway was just this vast white stretch of crushed up coral with nothing on it."

Rachael dipped into her grapefruit. "The Yacht Club's still there, but the old concrete airstrip is gone." She looked at Nate as she said it. Yes, he remembered.

Nate smiled sheepishly. "I was kind of hoping you'd forgotten that whole thing."

"What? You mean where my heart was broken for the first time?" She smiled and Nate couldn't help but laugh.

"Aw, come on," he said. "That's not fair! I was just a kid, and it was my first time, you were my first."

Smiley's eyebrows migrated sharply toward the top of his head.

"His first kiss, Smiley," she laughed. "Get your head out of the gutter."

And as a fragrant warm breeze wafted up from the sparkling sea below them, across the gardens, the infinity pool and the perfectly appointed deck area, they each receded into their own memories. And with each quietly mulling their own worlds, the mood of the small group slowly cooled, leaving all three gazing westward off toward Pigeon Island, toward the distant horizon, each silently but wholly snared in the net of the days that had led up to this one.

It was Nate who finally spoke, and brought them all back to the realities of the moment. "So, can someone take me into town? I need to rent a car."

Smiley cocked his head sideways. "Man, I would happily lend you one of my two vehicles, but since meeting you, both dun been ruined."

"Come," said Rachael. "I'll take you where you want to go."

Nate looked at her. "Rachael, where I want to go is to Ti Fenwe."

"I know," she said flatly. "I'm ready when you are."

The glass door at the house slid back and Rachael's housekeeper stepped out on the deck with a phone in her hand. "Miss Rachael," she said with an edge of concern in her voice. "Police at the gate. They demandin' to come inside." The round woman looked clearly shaken, and then, remembering the phone in her hand, walked stiffly toward Smiley. "And a call for you, Mr. Edwin."

Smiley put the phone to his hear and listened. "Sure," he said hollowly. "Mm hmm, I understand." He pushed the button on the phone to end the call, but remained staring at it, as if the handset was something vile.

Nate asked, "What is it? What's wrong?"

Rachael stood and wrapped an arm around her housekeeper's shoulders and muttered a few comforting words. The housekeeper smiled meekly and went back into the house.

"What's going on, Smiley?" Nate asked again.

"Dat was Peter Finch, my editor, also de General Manager—also de owner—of *The Word*." Smiley puffed his cheeks and blew a long slow breath of air out, gently shaking his head as he went. "An' I have been told to stop following dis story. Or any story dat has to do with Nate Mason, Rachael Stanton or events involving de De Villiers family now, three years ago, or back in 1976."

"Jesus, Smiley," said Nate.

"Finch say if I don't walk away right now, it will cost me my employment."

"This is Vincent's work," said Rachael acidly. "And the police at the gate."

Nate reached out and placed a hand on Smiley's shoulder. "You gotta go, then. And right now. This will all be over soon and I'll be heading home, but you have to live here, Smiley."

Smiley raised his head and nodded. "Nate, de police, dey here to take you for sure. And I cannot intervene." He shook his head; his frustration was obvious. "Rachael, can you get him out of here? Is there a way out past de police?"

Rachael bit her bottom lip, then, "There's the boat. Down at the beach there's a small pier. I have a boat there."

"Aright..." said Smiley, standing and extending his hand to Nate. "You mus' leave now. Forget about dis ting with the De Villiers. Dem playin' for keeps. Take de boat and go. Get to de airport and fly away, man. Jus' fly away. I'll go to de gate and keep the *jandam* occupied for as long as I can." He clasped both hands around Nate's. "Use de time well," he said gravely.

• • •

The Boston Whaler skipped cleanly along the swells, out of the tiny private bay at the foot of the garden pathway, and around the two iconic peaks, one higher than the other, of Pigeon Island. The boat was a fiberglass eighteen-footer, open hulled, and with a fixed helm at its center. Rachael stood behind a Plexiglas shield and controlled the output of the powerful Mercury 300 as it bit deeply into the water behind them. They quickly passed the sugary crescent of Reduit beach, rounded the headland, and pushed south keeping the island to their left. Nate held tight as the boat carved perfect arcs into the blue water beneath them.

The growl of the engine and the force of the wind kept the conversation to a minimum, but Nate felt the need to be clear. "I appreciate what Smiley was saying," he shouted. "But you understand I'm not leaving. I'm still headed to Ti Fenwe."

Rachael glanced sideways and forced a smile. "I know," she shouted back over the din.

Soon they passed the entrance to Castries harbor, and Rachael throttled back as they cut across the wake of a cruise ship that was steaming for the open sea. Once clear, she pushed the throttle forward again, and the Boston Whaler responded like a thoroughbred from the starting gates, digging into the water and lifting herself onto a plane with ease.

They passed deserted beaches and coves yet to be turned under the developer's back hoe and it made Nate feel good that there was still raw island out there, like it was in his youth. And as he thought it, Rachael brought the Whaler around a headland and face to face with a huge refinery. It had scrubbed the countryside clear of green and replaced it with acres of cement and steel pipe, great slabs of white concrete on vast pilings, with long, squat tankers connected to bulbous tanks by ugly red umbilicals. It was as if a section of the island's green coat had slid away into the sea, leaving an ugly scar and an unsightly skeleton never meant to be seen by the naked eye. Rachael saw the shock in Nate's face. "That's the refinery Smiley was talking about last night," she shouted through the wind and the thunder of the motor. "Pretty, isn't it."

The Whaler passed around the next headland and mercifully cut the sight short, resuming a coastland punctuated with idyllic beaches, swaying palms and colorful fishing boats. But for Nate, something of the island's beauty was now inexorably lost, whether he could see the Hersh oil refinery or not. Still they pressed on, running south, through the calm swells of the Caribbean Sea, past more yachts with their sails swollen and full, past fishing charters and scuba boats laden with holiday divers.

Finally Rachael throttled back and the sea behind them momentarily caught up with boat, gently lifting the stern. She motored into Marigot Bay at little more than an idle, and they turned into the naturally protected harbor, one that had provided mariners safety from storms for a hundred years. Nate immediately noticed the change. The Marigot Bay of his youth was a quiet inlet with a single stretch of so-so beach on a small, palm-laden sprit. There was one restaurant and maybe two or three private homes. It's most defining feature was an old fiberglass snail's shell, an abandoned movie prop used in the filming of the original *Doctor Doolittle*. It sat in the bush just off the beach, and kids would clamber around the six-foot structure that was, even then, in the process of falling apart. Other than that, Marigot Bay had been just a series of roughly constructed piers waiting quietly for the next glut of sailboats seeking shelter from a storm.

But now, as Rachael guided the Boston Whaler around the natural breakwater and into the harbor proper, Nate could see that it had become a developer's dream. The simple piers and jetties had been replaced with elegant boardwalks that tumbled down to the water's edge, designer condominiums clinging to the hillsides and stylish restaurants offering al fresco dining and drinks among million-dollar yachts. It was a different place now, one Nate felt he had never seen before. And as Rachael brought the Boston Whaler in to the dock, Nate had an odd moment of something he could only describe as nostalgic amnesia. The raped landscape of Cul de Sac Bay—now home to Hersh Oil, the new development in Marigot Bay—it all underscored an immense passage of time for him. What had he paved over in the last thirty years? The answer was ugly.

"Dennery's a straight shot across the island from here," said Rachael, tying a perfect cleat hitch to secure the boat at the dock.

Nate collected his small suitcase and hopped over the gunwale. All around him were shining condos and sleek yachts bobbing in their births. "Can we rent a car here?"

"No need. I own a few properties here for rent. Each has a car."

In half an hour, they were across the island in a small SUV. They sat at the edge of a rather nondescript turnoff from the main road that wound down into Dennery proper—a sinuous thoroughfare densely lined on either side with thick tropical forest that seemed poised to reclaim the asphalt at any moment. Nate tried desperately to recall it, to connect with some memory that might evoke the excitement and thrill he would have felt as a kid when Vincent's old Land Rover first made this very turn. But like his pursuit of memories of the police station after Richard's death, there was nothing.

"Are you ready for this?" asked Rachael.

It didn't matter if he was ready or not. He was here. And he was going. In the end he simply nodded.

Rachael swung the SUV onto the road and began immediately to climb up into the forest. The road was paved and nothing like the twin-rutted track it had been when he was a boy, and the trip was so much shorter than he remembered it to be. Back then he recalled a lurching, jarring roller coaster ride, an honest-to-goodness adventure that seemed to take a full day, but as they rounded the last bend in what was little more than a ten-minute drive, things began to drop familiarly into place.

The first thing he saw was the workers' huts. They seemed, impossibly, not to have changed. They were still uncertain structures haphazardly constructed of cast-off wooden planks, and they still seemed to be fighting off the advances of the surrounding forest at their backs.

Nate immediately gravitated to one in particular.

He could feel the air pressing up into the very top of his lungs and he had to remind himself to breathe. "Hold on, hold on," he said excitedly, and Rachael brought the vehicle to a stop. Nate stepped out of the vehicle and stood staring at the little lean-to, completely oblivious of everything else. In his mind he could see himself tumbling out onto the grass, locked in a flurry of arms and legs with Tristan, struggling and swinging but doing almost no damage at all. It made him smile.

He walked slowly over to the doorway, rested his hands lightly on the frame and leaned inside.

"I dun warn you once before," came a Creole voice scratchy with age but spirited nonetheless. "An' I can still reach you from 'ere!"

Nate jumped and pulled his head back, and the aged voice inside the shack laughed and laughed, and then began hacking and coughing. She quieted, and continued chuckling lightly. Finally Nate looked back inside.

"I'm sorry," he said apologetically. "I didn't mean to—" And then it hit him. He knew the woman sitting there at the table, that blue, chipped table. She was in the same spot she had been the last time he saw her more than thirty years ago. For a moment he wondered if she had been there the whole time, never moving, and the thought made him giddy. "Augustine?" he asked tentatively.

"De same," she said, nodding once. "You no come back for a long, long time, chyle."

Nate was astounded. She had been an old woman back then, maybe sixty or so he guessed, so she was easily ninety now. She was smaller now, much smaller, and her face seemed sunken— particularly around her lips. She smiled back and he saw there were only two or three teeth there, and her skin seemed papery and light. "You're still here," he said in wonder.

"Where I gone go? Dis me home!"

"No, I just…"

"You jus' can't believe me not dead yet!" she said, and then burst out laughing again, followed once more by more hacking and more coughing. Finally she stopped, and wiped her mouth with a white cloth clutched in her bony hand. "You find dem yet?" she asked casually.

Nate was confused and didn't understand her question. But then again, Augustine was old. Perhaps even senile now. Christ, she probably didn't even know who he was. He thought he should explain. "You probably don't remember me, but I was here once…"

"Tell me somethin' boy—why you so quick to see only pudding in de old woman's mind?"

"No, I…"

"You not changed in all dese years. Still quick to jump up. Yes, little Nate. De little boy from far, far away. I remember you fine. And I not de only one who remember you here," she said waving a finger that seemed all knuckles.

"We met once. Just once, and you can still remember my name."

"Mm hmm."

He shook his head in astonishment. "Augustine, you asked if I *found* them yet. Who did you mean?"

"I mean de boys you come for. Richard especially."

Something inside Nate sagged in disappointment. He should have known better—despite her ability to remember his name after three decades. She still believed Richard was alive.

Augustine continued. "Most all de boys gone quiet now. Most. But Richard…he still out dere by de river. Right where you boys lef' him."

Nate was flushed instantly cold. He had to reach for the door frame again to stop himself keeling over.

Augustine went on. "I unastan' why you don' come back 'ere. An' de place here, well, it unastan' too. But you a welcome soul 'ere, Nate. A welcome soul." She smiled warmly, but Nate was shaken, right through to his center.

"Sit, boy. Sit."

Nate obeyed robotically.

"Calm yourself now, chyle. I know you dun carry dat day wit you long time. An' I know you have no blame. So calm yourself."

Nate looked at the woman across from him and tried to steady his breathing. She just watched patiently, smiling and occasionally nodding. Finally Nate was able to speak. "What do you mean? You know what happened? Tristan told you?"

Augustine wiped her lips again with the white cloth. "No chyle," she said, gently shaking her head.

"So it was Pip—Pip came here, too? They never told me."

"No chyle," she said again. "Him never come back here, and I feel him never will. Never can." Augustine waved the white cloth in her gnarled old hand. "You remember you time 'ere, and what we talk upon dat night?"

Nate nodded. She spoke gravely, and her words were the only sounds in the world to Nate. "Everything dat 'appen on de estate is seen, chyle. Everyt'ing be watched."

"What do you mean? I don't understand."

"Are you ready to go on?" came Rachael's voice from the doorway.

Surprised, Nate turned and stood. "Sure, sure," he said, like a man waking from a dream and unable to explain that clouded moment between the two worlds. In front of him Augustine only smiled warmly at the woman in her doorway.

"Hello, Augustine," said Rachael. Her tone was respectful, but neutral.

Augustine nodded.

Rachael turned and went through the door with Nate behind her, and as he passed through the frame Augustine called his name just loud enough for him to hear. He stopped and turned.

"Calm yourself, chyle. Favors from de past will be repaid." And then she smiled, stood from her chair, and shuffled into the next room.

30

Darkness was close now.

The green mass of the rainforest was pressing in on the boys from every side. Tristan stopped them on the path, and from what Nate could tell they were about halfway back to the estate house, and somewhere near the clearing. Nate looked around, fidgeting incessantly with a small stick he had collected along the way, fighting the gnawing sense of anxiety that was mounting inside him. The gathering darkness seemed to be taking on a physical form, a wall of impenetrable black that was coalescing just behind the bushes closest to the path. Darkness was certainly part of it, but the grisly scene they had just left was weighing heavily as well.

"Nate, stay here," said Tristan in a tone so void of emotion that it caught Nate off guard. Nate simply nodded, and Tristan waved *follow me* at Pip, and then moved twenty or so paces up the trail.

Nate watched as the other two boys stood face to face further up the path, just far enough away that Nate was unable to make out any words. Tristan spoke, arms gesticulating wildly while Pip simply listened, never uttering a word. His physical form seemed to shrink as the boy in front of him drove home some point that Nate would never hear.

Finally Tristan turned away from Pip, and Nate could see the boy crying in a pitch almost too high to hear, and looking as hopeless as a person can. With an outstretched hand, Tristan curtly told Pip to wait, and then motioned for Nate to follow. The two jogged past Pip and then turned left off the path just twenty or thirty feet later, through a curtain of vines and leafy branches, and suddenly emerged into the open cathedral-like space of the clearing.

Nate followed Tristan over to the industrial-wire spool that served as the table, where they stopped and stood facing each other.

"I just wanna go. I just wanna go home now," said Nate. He was quaking uncontrollably, and his tone was something close to pleading. "Come on. Let's just get Pip and get outta here."

But Tristan, who was in complete control, simply shook his head.

"Please Tristan, let's just go. I just want to go back home. I just wanna be done with this."

"You can't," spat Tristan caustically. You're *in* this! You were there. You were part of it!"

Nate's panic overflowed. "No! I was—"

"We're all part of it. Especially you! You wanted to come out here again. It's your fault we went to the river at all!"

"What are you talking about?"

Tristan cut him off again, leaning forward this time, crowding Nate and pushing an outstretched finger viciously into his cheek as he ratcheted up his indignation. "This is all *your* fault! You're the one to blame! And when we get back my dad'll get you. He'll get you for this! For what *you* did!" Nate opened his mouth to object, but Tristan stopped him with an outstretched hand.

Something in Tristan was shifting, as if caught in a struggle between fury and control. Nate could only watch and wait.

Finally, Tristan took a deep breath and exhaled, seeming to gain control and some measure of calm. "Okay, look," he said, taking Nate by the shoulders. "What's happened here—it doesn't matter who did what. We're all in it. All three of us. Look at Pip," he said, jabbing a thumb over his shoulder. "He understands. He gets it. He knows we're all in it, but he also understands what separates us. I'm a De Villiers—*a De Villiers*, Nate—do you know what that means here? On this island? It means I'm untouchable. My father, my uncles and aunties—they own this place. The police, the schools, the judges, the lawyers…I can't be touched here—not on this island. But you," he said, his voice trailing off ominously. "Nate, you don't understand how the island works. What do you think will happen when I tell them it was you?"

Nate's panic unravelled him. He stuttered and faltered, tried to speak and managed only a few gurgled half words, a few unformed pleas. Finally his legs gave way, and he buried his head in his hands and began to cry.

"You have to understand, Nate," said Tristan, almost imploring him. "This is *my* island. But you...You and Pip..." He slowly shook his head and stepped away from the puddle of a boy before him.

Nate sobbed quietly, feeling the island and its ruling class press unseen shackles into him from every direction. "But it wasn't me, Tristan!"

The boy in front of him just shook his head. "That doesn't matter, Nate. It only matters what I tell them."

Nate's head dropped as that truth—that hard local truth—washed over him. Finally he looked up, his eyes wet, wide and pleading. "What do I do?" asked Nate.

"There's nothing you can do."

Nate sobbed. "Please Tristan. What do I do?"

And then, as if giving in to a costly favor: "There's only one chance for you. Just one."

Nate heard the sliver of redemption offered in Tristan's words and it lifted his chin.

Tristan slowly squatted down in front of Nate and placed both his hands on the boy's shoulders once more. "Maybe there's a way. One way I can help get you out of this."

• • •

Nate was shaken by the strange encounter with Augustine, but didn't have time to let it really sink in. Ahead of him, sitting high on a set of dark arches sat the old estate house. There was little change from the house he remembered all those years ago. It was still tall and somehow sinister, and the windows up in the attic—in the space where the nutmegs would roll and roll—were still black as missing teeth. It was clear, though, that the house had been partially restored to some degree. The paint was fresh and bright, and the red tin roof was mostly free of the rusty streaks that had once been such a dominant feature.

The day that swirled around them was much the same as any day on the island. The sun beamed warmly down, birds chirped and sang, and palms swayed in the breeze to the applause of their many fronds. Aside from a curdling sense of dread in Nate's gut, it was another perfect island day.

As the couple walked down the track—a track that was now carefully gravelled but still a track nonetheless—they passed a dilapidated square structure on their left, and Nate recognized it immediately as the old copra oven. Its roof had long since sagged and caved in, and the grass at its sides had grown tall and thick, like a million green fingers pulling it back down into the earth.

Up ahead, Ti Fenwe Estate stood waiting for them, and Nate stopped to take it fully in. The bank of windows was still there, lining the main bedroom, but the pole that held the battery they had shot at was gone. The doors and railings had been either replaced or refinished, and to those seeing it for the first time it might even seem quaint, perhaps even old-world charming. But even with its careful makeover, Nate still felt it emanating something else, something less welcoming, like a once flooded room that has never really lost the smell.

He couldn't peg it, couldn't quite understand what was bothering him. It wasn't the general creepiness of the place—it still had that in spades—but it was something else. Something, well, *structural*.

"Are you okay, Nate?" Rachael asked.

Nate caught her glancing down at the worn paper bag he held in his left hand. She never asked what it was. Not when he fetched it from his case in the car, not when they walked up the gravel track past the old copra oven, and not now.

"Are you okay, Nate?" she asked again.

"I'm not sure," he said softly, and then it hit him. "It's smaller. The house seems so much smaller than I remember it. Back then it was a mansion—it was this giant sprawling stately home. But now, up close from here, it's just a house. That's so damn weird."

They walked on toward the house until they were beneath the bank of windows and a few feet from the front steps. Nate put a hand on Rachael's shoulder and stopped her. "I want you to wait here. I really appreciate you coming, I do, but you don't need to go inside."

"Do you think that's wise? I mean, if there's two of us, he's less likely to do anything."

"Vincent's not going to do anything," said Nate reassuringly, but inside he felt less certain. What was about to happen was entirely unpredictable.

Rachael nodded without any more protest. Nate climbed the concrete steps to the wooden veranda, crossed the short span and knocked firmly on the door. As he stood waiting he cast his mind back to this very spot, and re-lived himself as a thirteen-year-old running headlong through the doorway, no actual door to impede him, out into the sunshine and down the stairs. They were headed to the clearing, and Nate's heart skipped a beat at the thought of that beautiful hollow, that natural dome of greenery out there in the forest.

He reached up and knocked again, then took a step back from the door, perhaps in deference, perhaps something else. Still no answer. Nate turned and looked out over the area in front of the house, marvelling at the fact that decades had come and gone since he'd stood there. It felt like the place had been waiting there, just for him, just to have him stand here once more. He was no longer the boy he had been, but in that moment—at the top of the steps on the landing at Ti Fenwe—adulthood could offer nothing to stifle the essence of thirteen that seemed to entirely possess him now.

Nate looked down at Rachael. Her arms were crossed tightly and her face was drawn and pinched, like someone fighting the urge to be sick. "Are you okay?" he asked. And then Nate realized that Rachael wasn't looking at him, but past him.

How the door behind Nate had opened without him hearing

it was unclear, but when he turned back to the house there was now a dark hollow where the door had been just moments before. Nate peered into the lightless opening, fighting the urge to take another step backwards. There was something there, in the shadow just inside the doorway, but it was hidden. All he could make out was what appeared to be the toes of two shoes peeking out of the darkness, strangely suspended in the air about four inches above the wooden floor. For a moment Nate thought of another pair of shoes—slippers, really—slippers lying just inside the bedroom door in his father's bedroom. Nate's eyes slowly adapted, and the shoes revealed themselves more fully, as did the metal footrests of the wheelchair in which the old man sat.

Finally the whole form shifted, and with a quiet squeak and the whir of an electric motor, the old wheelchair and the even older man moved a half turn through the doorway. "Why are you here?" The words were hissed more than spoken.

Nate took a reflexive half-step backwards, and as he looked into the old man's eyes he saw a flash of something he'd seen many years ago that day by the river. Back then it was Tristan, curling his lip in disapproval, but the man in front of him now—the man bent over and curled with age and clutching at the lever of his electric wheelchair—that man was undoubtedly Vincent De Villiers. "Why are you here?" he hissed again.

For a moment Nate was unable to answer, and all he could do was stare at the old man, at the bony hands protruding out from under his shirtsleeves, and at the brown and yellow blanket across his knees. His cheeks were bloodless and sunken, and an oxygen mask twitched against his face every time the old man drew a lungful. His eyes seemed to bulge slightly, as if panic was always nearby now, but beneath the pallid, exsiccated skin the architecture of the Vincent in Nate's youth—that towering, wondrous, pirate of a man—was still there. "Do you know who I am?" asked Nate. His voice came out much smaller than he intended, and he felt a wash of warmth at his collar.

The old man's hands came together and his fingers plucked at one another in his lap. "Of course I do," he said, his voice slightly muffled beneath the mask. "And you're not welcome here." He leaned slightly to one side and gazed past Nate toward the spot where Rachael was standing. "Neither of you."

In the shadows of the darkened room behind him Nate thought he caught movement, but as he glanced up he could see nothing. The old house still had a powerful effect on him, he thought, even after all these years.

"I suggest you climb back into your damn vehicle and be gone," continued the old man, his voice rattling like a pebble in a rusting tin can. "This is private property. And take that little whore with you."

"What did you just say?" He looked at the spiteful face gazing up at him. Rachael had already started to make her way back to the SUV. Nate suddenly felt that he had missed an important moment.

"Listen, Mr. De Villiers, I don't want any trouble."

"Is she your whore now?" He goaded Nate.

"What the hell's wrong with you?"

"Leave these premises now, before I have someone remove you."

Nate stared in amazement at the man. "You know, I never saw it back then, but I do now. Clear as can be."

Vincent lifted his chin slightly to match Nate's gaze, and a single bony hand reached up and momentarily pulled the mask aside. "What?" he spat. "What are you talking about?" Then he pushed the mask back over his mouth and nose and sucked the gas in deeply.

"When we were kids here, all those years ago, we all thought you were this great guy. You were Vincent De Villiers, you were this larger than life character who drove a Land Rover and owned a plantation and told great stories. And then you beat the shit out of your son—a little thirteen-year-old kid. You're a fucking bully. That's all you are."

The old man's face pinched tightly and his hand clutched at the black control knob on the armrest of his chair. He yanked it and the chair jerked backwards, clattering into the door frame and hooking the wheel.

Nate was angry now, more so than he expected to be, and he

stepped firmly toward the chair. Vincent dropped the knob and raised his hands defensively. His eyes cut a quick and nervous glance at the worn paper bag in Nate's hand.

"I'm not going to hurt you. But I do want you to tell me something."

Vincent simply stared up at him from the chair. He was breathing faster now, and Nate could see the old man's breath condensing momentarily inside the mask with each exhale.

"I want to know why you sent those people after me. All that nonsense with the dead chickens and the red paste. And then having someone run us off the road? What the hell's the matter with you?"

Vincent stared back acidly, and the two held each other's gaze. Finally Vincent broke away and reached out for the black control knob. He began to manipulate the chair with a gentle whirring of the electric motor, speaking to Nate as he did but without looking up. "I don't know what you're talking about. I know exactly who you are, and I've known you were here from the moment you set foot on the island. But if you've run into trouble here it's not been because of me."

The old man finally managed to free his chair and turn it to line up with the doorway. He rolled forward and then stopped just as his face dipped into the shadows. "Go home, Nate Mason. There's nothing here for you." The motor whirred again and the chair and its occupant slid into the darkness, leaving only a gentle swirl of dust particles that seemed determined not to be pulled inside. Nate watched as the door swung closed, and again his eyes played tricks in the darkness. Was something there? Something just inside and tucked deep enough into the umbra to be invisible?

No. It was just the house and its history playing with him.

Nate lingered at the top of the stairs. His hands hung loosely at his sides, the brown paper bag still clutched in his hand, his mind turning through the strange encounter with a man so different to the one propped up in his memory. Nate stared off down the track toward the old copra oven. He knew this was bullshit. It was Vincent, all of it—the Obeah, the attack, the police—all of it was the De Villiers closing ranks.

At the car, Rachael sat in the passenger's seat with her legs pulled up tight and her arms wrapped around them. "You okay?" he asked.

Rachael nodded unconvincingly.

"You know, I'm not sure he's your biggest fan."

"He never was. But the feeling's quite mutual." Rachael finally looked over and met his gaze, and then her eyes dropped to the bag he was holding at the sill of the door.

She let the moment stand, perhaps waiting for him to explain, but instead he pushed himself up from the window and began to walk back toward the copra oven.

Rachael slipped out of the car to follow. "Where are we going?" she called out.

Nate stopped on the track somewhere between the house and the copra oven and was craning his neck and searching for something in the bush that lined the side of the road.

"And what are you looking for?"

He stepped into the light bush and pushed the underbrush aside, let it fall back into place and repeated the motion a little further on. "Well, you're staying here, but what I'm looking for is— ah," he said with some level of satisfaction. "Here it is."

He stepped through the light scrub and onto a worn foot path. The path cut into the forest at a sharp angle almost parallel to the gravel track, making the entranceway almost indefinable from the gravel road. Without knowing it was there, a person could easily walk past it, covered as the entrance was with leafy bushes and tall grass.

Rachael watched from the path and Nate turned momentarily before pushing on. He knew the question she was not asking: "I'm going to the clearing," he said, and then turned down the path.

He followed the path at his feet, ducking under branches and pushing leaves and vines out of his way. The path was used less now, and the forest had narrowed it and claimed some parts almost entirely. Still, he was able to find the bare brown floor with enough regularity to keep pushing on. Finally he ducked under a swath of vines that were wrapping themselves into a stand of green bamboo, and found himself standing at the edge of that natural opening in the forest, still largely dome-shaped thanks to the trees that lined the edge and cast their branches up and over. It was darker now. The holes he remembered at its zenith were now filled in, and while light did still come into the natural room, it did so in shafts that cut their individual ways through and lit small pools of light on the earthen floor like puddles after a rainstorm. At the center of the clearing there was a cluster of small angular structures, and despite his edginess Nate was somehow thrilled to recognize them as old bits of furniture, some now just steel skeletons—a chair-back here, a coil-spring base there. And at the center, like a nucleus for the litter of rusting metal and softening wooden shapes sat the circular form of the old industrial-wire spool.

Nate walked into the clearing slowly, almost reverently, like a man entering a quiet church. He walked through the shafts of light, leaving swirling pools of dust to dance behind him, flitting in and out of the light like tiny pixies celebrating the return of some long departed king. The memories were coming fast now, and as he touched the edge of a slowly decomposing wooden chair, it was like electrifying a synapse, and his mind came alive with images of Pip, Richard, and Tristan, laughing that untroubled, carefree summertime laughter.

For a brief moment, he tapped into an incredible sense of lightness, that state of being unique to childhood where the day is limitless, where no rules exist to restrain, and no logic cinches around us to bound ideas. Nothing is impossible: not flight, not dragons, not warring armies, not magical armor. It hovered for a brief moment, and then it was gone. He was a man again, a man standing in the penumbra of a forest clearing surrounded by the relics of a single day in his childhood.

The laughter seemed far away now, little more than the lingering echo of something light and childlike coming from another room. As Nate approached the industrial-wire spool table, he felt a different sensation, one much less welcome but somehow seared more indelibly into his childhood memory. He remembered standing there facing Tristan, scared in a way that transcended a momentary fright. This was real fear—formative, life-changing terror. It reached past the moment, past its inception, and cast a shadow on how he would see the world from there on in. It was an awakening of sorts for Nate, a sickening realization that the world was not a safe, fun-filled romp, but rather a risky, uncertain landscape crammed with sharp edges over which a veneer of happiness and safety was thinly draped.

He looked down at the circular wooden table top, and was not surprised to see that the old wooden box, the one that had held the wrist rockets, was no longer there. The table was bare except for four small round spheres, each caked completely with brown rust, each sitting in the parallel seams of the wood that made up the table top. He reached out and picked one up, and rolled it into his palm. It was one of the ball bearings they had used all those years ago, and he looked automatically up toward the far end of the clearing where the white blocks of Styrofoam used to hang in the trees. Of course, there was no sign of them now.

But in their place, at the very edge of the clearing, stood a man.

"You got a little fat," said the man by the clearing's edge. He was wearing a pair of tan trousers, and a white linen shirt with sleeves rolled up to expose forearms wrapped in thick, conspicuous veins. As he spoke, locks of long, dirty blonde hair flecked with gray fell across a worn face, but his eyes were bright and clear. They cut sharp and nervous glances around the clearing. Nate noticed that his feet, all these years later, were still bare.

All Nate could do at first was look at him, at the deep lines carved in his face, at his slightly curled posture as if ready to spring away at any moment, and at the way his eyes cut anxiously around the clearing. Finally he was able to gather himself: "I heard you were dead. Some trouble out on a boat, I was told."

Across from him, Tristan twitched at a sound of a bird breaking cover, and his eyes stabbed at the brush all around the clearing. His gaze eventually came back to Nate, but he said nothing.

"You done having your fun with me? Your Obeah curses and all that?"

Tristan's chin pushed out and up. "What you want here? You were told never to come back."

Nate shook his head gently. "We were kids, Tristan."

Again, Tristan eyed the edges of the clearing. "You were given a way out. A way to wash your hands of what you did and—"

"What *I did?* You're a fucking psychopath, you know that?"

"—and now you force your way back into this sad, sad tragedy from so long ago. Back into something that was in the past. Dead and buried."

"Do you recall what happened, Tristan? Do you remember bashing your own cousin's head in? Does that sound familiar at all?"

There was no change in Tristan's timbre; he kept talking in that melodic West Indian cadence, and began taking small, tentative steps into the clearing. "I gave you many chances, both back then, and now in recent days. But you refuse everything I try do for you."

Nate felt a cold wave of realization wash over him. Tristan believed what he was saying. Over the course of thirty-odd years he had told himself the lie so many times, so convincingly, that in his mind, he had finally made it true.

Tristan continued on, still taking slow steps toward the center of the clearing. "And so now you force my hand, despite taking payment on our bond of silence all those years ago."

Taking payment, Nate said under his breath. He clenched his teeth and took a deep breath to steady himself. He looked down at the soiled brown paper bag in his hand. It had held its contents so long you could almost see the shape of it pressed forever into the paper—the knurling of the grip, the scalloped curves that would guide fingers into place and the curve of the steel as it emerged from the top of the handle.

Tristan was now only ten paces from where Nate stood at the table. He stopped, darted his eyes along the bush-line again, then squared his shoulders and jutted his chin out. "You should not have come here, to Ti Fenwe. You should not have come back to this island."

"What are you going to do, Tristan? Kill me like you did Richard? Or how about Pip? Or the reporter he was with."

"I can't let you leave from here. Can't let you spread lies 'bout that day."

The words struck Nate as hollow and toothless. He knew what the threat meant, but his mind never seated the words, never connected them with the possibility of the deed itself being carried out—not in real life. "If you think the story would end with killing me, well, you'd be wrong. I came here to do something I've needed to do since the day I left. Something for me. And if that helps set the record straight here then so be it. That's just a bonus. The story— the real story of what happened back there at the river—is being written right now, Tristan. It'll be front page news tomorrow. I've given my whole story to a reporter at *The Word*."

"You don't understand this island, Nate. You never did. Nothing will be published in *The Word*," he said snidely. "Not without my permission."

Nate matched his gaze. "Are you sure about that? You think you can buy your way out of that?"

Nate looked at the bag he was carrying, and then back at Tristan. "But you know what, I don't really give a goddamn. I'm just here to give this to you." And as he said the words, he reached into the paper bag with his right hand.

Tristan took a half step back, and thrust his own hand sharply into the right pocket of his baggy tan trousers. There was something about the gesture that made Nate instantly uneasy. He froze, right hand buried in the paper bag, eyes riveted on Tristan. In a fractured moment, Tristan pulled something black and compact from his pocket and Nate's mind flashed to the day the boys had all shot at the battery from the bedroom window of the plantation house. He remembered Vincent unfolding the cloth and revealing the little black gun, and the sense of awe that had seized them. He knew with utter clarity that the black shape in Tristan's hand was the old man's pistol.

In front of him, Tristan raised the gun in a single fluid movement. His thumb flicked out and drew back the hammer, and he squeezed the trigger hard.

31

Nate was pleading now. He was terrified, disassembled completely by the knowledge that Tristan was right; in a contest of pointed fingers, on this island, Tristan's would win every time. And so he was ready to do anything—anything that would promise relief from the madness whirling around him. The clearing seemed to be almost black now, and the forest was taking on a menacing quality. "What, Tristan? What do I do?"

Tristan stood, leaving Nate on his knees in a puddle of fear and uncertainty. The island boy towered over him, and his head bobbed up and down as if agreeing silently to some daring plan that might—just might—actually work… "Maybe there's a way. Maybe we can save you. One way I can get you out of this."

Nate's eyes pleaded in question.

"Silence," said Tristan plainly. "Silence is the only way."

"…What?"

"If you keep quiet—I mean not a word. Not a single discussion about this with anyone—especially those parents of yours—then maybe we can keep you from whatever it is my family and the police will do to you."

"But…people will…"

Tristan's rage flared. "You can never, *ever*, tell anyone what happened. Not your parents, not the police, not anyone. If they ask you, you shut up and look at the ground. Cry if you have to. If you talk…if you say it was me. Well, maybe I get a dirty look. But you, you'll die in some prison—if my father doesn't get to you first." He reached down and seized Nate painfully by the jowls. "You can never tell a soul. Never. Do you understand?"

Nate was trembling now. There was no other option: to his back, a line of dank stone cells deep underground, and the wrath of a family that was nothing short of island royalty. And in front of him, a simple lie to make it all go away. His eyes dropped and Tristan saw it.

Tristan reached over and snatched at the wooden box on top of the spool table. He flipped it open, upturned it and spilled the contents out. Two Wrist Rockets clattered onto the table. Tristan grasped one by the pistol grip handle and thrust in front of Nate's face. "You like this, right?"

Nate stared blankly ahead, confused.

"You want one—I know you do."

Nate just stared at the Wrist Rocket, unsure of how to react.

"Well *do* you?" hollered Tristan directly into his face.

"Yes! All right, yes!" blurted Nate, a fresh set of tears welling up.

"Then take it," snapped Tristan, jamming it harshly into Nate's hand. "You take this and you never say a word about what happened to anyone—no one at all. Do you understand?" Tristan looked down and saw that Nate had not taken hold of the Wrist Rocket, and it sat limply in his lap while Nate stared pleadingly into Tristan's eyes.

"Shit!" cussed Tristan. He reached down and snatched the slingshot, separated the two bands and slipped it over Nate's head, setting the Wrist Rocket around his neck like a necklace. "This is yours. Do you understand? It belongs to you now."

Nate just stared at him, terrified.

"*Do you understand?*" yelled Tristan.

Nate nodded at last. Tristan released him, and his eyes fell to the Wrist Rocket hanging around his neck. He reached up and touched it gently, then looked at Tristan.

"That's yours now," said Tristan. He stood back a step and let his hands fall to his side. His face relaxed, and he seemed to grow calm, almost in a daze. "Learn the lesson, earn the reward," he said.

Nate's face wrinkled in confusion. "What?"

Tristan dipped low and suddenly screamed the words into his face. "Learn the lesson, earn the reward!" And then he stood, blinking repeatedly as if caught in some waking dream.

Nate simply stared at him, shivering.

"Let me hear you swear it," said Tristan. "Swear you'll tell no soul."

Again Nate just stared.

"You have to swear it!" shouted Tristan, his spittle showering Nate's face. "Swear it!"

Nate flinched violently. "I swear it," he whispered.

"Louder!"

"I swear it!" shouted Nate, his tears running freely again.

Tristan took a step back and stared hard at the boy weeping in front of him. He let him cry, and waited until the sobs became hitches and snatches for air. "Good," he said at last.

And for Nate, there was a hint of comfort in the finality of that last word, something absolute and authoritative. It implied a way forward, a way out, a way to stop the horrors from coming true. He reached up and touched the slingshot around his neck again. It was cold and angular, and hideously powerful. And now it was his. *Learn the lesson, earn the reward.* It made almost no sense, and the words seemed angular and filled with jagged edges like a mouthful of nettles, but they also offered what he needed most: hope. And they offered it now.

Nate resolved to do exactly what Tristan had said; he would say nothing about what happened out by the river. Ever.

Tristan slapped him on the shoulder. "Now we can go."

• • •

Ten paces from Nate, Tristan raised the gun and pulled the trigger.

But in the instant that the hammer snapped forward, Tristan seemed to jerk sideways, almost as if reacting to the recoil of the round *before* it was discharged. In a single action the bullet let fly, streaking only inches over Nate's shoulder, and the gun fell from Tristan's hand and onto the ground.

Nate was transfixed. He had felt the bullet miss him, heard the air being ripped apart as the slug flew wide, but what he had just seen made no sense at all. Tristan was reacting to the odd moment as well. He was staring at his hand in confusion, as if it had somehow disobeyed him. His eyes were pinned wide open in a wild, almost unhinged way, and he began to frantically search the bush-line. But his dismay was short lived. He flicked his eyes to Nate and then back to the gun, and threw himself headlong after the weapon.

Nate's hands squeezed instinctively, and he became instantly aware that he was holding something in each. He opened his right hand and found a rusty ball bearing sitting in the center of his palm. He glanced to his left hand, but he already knew what was there. Nate shredded the brown paper bag and the Wrist Rocket slipped easily into his hand. The pistol grip with its scalloped finger guides fit his hand perfectly, and the leather pouch fell obediently open. In a motion that seemed entirely automatic, Nate slipped the rusty ball bearing into the pouch and drew the twin bands back the full span of his arms.

On the ground in front of him, Tristan was desperately clutching at the dirt in an effort to retrieve the gun, but something in the stillness of the man before him made him stop. He looked up and saw Nate, arms fully extended, hands shaking gently against the energy in the twin bands aching to be set free.

Tristan lay still, the gun just inches from his hand.

"If you reach for that gun I'll put this bearing through your head," promised Nate.

On the ground, Tristan held his position. The wheels were turning, and Nate could almost feel him weighing the odds. Could Nate make a clean shot?

"Nate, don't do it!" came Rachael's voice from the edge of the clearing.

Both Nate and Tristan glanced toward her; for Tristan it was all he needed. Like a coiled spring set free, Tristan snatched the gun from the ground and pivoted athletically onto his back, snapping the muzzle to bear on Nate.

Nate shifted his aim instinctively, almost imperceptibly, and released the pinch-grip he had on the leather pouch. The rusty ball bearing hissed through the air of the clearing, across thirty years of angst, and struck the side of small black gun like a hammer on an anvil. It glanced off the gun and tore on into Tristan's throat with the power of a bullet. Tristan went over backwards almost silently, his hands rising to his neck as he went, while a plume of crimson sprayed from him. The gun fell harmlessly to the ground. His legs flailed about as he clutched at his throat. Through the hole, he gurgled and frothed.

On the other side of the clearing from where Rachael stood with her hands cupped over her mouth, Nate thought he saw something move in the bush-line. It was almost nothing, just a branch swaying back into place, a few leaves swishing across one another. He turned back to Tristan.

The man on the ground had stopped writhing, and had taken on a state of relaxation that was even more frightening than the frantic thrashing that had preceded it. Nate dashed forward and dropped to his knees beside Tristan, and was staggered by the sheer volume of blood that had pooled around him. Tristan's face was vacant and ashen, and Nate immediately thrust his bare hands onto the wound to stop the bleeding. "Rachael!" he called out desperately. He looked over his shoulder but Rachael was still frozen, still fixed with her hands cupped to her mouth. "Rachael, quickly!"

Rachael ran to them, dropped to her knees and pried Nate's hand from the wound. She replaced it almost immediately, and turned her attention to Tristan's face. She lifted his eyelids, one after the other, and then slipped her fingers around to the other side of his neck, searching for a pulse. She drew her hand back slowly and settled on her heels.

"Do something!" said Nate. There was panic in his voice. "You have to do something, quickly!"

"Nate, he's dead."

"Go get help."

Behind them something in the bush broke cover. It briefly stopped them both and they followed the sound. It moved hastily, too far off to be seen, clattering its way through the bush in the general direction of the house.

Nate refocused on the man lying before him. "Now, Rachael, you gotta go now."

"Nate."

Nate exploded. "Go call for help now! Right fucking now!"

Rachael rose and ran back down the path, heading for the plantation house.

"Tristan?" Nate shook him lightly. But the man on the ground was relaxed in a way that went beyond sleep. Nate closed his eyes briefly to calm himself, and when he opened them a moment later, he saw that is was Richard lying there, sodden and still at the river's edge. Then it was Pip, then his father, and finally, Cody. He shook his head gently and the gathering quietly and obediently receded; in front of him was just a gray husk that had once been Tristan.

He moved his hand from Tristan's neck and looked at the wound; the bleeding had stopped, or more accurately, the bleeding had finished.

"I didn't come here to hurt you. I came back to put this where it belongs." He reached for the Wrist Rocket in front of him. Nate stood and walked slowly over to an old rusting kitchen chair near the clearing's center. He held the slingshot by one of the bands, stretched it and then ran it briskly back and forth along a jagged edge of the chair frame until the rubber finally parted.

The slingshot was useless now, and Nate placed it on the ground beside Tristan. "It's yours now," he said flatly. "It always was."

• • •

Nate followed the path back from the clearing, walking slowly toward the track that lead to the house. There was no rush anymore. No urgency. But legions of memories were calling for his attention. His childhood was so close he could feel the very fabric of thirteen. If he closed his eyes he knew he would see them all: Richard, Pip, and Tristan, racing ahead of him, laughing as they followed the twists and turns of green at full speed.

The pathway dissolved and the forest spilled him onto the gravelled track, and as he turned onto it he could see the car, and the house beyond. There was no sign of Rachael. She would be in the house, calling for an ambulance, perhaps the police. He looked down at his palms. They were smeared with Tristan's blood.

Rachael's voice, high pitched and tight with panic, shouted to him. "Nate! Come quickly!"

She stood ahead, with her arms raised on the balcony of the house. She called to him again and Nate broke into a run.

"What's wrong?" he asked, taking the stairs two at a time.

"It's Vincent."

She led Nate into the gloom of the main hall, and as his eyes adjusted he could see Vincent in his wheelchair at the room's center. He was slumped in his chair, as if asleep, with his head pitched back and his mouth open wide. Despite the dimness of the room Nate could see that the old man's mask was pulled down and hung loosely at his neck, and his lips were lightly tinged in cold blue. "Is he dead?" asked Nate in disbelief. He could see that Vincent's eyelids were half closed and still.

"No. He's still breathing. I've called the ambulance but his oxygen tank is shut off tight; I can't budge it."

"Let me try," said Nate, seizing the top of the green cylinder harnessed to the back of the wheelchair. He twisted hard on the cylinder valve but it wouldn't move. It held stubbornly fast, and Nate's hands, slick with Tristan's blood, couldn't find purchase. "Shit!" he cursed, standing back and looking around the room for a tool. "I need something I can put through the holes in the knob, something I can use as a lever."

Rachael ran to the kitchen and returned with a sturdy butter knife. "What about this?"

"Perfect," said Nate, sliding the handle of the knife through one of the holes in valve grip. Still the valve resisted, but with the new leverage it finally gave in, and the cylinder hissed lightly as the gas began to flow once more through the plastic tubing. Nate opened the valve fully. "Will he be okay now? Can you wake him?"

Rachael slid the mask in place and examined the old man in the chair. She checked his airway, his pupils and then shifted his hips downward slightly so his head wasn't lolling over backwards. Finally she made a fist and ran her knuckles up and down his breastbone. There was no reaction from the man in the chair.

"Well?" asked Nate, rubbing his hands against his shirt.

"I don't know. He's breathing, but he's unresponsive, comatose."

"But he's alive."

"Yes, he's alive."

In the distance a siren wailed, climbing its way up to the estate. Nate looked back at the cylinder behind Vincent. "What the hell happened to him? How did his oxygen get shut off?"

"I don't know," said Rachael, shaking her head. "He was right here when I found him, and it was only after I tried to wake him that I realized there was no flow to the mask."

Nate's face folded in question. "How the hell could that happen?"

"I don't know," she said again, "but the cyanosis—the blue around his lips—that worries me." Rachael checked again that the oxygen was flowing through the tube.

"Will he be okay?"

"We won't be able to tell until he wakes up."

Nate looked again at his hands, at the crimson stains there, and then thrust them in his pockets. Standing in that spot he did a slow circle, taking in the great room for the first time in more than thirty years. So much of it was familiar—the hall to the bedroom and the kitchen, the open windows where bats had swarmed in their thousands, and the stairs that led to the floor above, where the nutmegs would lay waiting to dry. That thought was linked inexorably to another, as it always would be, and he thought instantly of the Bolom. Nate turned back to Rachael. "Back there, in the clearing. The sound in the bush. Did you hear it?"

Rachael stared at him blankly. "It was an animal started by the shot. That's all it was."

"No," said Nate, softly, his mind turning back to the moment. "It was after that. It was right after you said Tristan was dead."

Rachael tuned to face him fully. Her tone was curt. "And what do you think it was, Nate?"

They stared at each other in silence. In the distance, the wail of the siren grew louder.

Finally Nate looked away and waved his hand dismissively. "Nothing, I guess. This place just gets to me."

Outside, the siren stopped abruptly and was replaced with the crunch of heavy tires on gravel. The ambulance had arrived at last.

32

In the days that followed, Nate spent hours going over the confrontation with Tristan. He still didn't understand what had happened. Why had Tristan twitched so violently with the gun in his hands? And what had crashed through the bush afterwards? They were questions that would come back to him again and again.

He stayed for four more days at Rachael's dazzling Cap Estate house overlooking the water. And although they never found each other in the way they had the night before heading to Ti Fenwe, there was something between them they recognized would never truly go away. They barely left each other's side for those four days, and perhaps it was the inevitability of their separation that kept them so close. Nate needed to go home, to face the demons of his present, having slain those of his past.

Smiley, unimpressed with the gag order issued by his boss, had ploughed headlong into the story. *The Word* was a small paper with a small press, and while his editor slept, Smiley marched in and literally stopped the presses before midnight to place his story on the front page. He gleefully told Nate that he had actually said those words, *Stop the presses!* and that's exactly what they had done. Nobody questioned it. It was, after all, Smiley. And his brother (he claimed) was the pressman.

The story broke and his editor fumed, but there was little he could do. It was the single largest print run in the paper's short history, and the tale of murder among St. Lucia's royalty went through the island like wildfire. The police quickly launched a murder investigation into the deaths of Pieter "Pip" Prinsloo and Desmond Bailey. Suspicion fell largely on Tristan—now confirmed dead instead of just missing at sea—and there was some speculation that Vincent also had a hand. Nevertheless, the issue would never see the inside of a courtroom. News of Vincent's death reached them on the second day. He never regained consciousness in the hospital, having finally succumbed to whatever injuries he sustained by being deprived of his oxygen.

But the news didn't stop there. On the third day Cornelius French arrived unannounced at the house in Cap. He was fat and sweaty and dressed in a two-thousand-dollar suit, and produced four copies of a thick document from a briefcase along with his business card. He represented the De Villiers, and the documents were the title to Ti Fenwe estate in Dennery.

With the passing of Vincent the estate would cede to Tristan, but with Tristan also now dead—and this time officially—and no children, the property would fall to his next of kin. And, having been blocked in her efforts to divorce Tristan, this meant that Rachael was now the sole remaining heir.

To her surprise, the De Villiers offered no resistance to the inheritance. It seemed they wanted to be rid of the place, and of the scandal that Vincent and Tristan had brought on the family. The documents would be signed and filed with the court, and Rachael would become the new Master of Ti Fenwe estate—the first woman to hold that title in the family's history. More royal scandal for *The Word.*

That same evening, on the heels of Cornelius French's departure, Ma Joop arrived. She sat with Rachael in the living room and talked in serious tones, while Nate sat outside by the pool largely out of earshot. It seemed Ma Joop was counseling Rachael on some level, and from her body language it was apparent that whatever the large woman with the booming voice was saying, it was being carefully weighed by Rachael. From his spot by the pool—and thanks to Ma Joop's strangely baritone voice—Nate could hear snippets of the conversation, words that his ears seemed tuned for. He heard *Ti Fenwe,* he heard *freedom ritual,* and he heard *Bolom.* He would not ask her about it, it was really none of his business, but he was left with a feeling that things, at last, were being put right.

• • •

Nate closed the door on Rachael's Beemer and the two stood facing each other in the parking lot of Hewanorra International Airport. It was the main tourist gateway in Vieux Fort at the south end of the island, and the day was another postcard-perfect tropical scene. The breeze was warm and light, and the bright sunshine made the carefully landscaped flower beds pulse with color.

Rachael started for the terminal, but Nate put his hand gently on her shoulder. "Let's say our goodbyes here," he said.

Rachael smiled and it hurt. Then she pressed herself to him and hugged him tightly. "I'll miss you, Nate."

"Me too," he said, fighting a rising lump in his throat. The strength of his reaction surprised him; he didn't want to cry and so he gently pushed her away, and then, to change the subject, "You know, I still don't know what happened back there at Ti Fenwe. Why did Tristan drop the gun? His hand just…I don't know, it kind of jerked down."

Rachael slipped her sunglasses on. They had had this conversation more than once over the last four days; there was nothing new here. "Who knows," she said glibly. "Maybe he had some kind of fit, maybe it was karma. Payback for the past."

Nate smiled awkwardly. "Sorry, I guess I need to get over it."

Rachael kissed him lightly on the cheek, opened the door and slipped into the car. She looked up at Nate and shaded her eyes against the sun. "Nate, do you know what *Ti Fenwe* means in patois?"

"I just thought it was a name."

"It means daybreak, the beginning of a new day." She smiled at him warmly. "Goodbye, Nate," she said sincerely, then put the car in drive and slipped away without looking back.

Nate recognized another part of his past had now been properly and finally closed. It was painful, but it was right.

And then it struck him.

What had she said? Payback from the past? Something in that was familiar, and as he considered it a series of thoughts aligned and snapped together like a shaken box of magnets. In his mind he suddenly saw Augustine, there at her chipped blue table, speaking those cryptic words as he left her lean-to: *Calm yourself, chyle. Favors from de past will be repaid.* And then his mind leapt to another time and place altogether, and in it he saw himself as a child. There was a gun in Vincent's hand and Nate remembered swinging his arm and crying *No!,* striking Vincent's arm and forcing the shot to run wide. And he remembered seeing the bushes move—leaves shuffling, branches swaying—as if someone or something had scurried away. Had he really seen that?

And then there was the movement he had seen in the clearing only four days ago. Was there something there as well? He remembered the way Tristan's arm had twitched, as if, well, as if something unseen had struck it hard, just the way Nate had with Vincent all those years ago. Was there really something there in the bush that night? Vincent had said it was the Bolom, and if it was— if it was real—had Nate's actions saved it? *Calm yourself, chyle. Favors from de past will be repaid.* It sent a chill up his spine that made him physically shudder.

No, it couldn't have been. Tristan must have simply had a fit, a convulsion at just the wrong moment. All those strange happenings at Ti Fenwe? Just the result of a creepy, dark forest and the wild imaginings of a kid. Obeah, black magic, Boloms. It was all nonsense. It didn't really exist.

Did it?

Maybe. No. It was the stuff of stories. It was fodder for a good book, or a bedtime story in the glow of a nightlight. And with no small amount of sadness he thought of Cody, and though he knew there would be no more bedtime stories, no more cuddles and tickles in his warm, darkened room, he felt that his boy would understand. And with that understanding, he could start again.

He slipped the old Wayfarers over his eyes, scooped up his bag and turned toward the airport terminal. Ahead of him was the return home. Behind him lay events that had unfolded at the old plantation house so many years ago. He would leave them there now, finally. He would leave this island and Ti Fenwe far behind him, and he would start anew. What had Rachael said Ti Fenwe meant?

That's right: it meant daybreak, the beginning of a new day.

ACKNOWLEDGEMENTS

The novel, when it's first born, is an unwieldy, legless beast that needs to be physically pushed around from place to place by people who care about it. And it's bloody heavy—so moving it takes the efforts of quite a few folks. This novel was no exception, and those who leaned in and put their shoulders behind it are people who will, from here on in, always be able to count on me for a cold beer. Maybe even two.

To my editor, Randall Klein—thank you for your unique and insightful perspective. You saw elements of the manuscript that were quiet, underserviced and begging to be teased out, and you were right. To Sarah Masterson Hally and Chris Mahon—thanks for bringing a sense of humor to the sometimes mysterious ways of publication, and for all the great advice along the way. To the rest of the talented people at Diversion Books, thanks for taking this project on and breathing a second life into it. I'd also like to thank my agent, Carrie Pestritto, whose infectious positivity and great book-sense are invaluable attributes. The way I see it, if Carrie's not your agent, you should probably keep looking.

And finally, I'd like to thank one of the most intelligent and brave people I know, and someone who has taught me something new every single day since I first met her: my beautiful wife, Laura. How I got so lucky as to have a fiery Irish lass like her in my corner, I'll never know.